LORI WICK

THE
RESCUE

HARVEST HOUSE PUBLISHERS

EUGENE, OREGON

All Scripture quotations are taken from the King James Version of the Bible.

Cover by Dugan Design Group, Bloomington, Minnesota

Cover photos © Rob Wilkinson, Rubberball, Linda Kennedy / Alamy

THE RESCUE
Copyright © 2002 by Lori Wick
Published by Harvest House Publishers
Eugene, Oregon 97402
www.harvesthousepublishers.com

ISBN 978-0-7369-2530-3

Library of Congress has cataloged the edition as follows:

Library of Congress Cataloging-in-Publication Data
Wick, Lori.
  The rescue / Lori Wick.
    p. cm. — (The English garden series ; bk. 2)
  ISBN 978-0-7369-0911-2 (pbk.)
  1. England—Fiction. I. Title.
  PS3573.I237 R47 2002
  813' .54—dc21

2002004553

Printed in the United States of America.

09 10 11 12 13 14 15 16 / RDM-CF / 11 10 9 8 7 6 5 4 3 2 1

This book is dedicated to my
Sunday school class, 2001-02:

Abby, Alexa, Ana, Andy, Drew, Erin, Ethan,
Joseph, Kevin, Lydia, Marissa, Micah, Molly,
Naomi, Nathaniel, Olivia, Rose, Sean, Sophia,
Tess, Tyler, and Zach.

Each one of you has touched my heart in a
deep and special way. I grew so much during
our study on the names of God, and you are
part of the reason. My prayer is that you will
long remember the truths we learned about our
great God—and that you will serve Him
with all your heart.

Acknowledgments

The title of this book, *The Rescue,* describes much more than the story within the cover. It also speaks of certain "rescues" in my own life. Below are the ones I need to thank for throwing me a lifeline.

Jesus Christ. I've never spoken of Christ in my acknowledgments before. I've never wanted to fall into some sort of mindless habit. But this time I would like to give Him praise and thanks for the ultimate rescue. Had God not interrupted me on my path of destruction, giving me the gift of His Son and eternal life, I would be lost indeed. I praise Him with all my heart for loving me so much.

The pastors at my church: Phil, Todd, Mark, and Darwin. I don't always want to hear what you have to say, but I'm so thankful for your faithfulness to the Word. I've been snatched from the brink of sin on many occasions.

My mother, Pearl Hayes. Thank you for your diligence in the Word, Mom. Like Anne's mother, you've always been a remarkable student of Scripture. Thank you for all you've taught me and for being one of my best friends. I love you.

The women at Denise's Bible study. Thank you for your prayers and listening ears. Your kindness and compassion have taught me so much. I'm so thankful for each of you.

Mary Vesperman. It's occurred to me, Mary, that you're one of my favorite people on the planet. This manuscript was such a challenge with the calendar and clock breathing down our necks, but we hung in there. Thank you for all your hard work and dedication. It's an honor working with you, my friend.

Bob Wick. You've rescued me so many times I think you must keep a life preserver in your pocket. Thank you for being there. Thank you for continued growth and support. And for acknowledging that sometimes we rescue each other.

Prologue

London, England
April 1811

"Are you all right?" Lenore Weston asked of her son, Robert Weston. The rain drizzled around them, falling from the tips of the large, dark umbrella that gave them some shelter.

"Yes," he answered quietly, but his eyes remained riveted on the casket at their feet.

"Mr Reynolds will be waiting for us at the house."

Weston sighed quietly. "Why must it be today?"

Lenore smiled a bit. "I don't know, but it always is."

"Very well," Weston said as he turned them both away. "Let's get on with it."

Mother and son made their way to the waiting carriage and were soon on their way to Berwick, the London home of the late Mrs Alice Dixon, Lenore Weston's mother. Not 20 minutes passed before they were in the library. Mr Reynolds, the family's solicitor, stood with his back to the fire, Mrs Dixon's will in his hand. Tea had been served, and once the businessman had enjoyed his cup, he began.

"It's all very straightforward," Mr Reynolds informed them. "Everything has been yours for some years now, Mr Weston, with the exception of certain privileges and revenues. The living rights to Berwick now turn to you, Mrs Weston, for as long as you live." He folded the papers and set them on the table. "Are there any questions?"

"No," Weston said, wanting to be alone with his thoughts.

It was a relief to see the solicitor to the door, thank him for his kind service and attention to detail, and return to the warmth of the library. Lenore was still in her chair, eyes on the fire, and Weston was confident she would want quiet as well.

He was wrong. He'd not been seated for more than a minute when she spoke.

"Did your grandmother ever tell you how much she wished you to live at Brown Manor?"

"At Collingbourne?" Weston asked in some surprise.

"Yes. She remembered how you loved it as a child. Did she never mention it?"

"No, never."

Quiet fell for some moments.

"What of the residents?" Weston asked.

"It's been empty for more than a year."

Weston shook his head in self-derision. "How did I miss that?"

"It's not been an easy year for you," Lenore said compassionately.

Weston didn't reply.

"Is it getting any better?" his mother asked, not certain if she should.

"It's been more than a year…"

An answer which was no answer at all, causing Lenore to fall silent.

"Why do you ask?" Weston asked finally, turning his head to see her.

"You haven't been the same since Henrietta canceled things between you. I assume you still care very much."

"I do still care. I don't hurt as I did, but I do care." Weston's gaze went back to the fire. "I've heard rumors that she moved to France."

"I've heard the same."

"So your wanting me to move out of London has nothing to do with the chance that I might bump into Henrietta here?"

"Yes and no. You don't have to see someone to be reminded of them. I just thought it might be a nice change, and I know the church there is very fine."

"I must be honest and tell you, Mother, that I have no wish to marry. I'm quite content as I am."

"I'm very glad for you, Robert; truly I am. You must know that even if it were in my power, I would never force or even pressure you to take a bride. My suggestion comes only with thoughts of your heart and, perhaps, the good a change could do."

Weston smiled at her.

"I'll think about it. Thank you."

With a tender touch to his shoulder, Lenore took her leave and retired to her room. She didn't think she would see her son until dinner, but he was knocking on her door just an hour later.

"I've sat for the last hour," Weston told his mother, "and thought and prayed about nothing but Brown Manor. I've never known such peace. It's not so very far from London, and I agree the change would be good."

Weston suddenly smiled. "I think it's time to leave the nest."

Lenore reached to hug him.

"When will you go?"

"I'll send Mansfield in a few weeks and follow later on. I'll secure affairs here and then go. Maybe you'll visit me?"

Lenore smiled. "I'll let you go and get settled. After that, nothing could keep me away."

Chapter One

Collingbourne, England
May 1811

"How are you?" Anne Gardiner asked as she slipped into the small cottage and embraced her friend, Lucy Digby.

"I'm very well, and even in my condition," Lucy rebuked her gently, "I can tell I'm getting more rest than you are."

Anne smiled tiredly at her very expectant friend and took a seat on the small sofa when Lucy urged her that way.

"Father isn't always this bad, Lucy," Anne explained when both women were seated. "But lately he's been very restless."

"And that means what for you exactly?"

Anne thought about the question for a moment.

"It doesn't necessarily mean more work in a physical sense, but he's on my mind more, and of course that can be very tiring."

"I saw him not too long ago and thought he looked very well."

"Yes, he does. He enjoys rather good health for all his absentminded ways."

"So he eats regularly?"

Anne chuckled a little before saying, "Not always at home, but I can tell that he never goes without."

Lucy could not say the same of her friend. Anne didn't look unwell or ill-fed; indeed, her color was very good, but Lucy couldn't help but wonder when Anne had last enjoyed a new dress, or even a pair of gloves or hat. Lucy's own husband was not a wealthy man, but one look at her friend told Lucy she had so much more.

The women visited until Lucy's two-year-old, Meg, woke from her nap. After spending a little time with the toddler, Anne went on her way. She wasn't in a hurry to leave, but hers was a long walk home.

❧ ❧

Levens Crossing

"Did you eat something, Father?" Anne Gardiner asked of her only parent, her eyes watchful of his face. The plate of food before him looked untouched. She had not made a large meal—it was just the two of them—but what little he'd served himself seemed forgotten.

Colonel Gardiner did not answer. He gazed across the room, his bushy brows making him look rather fierce. He wasn't. He was naturally kind at heart, but since his illness he'd become rather unpredictable.

"Father?" Anne tried again. This time he turned.

"Yes."

"How is your breakfast?"

"Very good," he said, sounding confident and reaching for his fork. "I need a good meal before I go on maneuvers this afternoon."

Anne knew that he would be doing no such thing, but she took it in stride. For years now she'd been accustomed to the unexpected in her life, so Anne only smiled a little and turned from his side. "I'll be outside if you need me. I need to fix that leak in the roof."

No answer was forthcoming, but then Anne had not expected any. Her mind on the task that awaited her, she slipped out the back door of the small home they occupied and took hold of the short ladder that stood nearby.

Water was leaking into the dining room. It had rained nearly all night, and in the morning the floor had been wet. The house was in need of great repair as it was—a soaked floor and ceiling would not help anything. Anne thought she might have spotted the problem, and with a prayer for personal safety, she set the wobbly ladder as best she could and began to climb.

Thankfully the roof was lower to the ground on this corner of the house. By standing on the very top rung of the ladder, some five feet in the air, Anne could reach the thatched roof with a stretch of her toes.

She was intent on her job when a small carriage approached. It was an open carriage, pulled by one horse, and carrying just one man: Robert Weston. Approaching the door of the cottage, Weston rapped several times but received no answer.

He wasn't lost, although this was his first trip to Collingbourne since he was a lad. He had stopped because he hadn't remembered the existence of this cottage. It sat some five miles from Brown Manor to the north—only two miles from town to the south—and Weston was frankly inquisitive about the owners.

He was eager to see Brown Manor, but curiosity drove him to stop. A noise at the side of the house sent him in that direction. He rounded the corner to find Anne on the ladder.

Unfortunately, Anne did not hear him.

"I say," he began, "would you be so kind—"

"Oh!" Anne started violently before he could complete his sentence, teetered a few seconds, and then completely lost her balance. One moment she was on the ladder, and the next moment she was in the arms of a strange man, her eyes looking up into eyes as large and surprised as her own.

"I'm terribly sorry," Weston began as he gingerly set her down, his hands making sure she was steady on her feet.

"Thank you for catching me. I simply didn't hear you."

"Anne?" a voice called from behind the couple. Anne turned to her father with a sinking heart.

"We have a guest, Father."

"Is this your intended, Anne?" the Colonel inquired.

"No, no, certainly not, Father. I'm sure I can explain."

"What are your intentions, young man?" the Colonel came forward, and for the first time Weston noticed not only his uniform but the large sword at his side. Up to that point he'd been ready to make light of the situation, but as the older man drew near, he read something in his eyes that sent frissons of fear down his back.

"Father," Anne tried again.

"It's all right, dear," he assured her in a tone she knew all too well. "I can handle this. Now, sir, you will tell me your name and how you plan to support my daughter."

Looking as thunderstruck as he felt, Weston made the mistake of hesitating. A moment later, the Colonel reached for his sword.

"Did I not make myself clear?" he demanded, the sword now pointed at Weston's broad chest. "I wish to know your intentions with my Anne."

Completely without fear for herself, Anne placed herself between Weston and sword, her voice and face calm, but every inch of her trembling.

"Father," she said sweetly, true to her very real nature, "I do not wish you to harm this man."

The Colonel calmed some. He lowered his sword point toward the ground and relaxed back on one heel.

"Of course you don't. You love him. And in light of that, I think the wedding should take place immediately."

"If you would let me explain," Weston spoke up, certain the man would see reason. "I'm just moving into the area. I'm sorry to have disturbed you this way."

"No disturbance at all," the Colonel said expansively. "Anne's intended is always welcome in my home."

"No, sir, I'm sorry you've mistaken me for someone else. Your daughter and I are not getting married."

The sword came back up with alarming speed.

Anne turned her back on her father and faced Weston.

"Please," Anne begged quietly, looking up at him with pleading eyes. "Please go along with anything I do. If you don't go along with this, he will harm you, I promise."

"Go along with what exactly?" Weston asked, his low voice matching hers.

"You'll have to marry me."

Weston looked at her in such horror that Anne's face flooded with heat. But this was no time to think of herself. Humiliated as she was, Weston was in real danger, and she was determined not to have him harmed. She turned back to her father and spoke firmly, hoping it would work.

"There is no reason to rush, Father. We have plenty of time. Did you finish your meal?"

"He had his hands on you, Anne. I won't have you treated with such disregard."

Anne knew there was no reason to continue. If he could have been distracted, it would have happened by now.

"Come along!" the Colonel demanded. "We'll take this carriage and go right to Croft's office. What time is it?" the Colonel, stopping, now asked his only child.

"Near noon," Anne said.

"Croft will be at home. We'll head directly there."

The Colonel strode toward the carriage but then stopped. He caught Weston's gaze with his own and motioned him forward, using the sword. He waited until both Anne and Weston started toward him before turning and climbing into the back. Weston, still in shock and walking slowly, looked to Anne.

"Is this some type of gag?"

"No, and I'm so sorry. I'll explain things as soon as I'm able."

"I would like an explanation now," Weston told her, his voice tight.

"Well, the last time—" Anne began.

"The last time?" Weston said, nearly losing his composure altogether. "What is the matter with you people?"

"Anne!" her father's voice boomed from the carriage.

Anne picked up the pace even as she attempted to draw a calming breath.

"I'm really most dreadfully sorry—I can't tell you how much—but if you don't wish to be harmed, you'll have to wait for your explanation."

Not waiting for a reply, Anne covered the distance to the carriage. A weaker woman would have been crying by now, but Anne had learned long ago that tears were very little help.

Weston followed a little more slowly but then sped up when he saw Anne trying to climb into the carriage unassisted. Her father, who was seated in the rear, made no move to help her. Anne turned to look at the man who had given her a gentle hand up, wondering for the first time who he was.

Weston climbed into the carriage but decided to try one last plea. When he turned and found the sword, three feet of polished, gleaming steel, laid across the Colonel's lap, he changed his mind and resigned himself to the nightmare.

"Where to?"

"Anne will show you."

The carriage jerked into motion, and with two quietly spoken directions from Anne, it stopped before a lovely home just a mile and a half away. The Colonel jumped down and strode to the door.

"Croft! Are you at home? Anne is to be wed!"

The door opened just before he could pound, and the Colonel strode in, clearly a man with a purpose.

Anne was climbing from the carriage when she felt Weston's hands assisting her. Once on the ground, she stood and looked up at him.

"Did you say you're now living in Collingbourne?"

"Yes."

Anne nodded with regret.

"If you were just passing through the area, you could probably leave now and this would all be over, but Father remembers things at the oddest times, and if you're making your home here, I'm afraid you're rather stuck."

Weston tried to tell himself that this was not Anne's fault. Clearly she was as helpless as he, but suddenly he was angry with her. He didn't care if the man tracked him or not. How could this woman stand there and expect him to go through with this?

Whether or not Weston would have made a run for it, Anne was not to know. Her father burst from Mr Croft's home just a moment later, sword on the attack, looking for the man who must marry his daughter.

"What's keeping you?"

Anne went forward into the house, not looking back but sensing that the man was wise enough to know he'd been beaten.

"Hello, Anne," Mrs Croft greeted as she stood waiting, her face filled with compassion. She was a woman Anne had grown up knowing, one who had been kind and known her mother.

"Hello, Mrs Croft. There was no persuading him, and I don't wish this man to be harmed."

"Of course not. Mr Croft is all set."

"Thank you."

"Welcome," Mr Croft, Collingbourne's oldest and most respected justice of the peace, greeted the man who had just entered his parlor. "I'm Mr Croft, and you are?"

"Robert Weston."

"Welcome, Mr Weston. If you'll stand right here...that's it. Anne, come stand beside him. Good, good." Having given these directions, he turned to the father of the bride. "Now I think, Colonel, that you can put that sword away," Croft said calmly, even as he remembered the last time and the horrible loss of blood. "This is a happy occasion; no need for force."

"Very well, but he was holding Anne very close, and I wish for the ceremony to commence."

"And it shall."

What happened in the next few moments was so stunning and confusing to Weston that he could barely think. He'd read of men who were shanghaied into the Royal Navy, and he thought about how it would feel to wake up and find yourself at sea. At the moment he thought he might be able to relate most keenly.

"Now then," Mr Croft suddenly said, the ceremony over. "You may turn and face the Colonel and my wife. Allow me to present Mr and Mrs Weston. We won't keep you. Feel free to be off at any time."

The Colonel came forward to shake Weston's hand and kiss his daughter. As he was giving Anne a hug, the justice pulled Weston to the side.

"Anne will explain everything to you. Just leave now and listen to her."

All Weston heard was the part about leaving. He found Anne at his side and turned for the door. His action automatic, he took Anne's arm, walked to the carriage, and helped her in. Once the reins were in his hands, he set off toward Brown Manor.

"Again, I'm so sorry," Anne said quietly. "Maybe you'd rather not hear the explanation just now."

When he said nothing, Anne fell quiet for a moment. A few glances at his stern profile kept her silent until she noticed that he was headed away from town, the horse moving at a brisk pace.

"If you'll just drop me here, Mr Weston, I can find my way back."

In all honesty Weston did not hear her. His mind was spinning with the events of the past hour, unable to make sense of any of it.

"Mr Weston?" Anne tried a little way down the road. "I wish to stop now."

Anne felt some alarm when he didn't even look at her, but compassion overtook her and she let him have his peace. She wondered how many miles she would have to walk to get back to town tonight. Not until she'd thought this through did she look up and notice they were almost to Brown Manor. Word of Alice Dixon's death had reached the village several weeks back, but Brown Manor had been empty for more than a year, and folks thought little of it.

She had just learned that the man beside her was Mr Weston, and for a moment Anne racked her brain to remember how he might be related to Mrs Dixon.

"Well, here we are." Weston said his first words in many minutes, and Anne watched as he climbed down, came around to her side, and, with an impatient hand, helped her to the ground. He took her swiftly inside one of the grandest homes she'd ever seen, but there was no time to admire. Once in the entryway, a man met them, and Mr Weston proceeded to speak more words than Anne had yet heard from him.

"It's taken me nearly the entire ride to figure you out," he said coldly, his eyes equally so before they turned away from her.

"Mansfield, this is my *wife*," he went on in a tone that kept Anne frozen in place. "Have you hired someone to clean?"

"Not yet, sir."

"Good."

Weston turned back now, his eyes fierce with betrayal.

"How many times have you and your father gotten away with this? How many times has he posed as a mad officer and used his daughter for financial gain? Well, it's not going to work this time. You want to be my wife? Fine! You can clean my home from top to bottom."

With one last blistering look, Weston turned back to Mansfield.

"As you can see, I've managed to gain a *scullery maid* for a wife." He gritted the words out. "Please see to it that she works hard. I'll return in less than a fortnight."

Not another word was spoken as Weston turned on his heel and strode back out the door. For a full 30 seconds the two stood and stared at the door that had closed in his wake. Anne was the first to look away, and she naturally looked to the manservant. He turned and spoke the moment he felt her eyes on him.

"Should I show you around, Mrs Weston?"

"It's Miss," Anne informed him quietly. "Miss Gardiner."

Mansfield's eyes were sharp and his hearing was excellent. There was no missing the tone of her voice or her ladylike stance and gestures.

"You are not a scullery maid, Miss Gardiner."

"No, I am not, but I do not blame Mr Weston for seeing me as such." Anne gestured rather helplessly. "He's upset."

Seeing she was going to give no thought to herself, Mansfield said, "I believe I should first show you to a guest room, Miss Gardiner, but I fear that you won't find it very clean."

"Well, maybe that's where I should start to work then."

The servant looked as though he would protest, but Anne held her hand up.

"It's the least I can do, Mansfield. Mr Weston has been very put upon, and I wish to make amends."

The tall servant disapproved with every line of his body but kept silent. Leading the way through the entryway and down the long hallways, he took the stairs that led to the bedrooms.

"Will this be comfortable for you?" Mansfield asked, opening a door that led to a spacious but sparsely furnished room.

"This will be fine, Mansfield, thank you. Now if you'll show me where I can gain cleaning supplies, I'll get to work."

"Miss Gardiner, if I may suggest—"

"Thank you, Mansfield, but I think this is best."

The servant gave up. He led the way to the stairs that went down to the lower levels and servants' quarters, the kitchen and spacious storerooms. Not ten minutes passed before Anne was armed with cleaning supplies and headed to work. She wished she would have been given a chance to explain and persuade Mr Weston to leave her close to the Crofts', but it was not to be. Accustomed to hard work, she knew right now she would have to make the best of things.

✺ ✺

"I half expected Anne to be sipping tea in our kitchen by now," Mrs Croft said to her husband that afternoon when she found him reading in the den.

"Did she never check back with you?" Croft asked.

"No. Do you think there's cause for alarm?"

"I don't think so. We certainly don't know this Weston chap, but Anne is resourceful. She's probably gotten a ride to the manse on her own. Weston might have taken her himself."

"I hope so. Are you certain she'll go to Pastor Hurst?"

"Nearly certain. He always steers her the right way."

Mrs Croft worried her handkerchief for a moment.

"I had hoped after the last time that this would never happen again."

"Anne did the right thing. The Colonel is not to be trusted. He was very upset when he realized he cut that last chap, but he doesn't feel that way until after the damage is done."

"But that last young man had a connection to the area," Mrs Croft argued. "This young man might be cut from a different cloth, and who could blame him if he wishes to press charges?"

Croft set his paper aside and looked to his wife.

"It might be the best thing that could happen. The village has put up with the Colonel's antics for years, and Anne wears herself out trying to keep up with him. Word of the last incident never got out, but one of these days he might seriously injure someone. We'll let this run its course."

That said, the man put his nose back into the newspaper. Mrs Croft thought he might be right, but that didn't stop her heart from wondering just exactly what had become of Anne Gardiner.

∾ ∾

Brown Manor

Daylight was fading and rain had begun when Anne made her way down to the kitchen. She had cleaned several rooms from top to bottom, and she was tired to the bone. If she didn't find something to eat soon, however, she was not going to have the strength to even climb into bed.

She was still approaching the room when the smell of food assailed her senses. Her mouth began to water so profusely that she was forced to swallow several times. She stepped into the room to find Mansfield, apron in place, working over a large pot.

"Miss Gardiner," he began at once, reaching to remove his apron. "I was going to bring you a tray."

The proof of this statement was on the table. A tray was fully laid: bread, butter, jam, tea and service, plus a large soup bowl, presumably to hold some of the contents of the pot still cooking on the stove.

"Thank you, but I believe I will sit right here and eat whatever you have to offer."

"I would be happy to deliver this above stairs," Mansfield insisted.

Anne did not answer. She sat down, bowed her head to say a brief prayer, looked up again, and reached for the bread and butter.

Mansfield could see that she was not to be swayed. He served her a hot bowl of thick beef soup just moments later.

"I'm sorry I do not have more courses to offer you."

"There is no need," she assured him, taking a spoonful of soup into her mouth and looking up in surprise.

"A manservant who cooks. Does Mr Weston know what he has in you?"

Mansfield nodded ever so slightly at the compliment. He looked pleased without smiling.

They didn't converse past this point. Weary as she was, Anne certainly had questions but knew that it was not her business how Mr Weston came to be in this home and why Mansfield was here alone. She realized she didn't want to stay for two weeks, but the house did need cleaning, and she still believed it was the least she could do under the circumstances. If she finished cleaning everything ahead of time, she thought she might ask Mansfield to take her into town. Indeed, that was preferable to meeting the irate Mr Weston again.

Mansfield, for his part, was doing his best to be invisible, knowing he could eat when the lady was finished. Something was not right. His master was not a mean-spirited or spiteful man. That he would leave this lady to clean his home meant he had truly taken her for some type of unscrupulous pretender. Mansfield believed that if Mr Weston had taken the time to get to know her at all, he would have seen otherwise. As it was, all of the answers to Mansfield's questions would have to wait.

"Thank you." Anne spoke quietly into his busy thoughts, and he turned to her.

"It was my pleasure. May I do something to make you more comfortable tonight? More tea perhaps?"

"Thank you, but I will be retiring. I would make one request of you in the morning. Should it be impossible for me to complete the house in the days before Mr Weston returns, perhaps you would be so kind as to give some direction. If it would be helpful for me to do some rooms ahead of others, I would like to know."

Mansfield only nodded to this request, his very being radiating with rebellion at the thought.

Anne took little notice. She was too tired to think about his feelings and wanted only her bed. Retiring to the room she'd been given, Anne looked at the dress she'd just removed, knowing that even with its dark color, it wasn't going to last through two weeks of the work she was doing. She washed out her undergarments, swathed herself in a spare sheet, and climbed into bed. She was tired and a bit achy but had a sense of having worked hard and done well.

She prayed for Mr Weston, wherever he might be, and for a chance to explain to him that she and her father were not ruthless charlatans. It occurred to her that he might have gone to the authorities, but she knew many people who would vouch for her father's mental condition. It was only to be hoped that when she explained, he would understand.

Still praying, she dropped off to sleep, never dreaming that her father would wake in the morning and do something he'd never done before.

As soon as it was light, the Colonel headed into town. He told each one he passed that his Anne had been married the day before. He couldn't remember the man's name, but married she was, and wasn't that a delight?

When asked where Anne was at the moment, his answer was simple: "With her husband on their honeymoon."

Chapter Two

Tipton

"How are you?" Marianne Jennings asked of her sister-in-law, Lydia Palmer, as she joined her in the large salon.

Lydia, very expectant with her fifth child and taking her ease, answered after Marianne leaned to hug and kiss her.

"I'm very well. Palmer wants me to go easy these days, so I can't even claim to be tired."

"So there's been no more sneaking around when he's not looking?"

Lydia laughed over this because she had done that very thing one day last week, been caught, and now knew the story had leaked out.

"How did you hear?"

"Palmer told Jennings," Marianne said with a smile, her own five-month pregnancy not very obvious at this point.

"And what did my brother have to say?"

"He thought you mad and would have scolded you had you been present."

Lydia smiled. "I'm glad I missed it."

"I assume that Palmer took it in stride?"

"He laughed, but I told him I wouldn't do it again."

"And what was it that you *had* to get done?" Marianne asked, a smile in her voice.

Lydia laughed again, and the women were still talking when they were joined by their husbands, Frank Palmer and William Jennings. The men kissed their wives and took seats, Palmer's face rather sober.

"I've news from town," Palmer told his wife with little hesitation. "Word is that Anne Gardiner was married yesterday and is now on her honeymoon."

"Oh, Palmer," Lydia said with great compassion. "What has the Colonel done now?"

"I don't know."

"Where is she really?" Marianne asked.

"No one seems to know."

"Who was this man?"

Palmer shrugged. "I wish I had more details, but I've told you what I know."

The foursome, who knew Anne from church, stared at each other for the space of several seconds. All were silently praying, but any further talk would have to wait. The voices of the Palmer and Jennings children, all seven of them ranging in age from five to thirteen, could be heard as they approached, and, at least for the moment, thoughts of Anne Gardiner had to be put aside.

∾ ∾

Brown Manor

"Mansfield?" Anne asked the morning of her third day. "I can't seem to locate any polish, and I want to do those mirrors in the hallway."

"I believe I can locate some for you. If not, I'll put it on my list for London."

"Benwick's should have it—in Collingbourne."

"I've not shopped in town yet. Is it on Main Street?"

"Yes, to the south in the center block."

"If I do go to town, is there something I can get for you, Miss Gardiner?"

"Well, depending on when I'm finished here, I would like to go back toward town."

"Are you from Collingbourne?" Mansfield asked in surprise, as this just now occurred to him. "Do you live around here?"

"Yes," Anne told him with her sweet smile. "I live at Levens Crossing."

"I would be happy to take you anywhere you wish, Miss Gardiner, at any time you wish. Indeed, we can leave this moment!"

Anne was surprised by his vehemence and didn't answer. Mansfield felt he must go on, albeit more calmly.

"Please do not feel an obligation here, Miss Gardiner. I'm certain that as soon as Mr Weston returns, he'll ask me to begin hiring a staff."

Anne shook her head. "Thank you, but I think I'd best finish."

Mansfield said nothing. He knew that many a man in his position would look down on this woman who did the work of a servant when she was a lady by birth, but he felt only compassion for a woman who was obviously stuck in her circumstances.

"Would you look for that polish now?" Anne asked kindly.

"Of course," Mansfield replied and went on his way.

Anne looked after him. She could see where his thoughts had been headed and knew he needed to be rescued. It was true she wasn't able to live in the style to which she'd been born, but she wasn't sorry for herself. Neither did she wish anyone else to be sorry for her. But more than that, she had to take her father into account. He may or may not remember her "marriage" when he saw her again, but if he did it wouldn't do to have him see her too soon without the groom in attendance. Even if she finished her work at Brown Manor, she wouldn't be headed for Levens Crossing; she'd be headed to the home of a friend where she could lay low for as long as she needed.

⮜ ⮞

London

"Mother, did you hear me?" Weston asked after he'd explained what had happened.

"I did, Robert, but it's just too fantastic to be real."

Weston took a seat, his mind having had the same thoughts, but he'd lived it and it had been amazingly real.

"What will you do?" his mother finally asked.

"What I should have done in the first place, go back and calmly ask Anne what's going on."

"That's her name—Anne?"

"Yes."

"Anne what?"

"I think the justice of the peace said Garden or Gardiner."

Lenore nodded but didn't comment.

Weston caught his mother's look and questioned her.

"What are you thinking?"

Lenore hated the tears that came to her eyes, but her compassionate heart overflowed.

"I'm sorry this awful thing happened to you, Robert, and if it turns out to be a huge masquerade, I'll know I wasted my sorrow on this young woman, but I can't help but think she was just as trapped as you were. More so."

"I did think of that, but not until I was much calmer."

"Why did you not go straight back?"

"In my panic, my first thought was to return to London to see my solicitor, something I decided not to do. On top of that, by the time I could think clearly I was almost here and wanted you to hear what happened from me before any word floated back this way."

"I appreciate that, but I'm glad you're going back. I so wanted you to fit in and enjoy that community."

"I'm returning in the morning."

"Would you like me to come with you?"

"Thank you, Mother, but I want you to visit under better circumstances."

"Write to me." She put a hand out and he took it. "Keep me informed, and when the time comes, invite me for a visit."

"I'll do that, I hope, very soon."

❧ ❧

Brown Manor

The fifth day had arrived, and Anne was nearly certain it would be her last. If walking back to the village was necessary, she might not be able to manage that until morning, but she was confident of finishing her work by bedtime. The 15-hour days were starting to wear on her, but she hoped the end was in sight.

"Miss Gardiner," Mansfield said, interrupting her cleaning of the fireplace in the library, "I'm going to Collingbourne. Would you care to join me?"

"You're leaving now?"

"Yes, unless you plan to join me and need some time. In that case I'll wait as long as you like."

Anne smiled at him.

"I'll remain here, but I believe I'll be finished today and on my way tomorrow."

"As you wish," Mansfield forced himself to say, wishing he could persuade her otherwise.

"You won't forget more polish, will you?" Anne now questioned him.

"No, I will not," Mansfield forced these words out as well, having learned in the last five days that he was not even able to stay in the room while she was cleaning. "Is there anything else?"

"I don't believe so. If I had to stay longer I would need some things from home, but I do think I'm nearly finished."

Mansfield bowed his head in answer and moved to the carriage he had waiting. He was not in the least put out about doing for himself when he was accustomed to ordering other servants about, but the situation with Miss Gardiner was almost more than he could tolerate. That she had kept her appearance fresh, her hair neat and out of her face, and her manner kind and congenial, was amazing to him, but it wasn't enough. This woman was a gentle creature. She had no business cleaning anything.

❧ ❧

Levens Crossing

Weston rapped on the door of Anne's house for a full minute before going around the back. Fearful of meeting up with her father, he moved cautiously but found no one. The back door was standing ajar, and Weston took the liberty of checking inside. Completely missing his surroundings and noticing only that no one answered his calls, he slipped back out the way he'd come and into his carriage.

He had half expected to find someone at home and was let down over the outcome. It passed through his mind that the woman he supposedly married was still at Brown Manor, but that seemed too preposterous to be true.

Ah, well, he thought silently. *I'm sure to have bridges to patch with the way I left, but I hope Mansfield can tell me where I'll find the Colonel and his daughter.*

❧ ❧

Brown Manor

"Welcome, sir," Mansfield greeted his master in the heat of the afternoon. "How was your trip?"

"It was fine, Mansfield. Are you alone here?"

"No, sir."

Having dreaded that answer, Weston looked into the eyes of his servant.

"So she's been here since I left?"

"Yes, sir."

"Doing what?" Weston made himself ask, fearing the answer with all his heart.

"Cleaning," Mansfield informed him, not able to keep the tensity from his voice.

Weston studied him.

"She's not a maid, is she?"

"Not remotely, sir."

But then why? The question reverberated in Weston's mind concerning several aspects of this entire ordeal, but he didn't voice his confusion. The only person who could give him answers was inside.

Handing his hat to Mansfield, Weston went that way.

ᔥ ᔧ

The first mirror Anne polished in the downstairs hall looked spectacular, until she dropped her eyes to her own reflection and winced with regret. Time in front of the mirror had not been a high priority in the last few days. Anne knew that it would be obvious to anyone who looked at her.

"Oh, well, keep going," she said quietly to herself, and moved to the next gilt frame. She was half done with it when movement in the glass told her someone had come up behind her. In the mirror she met the gaze of the man she'd "married." Her heart plummeting to her toes, she turned, keeping her back to the wall as she balled the cleaning rag in her fist.

Weston came a bit closer but saw the uncertainty in her eyes and kept some distance between them.

"I stopped at your home but found it empty."

"Did you?" Anne asked, her voice a little breathless.

"Miss?"

"Gardiner."

"Miss Gardiner," Weston started kindly, "I can't tell you how sorry I am to have left you here the way I did. Truly, I never wished for you to work. I deeply regret my words and actions."

"Please, Mr Weston," Anne cut in, "it is I who owe you such a great apology. I'm so sorry for all you had to go through. Father is not a well man, and I feared you would be harmed. I wish I could have presented another way, but he was most determined."

Weston nodded, not certain what to say next. The woman before him looked exhausted. He had not taken time to look around when he'd dropped her off, but if she'd been cleaning since he left, she was quite naturally spent.

"Mansfield tells me you've been working."

Anne looked away.

"I felt it was the least I could do."

"I'm sorry I placed that burden on you. Please allow me to take you home, Miss Gardiner."

"Weston?" a soft feminine voice floated to the couple from around the corner, coming from the entryway that led to the front door.

"Henrietta," Weston breathed softly, the woman before him forgotten. Without a glance in Anne's direction, he moved toward the voice.

"Weston!" the woman cried in delight.

"Henrietta! What are you doing here?"

"I've missed you so."

That was all Anne stayed for. Slipping down the hallway and finding the stairs, she set her cleaning supplies on a table in the kitchen. Mansfield was nowhere to be seen, but that didn't stop her. She went to the door, skirted the large manor house, and started up the driveway that led to the road. It was time to go home.

≈ ≈

"Weston?" Henrietta asked cautiously, realizing she was hugging him but not being hugged in return.

"How are you, Henrietta?" Weston asked with more calm than he felt, his hands still at his sides.

"I'm well. I missed you. Did you not miss me?"

Weston hesitated. He had only just remembered the way he'd left Anne in the hallway, and for a moment was bereft of words.

"It's nice of you to stop by," Weston finally managed, sounding inane even to his own ears.

"Stop by?" Henrietta said on a laugh. "I'm here for a visit. Surely you didn't think otherwise."

"That's impossible, Henrietta." Weston felt he had to be direct. "The house is not ready for guests, and on top of that, I'm here alone."

Henrietta's look turned playful. She walked around her host, her eyes taking in every detail of Brown Manor.

"Things don't look needy in the least, Weston," Henrietta said as she walked away from him. "Why don't you ring for tea and invite me to join you?"

Weston trailed in Henrietta's wake, knowing that for the moment he would simply do as she asked. His head turned in all directions for a glimpse of Anne, but he didn't spot her.

Once in the square salon, Weston rang for Mansfield. That man found him less than two minutes later, and Weston requested tea.

"Mansfield bringing the tea? When you have a guest? You *are* alone here."

Weston didn't answer. Henrietta pretended not to notice and began to study the room.

"I remember visiting here with you when we were children, Weston. I was so thrilled to hear you were moving to Brown Manor."

"I heard you had moved to France."

"That's true," Henrietta said, some of the pleasure missing from her voice. "I didn't expect to miss London as I do."

Silence fell thick and uncomfortable between them. Henrietta had pictured Weston nothing like this, and Weston remembered her as being quite different.

"Why have you come, Henrietta?" Weston put it on the line as soon as Mansfield had served them and vacated the room.

Henrietta put her cup aside. She stood and moved to the window. She spoke with her eyes on the prospect beyond.

"Andre has asked me to marry him. I wanted to say yes, but you kept coming to mind." Henrietta looked back at Weston. "I began to doubt my reasons for breaking off with you. I wanted to see you so badly. I told Andre that I couldn't marry him until I was sure."

"And are you certain now?"

Henrietta shook her head miserably.

"You're not the same, Weston. You were supposed to still love me."

"It's been a year, Henrietta," he said reasonably. "And you were the one who left me. I have no wish to be cruel, but how could I trust you to know your feelings from this time forward? You're seeing this Andre chap now, but after you left me I heard that Perry was pursuing you and that you were not running."

Henrietta looked guilty and miserable at the same time.

"I'll always care, Henrietta," Weston said quietly. "But I can't trust my heart in your hands—they're much too careless."

The woman across from him bit her lip and turned back to the window to compose herself. Weston had not wanted to hurt her, but he felt he must be honest.

"I think I must go," Henrietta said after some moments of quiet. She turned to look at Weston now, seeming to be in control once again. "I believe I'll go on to Bath for a few weeks. My aunt is still there and wrote me recently."

"Give her my greetings," Weston said, wanting to set their relationship back on a kind footing, but even as he said this, something came to mind, something that Henrietta had said to him when she'd broken off the relationship.

"Have you found a good church in France, Henrietta?"

In the front hall and nearly to the door, she stopped, looking surprised.

"I haven't looked. Why do you ask?"

"I just recall something you said to me many months ago. I'd not thought of it until this moment, but now I'm wondering what you meant when you said it would never work between us since I took religion more seriously than you did. I barely heard you at the time, but now I do wonder what you meant."

"It's not complex, Weston," she told him, a bit of irritation showing. "Your very question just now proves my point. Of all the things you could ask me, you speak of religion!"

"Not religion, Henrietta, but of being involved and a part of a church body. How else is one to grow and change to be like Christ?"

This statement, although said kindly, seemed to agitate Henrietta in a way that Weston had never seen before. He watched as her chin went in the air and her eyes raked him.

"I can see now that you think yourself somehow superior to me. I never noticed that about you before, Weston, but I'm very glad I saw it in time."

"That's enough, Henrietta," Weston said, his voice still quiet and calm. "We both know that this is between you and God. Do not start hurling accusations at me to make yourself feel better."

Henrietta had the good grace to look shamed.

"I'm going now, Weston," she said, all fire gone, her eyes not meeting his. "I wish it could have been different between us, but I can see now that it would never work."

"Please take care of yourself, Henrietta, and know you're in my prayers."

This was too much. Henrietta bit her lip and dashed for the door. Weston's heart broke over her upset, but he couldn't see any way around it. She was still so lovely, but she was not the woman for him. That was only too obvious now.

"You rescued me, Lord," Weston stood in his place in the entryway and prayed in wonder and awe. "I ached for Henrietta when she left, fully believing she loved You as I do, but You knew. You took her away with her fickle heart and saved me heartbreak. Thank You, Father. I still hurt. I still care for her. But she doesn't love You, not as she needs to, and a union between us would have been a disaster."

Weston's hand went to the back of his neck. Relieved as he was, he suddenly realized he was tired. He leaned against the wall, starting to wonder if moving to Brown Manor had been a good idea. That thought only lasted a moment. He had a townhouse in London, but this was the first time he'd ever lived in a home of his own.

Weston began to walk slowly down the hall. The detail and layout of this house were favorites of his. The hallways were low-ceilinged, making the first step into high-ceilinged rooms all the grander. The carpets were intricately patterned and still in fine shape. He suspected that the last tenants had done some painting, and he planned right then to continue wherever there was a need. His own furnishings would be coming as soon as he sent for them, but there would also be plenty of time to shop and add things to his liking.

And everything was so clean! Mansfield had certainly been busy. Weston wondered if he'd found help from the village. The thought stopped the owner of Brown Manor in his tracks. Anne! Where had she gone? Had she done all of this cleaning on her own? He must find Mansfield and gain some answers.

"Mansfield!" Weston called, finally running him to earth in the kitchen.

"Did you ring for me, sir?" that servant asked plainly, not having ever heard Weston shouting for him.

"Where is Anne? I mean, Miss Gardiner?"

"I believe she may have left, sir."

"Are you sure of this?"

"I am not. I was unwilling to search for her while you still had a guest."

"Miss Rooke has left. Let us ascertain whether Miss Gardiner is still on the premises and then go after her if she is not."

"Very well. I shall ready the carriage and prepare something for her to eat and drink."

"Did she not eat today?"

"Not since breakfast early this morning."

Weston forced himself to remain calm as he looked around, calling Anne's name from time to time. When he gained the kitchen again ten minutes later, he saw what Mansfield had seen some time earlier: Anne's polish and cleaning rag had been left on the table.

"Are you ready?" Weston asked of Mansfield, clearly eager to be off.

Mansfield was not one to keep his master waiting. They left just moments later.

Chapter Three

Anne was off the road and sitting in the shade of a tree when Weston and Mansfield went past in Weston's large, open carriage. It was disheartening to say the least, but she had resigned herself to walking and would continue to do so as soon as the sun dropped a bit more. She would barely make it home before dark and would have no choice but to stay there overnight, but hopefully her father would have forgotten the events of the last week.

Anne thought about lying down but suddenly heard another carriage, this time from the direction of town. When she saw that it was Weston again, she stood but remained under the tree. As she watched, the carriage pulled off and both men alighted. Weston started toward her, and Mansfield came as soon as he had gathered a hamper and blanket.

"Hello, Miss Gardiner. Are you well?"

"Yes, thank you."

"May I join you?"

"Certainly."

"This is a fine spot," Weston proclaimed, his head tipping back to see the trees just as Mansfield began to lay out the blanket.

"Are you having a picnic?" Anne asked of him, stepping aside so the blanket could be smoothed at the corner; it had been literally laid at her feet.

"*We,* Miss Gardiner, *we* are having a picnic. Mansfield tells me you have not eaten recently, and my last meal is but a memory, so we shall partake. Then I will deliver you in the carriage to wherever you wish to go."

"That's very kind of you, Mr Weston, but you didn't have to bother."

"No bother at all. Come. Have a seat, and we'll see what Mansfield has packed."

Anne sank onto the blanket, not wishing to seem ungrateful but suddenly embarrassed in front of these two men. Collingbourne was not London, and Anne couldn't help but notice how elegantly Mr Weston was dressed. Mansfield himself was outfitted in some of the finest attire Anne had ever seen. Her own simple gown—not nearly as fresh as she would have liked—seemed like a rag in comparison.

"Let me begin by offering my most sincere apology to you, Miss Gardiner. I left you standing in my hallway in a rude fashion. My guest was most unexpected, but that doesn't excuse my behavior. I am sorry."

"It's all right, truly. I understood."

"Do you enjoy fruit?" Weston asked without warning.

"Yes, thank you," Anne answered automatically. "Anything will be fine."

The twosome dined in silence for the next several minutes, but when Anne had refreshed herself with lemon water and some of the food from her plate, Weston began to question her.

"Has your father been confused for long?"

"More than ten years now," Anne answered, happy to explain her parent's actions. "He ran a fever that nothing could break. It lasted for days. I was sure he would die at any time, but he seemed to cling to life with a fierce tenacity. When he awoke and asked for water, he didn't know who I was. He eventually remembered me, but many things have slipped away from his mind. I think I'm one of the few things he does remember, so he tends to be rather protective." Anne blushed at the thought of all her father had put this man through and ducked her head under the guise of reaching for more food from her plate.

"How long have you lived at Levens Crossing?"

"Just a few years."

"And before then?"

Weston's voice was so gentle that Anne found herself sharing.

"We lived at Stone Hall. Do you know it?"

"Yes. Brown Manor was my grandmother's home. I visited here often as a child and know many of the homes."

"Mrs Dixon was your grandmother?"

"Yes."

"We heard of her passing. I'm sorry for your loss."

"Thank you."

Silence fell yet again, but Anne didn't notice. Not having felt particularly hungry, she now realized how wrong she had been. It was kind of Mr Weston to offer her a ride, but in truth she now felt refreshed enough to walk the distance.

"That was lovely," Anne said as she put her plate aside. "Thank you."

"Can I offer you more?"

"I'll just finish my water and be fine. Thank you again."

Weston nodded, and wishing to return Anne safely back to her life as soon as possible, finished his own food.

"Mansfield," Anne turned to him, "did you find the cleaning supplies I left?"

"I did, Miss Gardiner. Thank you."

Anne was opening her mouth to thank him for his kindness of the last days when yet another carriage was heard in the distance. Anne looked with curiosity—this road not being heavily traveled—until she saw the occupant of the fine coach.

"Oh, it's Mr Daniels," she said under her breath, just before ducking her head.

Both men heard her, but their eyes were on the man who had nearly poked his head from the carriage to gawk at them.

Weston waved before looking back to Anne. Only then did her comment make sense to him. Anne had angled her body in such a way that her face was turned completely away from the road. That Anne had known the rider was now fully clear.

"Did you say his name was Daniels?"

"Yes."

"And you know him?"

"I do, yes."

"I think you did not wish him to see you."

Anne now looked into her host's face, her eyes showing dismay.

"I am not certain what conclusions he would draw from our situation just now, and he is not a man afraid to tell what he has seen."

It didn't take long for Weston to understand. Anne's reputation was at stake. As for him, he was new in the area and not yet known. Except for...

"I'd like to ask about Mr and Mrs Croft. Will they be more discreet?"

"Absolutely. Had the ceremony happened in town, it would have been out of their hands, but they are not in the habit of divulging private matters."

Seemingly calm, Weston nodded but said firmly, "I think we must get you home."

"Thank you" was all Anne replied, coming gracefully to her feet.

Once in the carriage, silence fell yet again. Anne found herself wishing she could go home under cover of darkness. She might have been surprised to know that Weston was having the same thoughts, but he knew that taking her back to Brown Manor after dusk could make things even worse.

"To your home?"

"Yes, please."

"When I stopped there, your father was not at home. Will he be there now?"

"It's hard to say. If he's remembered the incident, I rather hope he isn't, but I honestly can't tell you what to expect."

"So he might have forgotten what happened?" Weston had not considered this.

"Certainly. He may remember it forever, or it may have been gone that very day."

"If he has not forgotten, will he welcome you home?"

"Oh, yes."

"And he won't wonder why you're back?"

"I'm not staying. I'm only gathering some of my things."

They were coming to Levens Crossing, and the house was in view just minutes later. Weston helped Anne from the carriage and spoke.

"We will wait until you have what you need and then deliver you wherever you wish to go."

"No," Anne said firmly. "You have been very kind, but I assure you, this way is best."

Weston thought for a moment.

"You will gather your things. Mansfield will take you wherever you wish, and I will remain here. When he has delivered you, he will come back for me."

"No, Mr Weston, it is not necessary, I assure you."

Weston looked about. He couldn't be sure what was over each hill or mound, but from where he stood there was not another home or even a building in sight.

"You mustn't walk laden down with your belongings. Mansfield will take you. You must let me do this, Miss Gardiner. I owe you that much."

"Mr Weston, you forget. It was you who was set upon by my father. You owe me nothing."

"My mind is quite made up. Now gather your things so you and Mansfield can be off."

"And what if my father returns?"

"If he remembers me, I'll tell him the truth: You're visiting friends, and I'm waiting for the carriage." Weston smiled. "He might even offer me tea."

Anne smiled. She couldn't help herself.

"Go along now," Weston said quietly, his eyes watchful.

Anne moved to the door without another word. When she was inside, Weston turned to his manservant.

"Was she this sweet and unspoiled for the last five days?"

"Yes, sir," Mansfield answered quietly.

❧ ❧

The Manse

Anne gladly returned the hug Judith Hurst gave her the moment she was safely inside her pastor's home.

"We've been concerned," Judith offered, holding the younger woman at arm's length so she could study her. Pastor Hurst was next in line, hugging Anne and welcoming her to a comfortable chair.

"Are you all right?"

"I am, yes."

"Would you like something?"

"No, I've just eaten."

"Can you tell us about what has happened, Anne?" the pastor asked kindly.

With a certain measure of relief, Anne did just that, finding that it did her heart good to speak of it.

"You say that when Mr Weston returned, he was calmer?" Pastor asked when the story had been unfolded.

"Yes, even apologetic. I was somewhat amazed."

"How old a man is he?"

"Mid-twenties, I would guess."

"Do you know him, Frederick?" This came from his wife.

"I'm not certain. Maybe I'll have a chance to meet him and find out."

The threesome fell quiet for a few minutes, and then Judith spoke again.

"Anne, we do not have good news for you."

"My father?" She looked pained when she asked.

"He is well, but the day after the incident he went into town and told everyone you'd been married the day before and that you'd gone away on your wedding trip."

"Oh, Father," Anne said quietly, the color draining from her face, her mind scrambling with this new information. Two other times she'd been forced into this same type of "marriage" to satisfy her father's heart, but never had she left with the man. She had certainly never spent five days in his home. Because of her father, Anne's station in town was something of an oddity, but her reputation had never been questioned.

It would seem this would no longer be the case.

"May I stay here?" Anne asked next.

"Of course you may. Judith made a room ready when the news reached us."

"Thank you."

"I think a warm bath..." Judith suggested, and Anne looked so relieved that the older woman smiled. From that point on, even during her bath, Anne bent her mind to dealing with her father.

~ ~

Mansfield returned to Levens Crossing to find Weston waiting patiently on the stone bench in the front yard. Clearly Anne's father had not returned.

"Where did she wish to go?" he asked as soon as the carriage was in motion.

"A manse."

Weston's brows rose.

"At the church were Pastor Hurst ministers?"

"I'm not certain."

Weston described the building, and Mansfield agreed it was the same. The men rode in silence for a time, but Weston had made up his mind just before reaching Brown Manor.

"I'm off to a rocky start here, Mansfield, but I'm still making this move. I'll be starting a list of what I want from London, as well as the shopping I wish to do. Figure out which staff you want to remain in London and which is to come here. Hire whomever you, Cook, and Sally need to run this house."

Mansfield didn't comment, but he was quite satisfied. He felt that Brown Manor suited Mr Weston very well.

ᔥ ᔦ

Tipton

"Hi," Palmer said quietly to his wife on Saturday morning. Lydia was still in bed, having just awakened. "You didn't sleep well."

"No, I didn't. I'm sorry I disturbed you."

Palmer leaned forward and kissed her stomach.

"I'll scold this little person as soon as I meet him."

"You're still certain it's a boy?" she asked with a smile.

He smiled back at her and said only, "Anne is at the manse."

Lydia's sigh was heartfelt.

"You spoke with her?"

"No, but I saw Pastor, and he told me."

"Did you and Jennings have your Bible study already? What time is it?"

"We did study, but it's early. I wanted to get home to you."

"Palmer, I'm sure I can manage church tomorrow. Say you agree."

"Why don't I see if Anne can come here to visit you?"

"But I want to go to church. I can stand in the rear if my back hurts."

"Then everyone will think your pains have started, and no one will be able to concentrate on the sermon."

Lydia was disappointed but understood. She liked the idea of Anne coming to visit, however, and grabbed onto the idea with vigor. She reminded Palmer that he was going to invite Anne right up to the moment he left for church the next morning.

∾ ∾

Collingbourne

The Colonel had not been at home when Anne arrived Saturday morning. The kitchen had been very clean, and she could see that he'd done some marketing, but even though she'd left the manse almost as soon as she'd risen, Anne found her father gone from Levens Crossing. She'd debated her next move until she came to the fork in the road. One stretch led into town and one led back to the manse. She was now in Collingbourne, her father's whereabouts filling her head.

"Mrs Musgrove," she said, stopping that woman on the street. "Have you seen my father?"

"Well, Anne," the woman said quietly, her brows arched. "We'd heard news of your nuptials. Where is your husband?"

Mrs Musgrove made a show of looking around, causing Anne's heart to sink with dread. That Mrs Musgrove was not one of the kinder individuals in town was something to be taken into account, but this first meeting did not bode well.

"Have you seen my father?" Anne asked again, accustomed to dodging questions.

"No, but we've been wondering about your whereabouts."

"Thank you for your concern," Anne said, having to force the words out. "I won't keep you any longer."

Mrs Musgrove, looking smugger than ever, turned to watch Anne move on her way.

Anne walked slowly. Clearly she was going to have to be careful with whom she spoke, and that only made her task more difficult.

With a prayer for wisdom she carried on, careful about catching the eyes of some and working not to imagine condemnation when there was none.

"Miss Gardiner," a whispered voice stopped her when she was halfway down the center block.

Anne looked about and found Tommy Benwick motioning to her. She went to him where he had a door partially open at the side of his father's shop. Anne slipped inside.

"My father wants to see you."

"Oh, Tommy, can it wait? I'm looking for my father."

"I think it's about your father."

Anne followed Tommy without another word and found herself in Benwick's storeroom. She had been in this room a few times over the years and always found it a bit awe-inspiring. Benwick's store was as neat and tidy as anyone could imagine. But the storeroom was another story. Anne had known Benwick to disappear to this room and return to the front just minutes later with a requested item, but how he knew where to look was anyone's guess.

Bolts of fabric were stacked in confused and chaotic disorder, and crates of unknown objects were strewn about. The room was lit by two small windows, with shelves lining every available portion of the walls. Items hung from even the rafters. Anne was still taking it all in, her attention catching from time to time on a certain object, until Benwick himself entered the room.

"Miss Anne," he said, immediately at his most solicitous. "How are you?"

"I'm well, Mr Benwick. Tommy said you have news."

"Indeed, I do. Your father had a bit of a mishap on Wednesday. It's only a sprained ankle, but very painful and swollen. He's most put out about it, but Dr Smith has kept him at his office since it occurred."

Anne's relief was great.

"I'll go there directly, Mr Benwick. Thank you very much."

"You are welcome," he said kindly, but Anne caught a hint of hesitancy in his eyes.

"Maybe it would be best if I exited the way I came."

Benwick's chin jutted suddenly.

"Never, Miss Anne! You are as welcome in my shop as my own family."

"Thank you," Anne replied, giving him a grateful look, "but if I go out the side door," she still felt he needed a rescue, "I'll nearly be at Dr Smith's door."

"As you wish, Miss Anne, but I hope to see you soon."

"And you shall."

Anne went on her way, Benwick holding the door and smiling at her in genuine warmth as she exited. Anne's heart was cheered that at least Benwick did not believe the worst of her reputation. She set her mind to seeing her father, checking on his health, and ascertaining whether he remembered the events of the past week.

≈ ≈

"Palmer," Anne said patiently from her place in the church pew, "you don't know what you're asking."

"I do, Anne," he said with a smile. "Liddy is most eager to see you, and I hate to disappoint her."

"I fear that her disappointment will be the lesser of your problems if I show my face at Tipton."

"You can't honestly think that we believe poorly of you, Anne."

"No, I do not, but I was in town yesterday, and more than one person has made it clear that life in Collingbourne has changed for me." Even as Anne said this, she remembered Mrs Smith's words. She was not an unkind woman, but she was outspoken and had told Anne in plain terms that if she wasn't willing to say where she'd been all week then, indeed, her virtue was in question. Anne had remained mute. Mr Weston was new to the area, and much as Anne hated having aspersions cast upon her, she needed to give Mr Weston a chance to establish himself.

Palmer tried for several more minutes, having taken a seat next to Anne near the front, but she would not be swayed. He was left with no choice but to tell her that if she did change her mind, she would always be welcome. Squeezing her hand, he returned to sit with his children.

Judith Hurst joined her soon after Palmer left, but at the moment Anne's heart was too heavy to speak with her. It was a relief to have Pastor Hurst step into the pulpit a moment later.

"Good morning, friends. I'm going to start in an unorthodox and, for some of you, cryptic manner this morning. If you have not heard rumors from this last week, then there is no cause for worry. If you have heard the rumors that are spreading about one of our own, you need to know firsthand that there is no value or truth to these rumors. If you have not had contact with me or one of the elders, and you do have questions, I hope you will contact one of us today.

"I'm not going to preach on gossip or the evils of it. We've talked enough about that subject to know where God's Word stands, but my words today are simply to warn you to be on guard. Should you hear slander toward one of us, you must speak up and put a stop to it. If you have been talking without information, you must stop. And if you are at all tempted to shun any of our own without due cause, you must repent of that immediately.

"As I said, we are here to help. Come to us with any questions and concerns, and keep this small church body in your prayers lest Satan use this to tear us apart and destroy our unity."

Pastor Hurst paused, his gaze taking in the congregation gathered that morning. There were no visitors or first-timers—he had already checked—but he now took a moment to establish brief eye contact with each one.

"Let us stand now," he said when he broke the silence. "Open your hymnals, and we'll raise our voices in praise to God."

From where Anne was sitting, she had felt Judith squeeze her arm but only nodded in acknowledgment. She feared that if she had eye contact she would become emotional. Neither did she join the singing when the flock began the first hymn. She was too busy praying.

Please, Father, please don't let this congregation suffer for my father's imprudent words or my actions. I see now that I was caught off guard and should not have stayed at Brown Manor all those days. Mr Weston didn't slow down and think about his response before leaving me so abruptly. You know that while at Brown Manor I did not act improperly with Mr Weston—in that we are innocent—but my largest concern, Father, is for the church family. Regardless of how the community views me, please help people to see that this church is fully committed to You.

Anne prayed through the entire first song, finishing up by thanking God for Pastor Hurst and the church family and working to prepare her heart for the message.

She was completely unaware of the fact that Robert Weston was running late this morning. Just before the song ended and everyone took a seat, he slipped in to sit in a rear pew.

Chapter Four

The sermon ended with prayer, and almost before Weston could open his eyes, Palmer was there to greet him.

"Welcome to Collingbourne," Palmer said to Weston as he introduced himself.

"Thank you. Robert Weston," Weston filled in as they shook hands.

"Are you passing through?"

"No, I'm moving into Brown Manor."

At Palmer's questioning look, Weston informed him who he was.

"Alice Dixon was my grandmother."

"I'm sorry for your loss. I hadn't seen Mrs Dixon in years, but my memories of her are very fine."

"Thank you. I feel the same way."

"It's marvelous news about your joining our community, Mr Weston. I haven't visited Brown Manor for some time. Will you have many repairs?"

"No, the former tenants valued the property as my family has, and things are in fine order. You'll have to come and visit when I get settled."

"I'll do that. Oh, here's my eldest. Frank, come and meet Mr Weston."

Introductions were made and the threesome visited for some moments. Frank had ridden his horse near Brown Manor some weeks earlier and was able to converse articulately about the land. While they visited, the three other Palmer children joined them.

"Walt is my next eldest," Palmer explained. "And this is Lizzy and this is Emma."

"It's a pleasure to meet you," Weston said, and he meant it. He liked children, and the ease with which these children approached their father told Weston that the relationship was a good one.

The group talked all the way out to the carriages and horses, and before Weston went on his way he repeated his invitation to visit, even going so far as to tell Palmer to visit anytime.

"Who knows how long it will take for the dust to settle, but if you don't mind the disruption, feel free to stop in."

"I'll plan on that. Thank you."

They parted company, Weston well content, but Palmer with a niggling thought in the back of his mind. Lydia was sure to be disappointed in Anne's refusal to visit, but something told him she would find Mr Weston's presence today as curious as he did.

≈ ≈

Tipton

"What reason did she give?" Lydia asked as soon as she saw her husband's face.

"She does not want our reputation to suffer with her own."

"Is it that bad, Palmer?"

"Yes. Pastor even addressed the issue before the congregation," Palmer said, before giving her a brief account.

Lydia looked crestfallen.

"Does she think that we—" Lydia began, but Palmer shook his head.

"No, but she's being protective of us and would not be swayed."

"What are we to do?"

"We're going to go on praying for her and keep befriending her. Maybe the children and I should stop by Levens Crossing and pay a visit this week."

"She's not at the manse?"

"Not after today. Her father was staying in town, but he's going home tomorrow and she'll go and be with him."

"Did the Colonel remember?"

"Not a thing."

Lydia shook her head, still a little amazed by Anne's eccentric father.

"We had a visitor this morning, a Mr Weston. He came in rather late and sat in the rear."

"You met him?"

"Yes, he's Alice Dixon's grandson. He's moved into Brown Manor."

Lydia was opening her mouth to ask another question but stopped. Palmer watched her.

"What exactly do we know about the man Anne was forced to marry? Did any further information come out this morning?"

"No."

Lydia looked at her husband.

"Would a man who'd been through that sort of ordeal actually come to church in this community without a qualm?"

"That all depends on the circumstances, and we don't know those."

"But you wondered about it as well, didn't you, Palmer?"

"I admit I did, but only for Anne's sake."

"What do you mean?"

"I mean that Anne has been very closemouthed about this, which leads me to believe she's protecting someone. I'm not sure she would do that if the man in question was passing through. Now Mr Weston moves into the area just after the occurrence. You and I are doing our speculating behind closed doors; others will not be so discreet. They will think they've figured it out and be very vocal about it..."

"And Anne's reputation will suffer all the more," Lydia finished for him.

Palmer only nodded, his face grim. The couple was quiet for a few moments before Palmer suggested they pray. Before they had a chance, however, the children came to check on their mother.

❧ ❧

The Manse

"Here, John," Anne offered the youngest Hurst child. "Let me hold that bowl for you."

"Thank you," the five-year-old answered politely while he scooped some potatoes onto his plate.

"I understand you have some good news," Anne prompted.

The little boy nodded, a smile coming to his face.

"Margaret is coming home on Wednesday. Jane too!"

Anne smiled at his enthusiasm. Margaret was eight and Jane was 11, and clearly the little boy had missed his sisters terribly.

"And what of Jeffrey?" Anne asked of the Hursts' oldest, who was 13.

"Next week, I think."

"That's right," Judith put in. "But the best part will come in the fall. All the children will remain home for their schooling."

Anne looked surprised, so Pastor explained.

"Jennings wanted to give it a try with his children, and Palmer liked the idea too, so we've joined them. The children will go to Thornton Hall for history and geography with

Jennings, to Tipton for mathematics with Palmer, and I'll be
tackling English studies here at the manse."

"That sounds marvelous. Will they be at each home each
day?"

"No. A day with each subject and then Friday mornings
for study time. Friday afternoons will be for outings and indi-
vidual learning sessions."

"Where do I sign up?" Anne asked, clearly impressed with
the idea.

"It does sound fun, doesn't it?" Judith agreed.

"Indeed. Will you be doing some schoolwork also, John?"

"Some. So will Lizzy Palmer."

Anne smiled into his soft brown eyes, her heart melting
a bit when he smiled back.

"Are you going to stay with us until Margaret comes?"
John asked.

"No, John. I'm going home tomorrow."

"Are you about finished, John?" Pastor Hurst asked of his
young son, seeing that his plate was nearly clean.

"Almost," John said, not having caught on to the fact that
his father wanted some time for private conversation. The
little boy calmly spooned the last bites into his mouth and
reached for his glass of water as though he had all the time
in the world.

Anne put a napkin to her mouth to keep from laughing,
but he was so delightfully charming it was almost impossible.

"Miss Anne," John asked suddenly, "will you play a game
with me?"

"I will, John, but not just yet. I'll find you later, and we'll
play whatever you like."

"All right."

"All done, John?" his mother prompted, and the little boy
nodded. Judith saw him on his way and returned to the table
shaking her head.

"To be young and unaware; sometimes I envy him."

The adults were silent for a moment. Phoebe came and filled teacups before Pastor leaned back in his chair and looked to Anne.

"How do you think it went this morning?"

"Very well. Several folks checked on me, and they were all quite gracious."

"Did anyone come to you, Frederick?" Judith asked her spouse.

"Yes, and, as with Anne, they were all very positive. Some had heard rumors and others needed clarification, but all were very confident of Anne's innocence."

"I'm glad to hear that."

"Did you get to the rear of the church at all this morning, Anne?"

"No, I came and went through the side door down front."

"We had a visitor."

Both women stared at the pastor.

"I thought you were going to postpone your words if someone visited today," Judith mentioned, trying not to panic.

"He was late. He didn't come in until the first song."

"He?" Anne questioned while an odd feeling started around her heart.

"Yes. I didn't get to meet him, but he seems familiar to me. I can't help wondering if it wasn't Mr Weston."

"Well, if it was, then I'm extra glad Father has forgotten everything. The Crofts have been silent concerning the whole affair, and although I'm under scrutiny in town, there's been no mention of Mr Weston."

More concerned for Anne than anyone else, both Hursts kept silent. It was like Anne to think of others first, and they knew her visit to town the day before had been very hard, but Pastor and Judith feared that when all was said and done, it might not prove to be so simple.

Anne caught no undercurrent of this. Some minutes later she remembered that John had wanted to play a game, so she dismissed herself and went on her way. For more years than anyone could remember, life had never been anything but difficult for Anne Gardiner. She expected little else.

≈ ≈

Levens Crossing

"How is he doing, Anne?" Dr Smith asked on Wednesday morning, his carriage parked before the house.

"He's willing to stay off his feet, but he's been rather quiet."

"Well, I'll have a look. He wasn't at all feverish when he left, but I want to keep an eye on him."

"Thank you."

"You look tired," the doctor stated plainly. Anne only smiled at him.

The man grunted before going on his way, Anne following slowly. She had been home for only two days, but as the doctor had read on her face, they had been weary hours.

Her father had been off his feet and little trouble, but the rain had come through the roof at a steady rate, and mold had started to spread in one corner of the dining room. The leak she had been trying to fix when she found herself in Mr Weston's arms was now repaired, but getting things dry and clean indoors had been a tougher task. A small table and some linens had been ruined.

Anne went to the kitchen to make a pot of tea for the doctor and her father, and made the mistake of sitting down. In less than a minute she was sound asleep. She had no idea how long she'd been out when the doctor was there, touching her shoulder and calling her name.

"You can't go on like this, Anne," he said.

Anne blinked as he put a cup of tea in front of her and sat down across the table, his own cup in hand.

"Did I fall asleep?"

"Of course you did!" he said brusquely to cover his deeper emotions; her tired, confused face tore at his heart. "You can't push yourself this way."

"Well, it won't stay like this, Dr Smith. I've gotten a lot done, and things won't be so busy now."

"Only until he does it again, Anne," the doctor said more quietly. "Only until your father runs foul again and gets it into his head to marry you off."

Anne sipped her tea and tried to think clearly. The doctor was probably right, but what else was she to do?

A noise at the door made her forget her immediate problems. The sound of metal on wood prompted her to look up and see that her father had used his sword for a cane.

"My ankle's better," he stated. "I'll have my tea in here."

And as steady as though he'd never ailed a day in his life, the Colonel joined the twosome at the kitchen table, his teacup in hand.

They had only just settled in for a visit—the Colonel quite lucid as he asked the doctor about a difficult case—when they heard a horse outside.

"Is the doctor here?" a voice yelled as the front door burst open.

What followed in the next few minutes was an excited Tommy Benwick, whose sister was in labor, pleading with Dr Smith to attend her. The doctor had gone on his way, Tommy having already ridden ahead, when the Colonel spoke.

"You better go on, Anne."

Anne stared at her father.

"It's your friend, Lucy, isn't it?"

"Yes, Father, it is."

"Well, go on. I've food enough to last me out. Go and stay as long as she needs you."

"It could be several days," Anne said, speaking from experience.

"Go."

"You'll stay here?"

"Certainly," the Colonel answered as though nothing else had ever occurred to him.

Lucy Digby was a good friend, and Anne did want to be there. She put a hand on his arm, a gesture of thanks, and went to pack a bag. It would have been nice to sleep in her own bed another night, but Lucy was too dear to ignore. Satchel in hand, Anne left for Collingbourne not 15 minutes later.

❧ ❧

Brown Manor

"Cook has a meal hot and ready for you, sir," Mansfield informed Weston late in the day on Wednesday, his voice firm with resolve. Weston had been working all day in his study, and Mansfield was starting to fret.

Weston looked up and felt for the first time that his neck had become stiff. His grandmother had always dreamed and talked of adding a conservatory to Brown Manor, and Weston had determined to do it now. He'd been drawing and poring over plans all day, barely touching the tea and plates of food that had been offered.

"I could use a meal," Weston said. "I'll be along shortly."

Mansfield hated to take his word for it, but did. He closed the study door quietly and started toward the dining room, passing one of the new maids in the hall. She was a pretty little thing, managing to turn the heads of several coachmen, but Mansfield knew she was also a good girl and would brook no disrespect from any of the men.

A certain amount of interaction was to be expected among the servants in any household, but Mr Weston had high standards and would be very hard on any of the men who didn't hold with his view that, while a part of his household, interactions of a more personal nature were for marriage alone.

He set the same standard for the women. They were expected to comport themselves with self-respect. It never took long for word to get out that the female servants in the Weston household were treated well, not just by the Weston family, but by the male servants as well, something many women found desirable.

Mansfield had only just arrived in the small dining room, checking to see that all was in readiness, when Weston joined him.

"Something smells good," Weston commented as he took a seat.

"Onion soup, sir, and fresh bread. The hour is late, so we kept things light, but there is treacle for pudding."

"Splendid, Mansfield. You always know just what I need."

Mansfield inclined his head modestly, but he was pleased.

"I'm going to head into town in the morning and do a bit of shopping. Have you word on the arrival of the furniture?"

"Everything should be here Friday."

"Good. I'm not going to have work on the conservatory start until we're a little more settled, but I'm eager to get things underway."

"Will you hire from London, sir, or locally?"

"I'm going to do a little inquiring when I'm in town tomorrow. I may check with a man I met on Sunday."

"Very good, sir. More tea?"

"Yes."

Soon after that, Mansfield left Weston to eat alone, but Weston barely noticed his departure. He was once again mentally walking through the conservatory, his mind taken up with the building, the plant life it would include, and just how long it would take to complete the work.

The meal before him was very good, but Weston ate distractedly. When Mansfield returned he was satisfied to see that Weston had eaten all the soup and bread, but he hadn't waited for dessert.

Mansfield thought—not for the first time—that the man needed a wife, a loving woman who shared his beliefs and would see to it that he ate properly and gained the proper amount of rest.

Mansfield ordered the table cleared and eventually took himself off to bed, a wife for Mr Weston still on his mind.

∾ ∾

Collingbourne

"Oh, Anne," Lucy panted weakly. "I can't go on much longer."

"You're doing splendidly, Lucy. It won't be long now," Anne encouraged as she wiped the other woman's brow. Anne's arm was bruised where Lucy had squeezed it, but that was of little consequence. The doctor had not been back for more than an hour, and Anne so wanted this baby to arrive safely.

A shadow passed over the bed just then, and both women looked up to see Lucy's husband, Billy Digby.

"Oh, Billy." Lucy was apologetic, her face flushed and hair limp with perspiration. "I'm sorry it's taking so long. You won't get a bit of rest tonight, and you have to work in the morning."

"You silly girl," he said lovingly as he took a seat on the bed. "You're all I care about."

"The baby too?"

"Yes, the baby, but you most of all."

Anne knew she must be tired when she felt tears coming to her eyes. She ducked her head and blinked rapidly to dispel them but felt more coming on when Billy leaned close and kissed his wife. A pain gripped Lucy a short time later, and Billy fled, but Anne saw her through, praying again that the doctor would check on her soon.

As it was, Dr Smith had a second delivery keeping him up this night and didn't arrive back until Lucy's baby had let out her first loud cry. It was a girl, red and wrinkly, with robust lungs announcing to everyone that she had arrived.

After the doctor came on duty, Anne slipped from the bedroom into the kitchen and sat by the stove. Benwick, a grandfather for the second time now, pushed a mug of tea into her hands, and Anne drank gratefully. No one disturbed her or said a word when she fell sound asleep in the chair.

Tommy, up well past his normal bedtime, covered her with a blanket before going in to see his new little niece.

℞ ℳ

"Would you like some more, Meg?" Anne asked of Lucy and Billy's daughter, who was spooning porridge into her mouth with a fair amount of accuracy.

"Yes, please," she said, her little mouth still half full.

Anne did the honors, adding extra sugar to make it special.

"I want Mama," the little girl said before she was through with the second bowl, and Anne was as honest as she had been the first two times the toddler had requested her mother.

"Mama's resting. We'll check on her later."

"And baby Liz?"

"And baby Liz," Anne assured her, pleased when she went back to her meal.

There was not a lot of room in the Digby cottage, but well after midnight when Anne had found herself asleep in the kitchen chair, she had slipped into Meg's room and climbed into bed with her. Lucy had needed her only once in the night, and other than that she'd slept hard until Meg woke and found her company in the morning.

Always happy to see Anne, the little girl had squealed with delight, and Anne had woken to a tight hug around the neck. Now the two breakfasted together—it was still very early—while Lucy found some extra sleep.

This worked until a small cry was heard from the bedroom. Anne made certain that all porridge was washed from Meg's little face and hands before explaining that they would go in quietly in case Lucy was still asleep.

Meg, her face alight with excitement, agreed to all of this until she saw her mother. The toddler flung herself onto the bed and into Lucy's arms, who laughed in delight.

"We tried to be quiet," Anne explained, having gone to the cradle to scoop the tiny infant girl into her arms.

"It's all right," Lucy said wearily. "That kind of welcome is always worth waking up for."

"How are you?" Anne asked, gentling bouncing a still crying Liz.

"I'm lying here worrying about seeing to both Meg and Liz. Can you stay a few days, Anne?"

Making it sound like the simplest task in the world, Anne said, "Of course I can."

Lucy smiled and said, "Then to answer your question, my friend, I'm fine—very fine indeed."

Chapter Five

Weston started his morning in Collingbourne at the office of Mr Vintcent, an architect. He explained what he was looking for, even going so far as to show the man his rough sketch, and was encouraged when the architect became animated with ideas. Weston knew he would not agree to anything today, even if the man offered references, but in an hour's time, Weston was certain that Mr Vintcent knew exactly what he was looking for.

"I can come out later this week to ascertain the exact location. Once I have that, I can put an estimate on paper for you."

"Excellent. I'll plan on that."

"Brown Manor, you said?" Mr Vintcent took notes as he asked.

"Yes. Friday morning would be good for my schedule. May I expect you then?"

"Eight o'clock?"

"Perfect."

The men parted company, Weston well pleased with the meeting. He was finished earlier than he'd planned, and the moment he walked from the architect's office, he knew he wasn't ready to head home. He hadn't been in Collingbourne for any length of time in years and had a sudden yearning to explore.

Not bothering to climb back into his carriage, he told his driver to meet him at the other end of town and began walking down the street. He had no particular plan in mind, but as soon as he saw Benwick's, he remembered Mansfield mentioning he'd been there. Weston made directly for the door, stepping inside to the soft chime of a bell.

Things were quiet—the bell didn't appear to rouse anyone—and Weston began a slow tour. He hadn't been in the first aisle two minutes when the chime sounded again, but he was too busy with the contents of Benwick's shelves to give it much notice.

Just moments later a female voice floated over to Weston's aisle. "What are you looking at?"

"Oh, nothing, really," a second voice answered, sounding distracted. "I just spotted this bit of tapestry and thought it pretty."

"It is pretty, but finish your story first."

"Well," the woman launched back in without further prompting, her voice growing dramatic. "She was gone for *days* and isn't saying where she was or *whom* she was with."

The first woman sighed. "She won't be showing her face around town very soon."

"That's just it. She's in town! Lucy Digby's just had a baby, and she's here helping her."

"A gentleman's daughter—a military man no less—acting as a midwife for Lucy! And shopkeeper's daughter or not, we both know that Lucy married below herself. If they aren't two of a kind, I don't know who is!"

"Good morning, ladies." Having come from his back room, Mr Benwick himself cut into the conversation, not having any idea what they'd been speaking about. "May I help you with something?"

Still in the next aisle when he heard the other man's voice, Weston realized he'd been standing there listening. He gave himself a little shake at his own stupidity and returned to browsing. He was vaguely aware that the threesome was speaking across the way, but he'd spotted a slim volume that held some of the more popular works of Shakespeare and thought his mother might enjoy it. Her birthday was months away, but that didn't matter. He had plucked it from the shelf and was studying the pages when Benwick found him.

"Are you finding everything, sir?"

"I am, yes."

"If you need anything wrapped, we can do that at the counter."

"Thank you."

Benwick left Weston on his own, turning to check on a woman who had just entered the store. She was a handful, wanting items he didn't stock and would have to order from London, but the shop owner was patient, as were some of his other customers. When he had the woman settled, packed up, and out the door at last, he found Weston at the counter. Weston had selected the book of Shakespeare, an intricate German-made clock, and some of the finest linen handkerchiefs the store carried.

"Did you find everything you needed, sir?

"Yes, thank you."

"Do you want these wrapped or delivered?"

"Just wrapped. I'll be taking everything with me."

Benwick, an old hand at the task, had Weston out the door in little time, wishing him a fine day and inwardly hoping he would shop there often.

"Who was that man, Mr Benwick?" one of the gossiping women asked the moment Weston left.

"I don't know, Mrs Stanhope. He didn't give his name."

The women, who had been doing more visiting than shopping, exchanged glances, neither one the least bit ashamed of her unnecessary interest. Benwick was used to such behavior and took it in stride. He truly didn't know who the man was, but even if he had, he would have been very closemouthed to Mrs Stanhope and her companion.

"Baby Liz is crying!" Meg announced, running to Anne where she worked at the stove.

"I hear that," Anne answered calmly. "Shall we check on her?"

This time Anne was able to creep into the room, take the howling Liz from her cradle, and leave Lucy asleep. The night's work had finally caught up with the new mother, and she was sleeping soundly.

Meg started to cry when Anne changed Liz's wet clothing. The baby was turning red in an effort to be heard, and Anne laughed at the two of them.

"Well, this sounds interesting." Billy had come in the door and spoke from behind Anne.

"Oh, Billy," Anne said on another laugh, "will you comfort Meg and tell her that Liz is fine? She seems to think she needs to commiserate."

Billy was smiling hugely when he scooped his two-year-old into his arms and let her bawl against his shoulder.

"How's Lucy?"

"Sleeping soundly," Anne told him as she transferred the now-dry baby to her shoulder. "I'm going to get a little sugar water into this one and see if I can't buy Lucy a little more sleep."

"You're a treasure, Anne."

"Do you think?" Anne teased him.

Billy ducked his head, a bit of his old shyness surfacing, before turning to comfort his daughter.

"I saw a kitten today," he said, attempting to distract her.

Meg turned to look at her father. She sniffed, but the tears were abating. The two sat at the table, Meg on the table surface and Billy in a chair, facing each other so they could talk.

Anne settled Liz by dipping a soft towel into sugar water so she could suck, and when she seemed satisfied, rocked her back to sleep. She put her in a basket nearby and then readied lunch to go on the table.

The simple everyday action caused her to wonder if her father was getting his meals. In the past he'd fared well on his own, but she wasn't so confident now that he'd hurt his leg.

He always lands on his feet, Anne reminded herself, knowing it was wrong to worry.

Had Anne's friends—especially those from the church family—known the direction of her thoughts, they would have advised her as they had in the past: to see to her own needs more often.

❧ ❧

Weston went home by way of the church. It wasn't actually on the way home, but he'd not met Pastor Hurst on Sunday and wanted to rectify that before he attended church again.

Pastor Hurst was in his study and heard the church door opening. He met Weston halfway up the aisle.

"Welcome."

"Thank you. It's Pastor Hurst, isn't it?"

"Yes. Did I see you in the back row last Sunday?"

"Yes, I was here. Robert Weston."

The men shook hands before Pastor invited Weston to join him in his study. That book-lined room was warm and comfortable, and Weston felt remarkably at ease.

"I've just moved onto my grandmother's estate, Brown Manor," Weston explained.

"How is your family doing with Mrs Dixon's passing?"

"Well, thank you. It was not unexpected, and she left her daughter, my mother, well provided for."

"Through you, Mr Weston, or is there an older son?"

"No, I'm an only child."

Pastor nodded, hoping that this young man would talk about his first days here but knowing that some type of relationship might need to be established for that.

"My visit today is twofold in purpose," Weston said. "I didn't have a chance to meet you on Sunday, something I wanted to do, and I also wanted to ask about someone I believe to be part of your parish."

"All right."

"Do you know Anne Gardiner?"

"I do, yes. She is a part of our church family."

Weston nodded, feeling some relief.

"Miss Gardiner was one of the first people I met when I arrived, but it was under rather trying circumstances. I was hoping you could tell me if she is well."

"She's fine, Mr Weston, but I think it only fair to tell you that she informed us of her predicament."

Weston nodded, his face pained. "It was most unexpected. If I had it to do over again, I hope I would do things differently, but I must admit that it came as quite a surprise."

"Are *you* all right, Mr Weston?" the kind pastor asked.

Weston laughed a little. "At times I'm still trying to believe this marriage actually happened. It was all rather dreamlike, if you catch my meaning."

"I do indeed, Mr Weston. The Colonel is not a well man. If you haven't dealt with him, it can be most alarming."

"But Miss Gardiner does it every day."

The pastor smiled before saying, "Miss Gardiner is a very special person. She looks like a stiff wind could carry her away, but she's actually very strong—on the inside, where it counts."

"I'm glad to hear she's well."

"She tends to be rather protective," Pastor added next, working to be as subtle as possible. "She tends to put the needs of others above her own, sometimes to a fault."

Weston nodded, finding that easy to believe. In his short acquaintance with Anne, he saw that she was very kind and unassuming.

"My man dropped her at the manse last week. Is she still staying with you?"

"No, she's gone home."

"And her father, is he well?"

"I assume so. I've not heard otherwise."

"I'm glad to hear it," Weston said, making to rise. "Thank you for taking the time to see me."

"My pleasure. Will we see you on Sunday?"

"I'm planning to be here, yes."

"We'll look forward to it."

Pastor Hurst saw Weston out to his carriage, all the while asking himself if he should have been more blunt. He waved the younger man off, knowing he was completely unaware of the way Anne's reputation had suffered from the incident, and that Anne herself was protecting him without regard for her own standing in the community.

It was with a prayerful heart—one that fervently asked God to make heads or tails of everything that had happened—that Pastor Hurst returned to his study to work on his upcoming sermon.

∾ ∾

Levens Crossing

"Father, are you here?" Anne called to the empty house on Saturday afternoon. She received no answer. The stove in the kitchen was cold, and the rooms had an empty feel to them.

Knowing her father would return in his own good time, Anne began to make the house homey again. She fixed a meal with the stores she found in the pantry and brewed a

large pot of tea. She had only just finished with her meal,
deciding a bath was in order next, when someone knocked.

"Well, Emma," Anne said with pleasure. "How nice to see
you."

"We're all here," Emma Palmer informed her. "Everyone
but mother and Frank."

"Come in. Come in," Anne welcomed, glad to have visitors.

"Hello, Anne," Palmer greeted her. "How are you?"

"I'm well. Please sit down, everyone. Make yourselves
comfortable."

"We heard you were in town with Lucy Digby," Palmer
said from the davenport. "How is she?"

"She's well, and the baby is precious."

"What did they name her?"

"Liz."

"Did you hear that, Lizzy?" He turned to his daughter.
"Another Liz!"

"Is she a good baby?" Lizzy wished to know.

"Very good. She slept almost all night last night."

The children smiled at her, and Anne was reminded of
their mother.

"How is your mother?" she asked.

"Tired," Walt gave this information matter-of-factly.

"Is she getting some extra rest?"

"Father says she must."

Anne smiled down at Walt and then over at Palmer, who
smiled back.

"And tell me, Palmer, how is your sister-in-law faring?"

"Marianne's well and very calm. Jennings is a bit hen-ish
about the whole thing, but Marianne keeps on and he keeps
trailing after her. Come and see us, Anne," Palmer slipped
these words in at the last minute.

"As soon as I can, Palmer," Anne said, her voice soft with
conviction.

Palmer's look told her he wanted it to be today, but with the children sitting among them, he let the matter drop.

"Emma," Palmer turned to his youngest. "Did you give Anne the basket?"

"No."

"Where is it?"

"In the carriage."

"But you insisted on carrying it," Walt reminded her.

"It was too heavy."

Palmer hid a smile.

"Go ahead, Walt," his father instructed. "Bring it in, will you?"

Walt accomplished this task in little time and laid a large hamper at Anne's feet.

"Lydia says she knows you're busy and might be behind on your baking," Palmer explained.

"Oh, my," was all Anne could say as she peeked under the linens to find loaves of bread, scones, biscuits, and muffins. "Really, Palmer, you must tell her it's too much."

"She won't listen," Palmer said lightly, well pleased with what they'd done. "And you wouldn't want to get me in trouble by sending any of it back."

Anne was still shaking her head at him when Walt spoke.

"How is Colonel Gardiner?"

"Thank you for asking, Walt, but I don't know. I've not been back from town too long, and he wasn't here when I arrived. I assume he's fine."

"I like his sword."

"He would enjoy showing it to you. We'll have to plan on that some time."

"Does he polish it each day?"

"Not every day, but often."

"We have a sword, but it hangs on the wall."

"I've seen the one you mean. It's very fine."

"Yes, but we can't touch it."

Anne smiled at his obvious regret over this, and at the same time she felt very tired. It had been a long few days. She found herself relieved when Palmer told the children it was time to go home, but her thanks for their visit and the basket were genuine.

"Take care of yourself," Palmer told Anne, hanging back a moment before climbing in the carriage to join the children.

"I will, Palmer. Thank you."

"Get some rest."

Anne had no problem agreeing to that. She had just finished her bath when the Colonel arrived home. He was happy to see her but didn't remember where she had been. She filled him in, but other than telling her she looked tired, he had little to say.

Anne told him where he could find his dinner and that the tea was still hot, and without guilt she took herself off to bed at an early hour.

᙮ ᙮

Weston was on time Sunday morning and met several parishioners before the service began. He even had a few moments with Palmer, as he'd hoped.

"Have you had any dealings with Vintcent, the architect in the village?"

"Yes, I have. He's never designed anything for me personally, but we've met and he's done work for James Walker. The man you just met—Jennings—is Walker's son-in-law. You should talk with him about Vintcent."

"Could you introduce me to Walker?"

"If he's here this morning, I'd be happy to."

The bells began to ring just then, and Palmer said he would find Weston after the service.

❧ ❧

"I have a message for you," Marianne Jennings told Anne as soon as the service ended.

"Have you?" Anne asked but was quite certain she knew who it was from.

"Yes. Lydia wishes for you to come to tea tomorrow morning."

Anne smiled.

"It didn't work to send Palmer, so now she's sending you."

Marianne smiled but still said quite earnestly, "I know she wishes to see you, Anne. Please go."

Anne was about to accept, seeing the entreaty in Marianne's eyes, when she caught sight of Mr Weston. He wasn't looking her way but was in conversation with several men, including Marianne's father. Seeing him, she was starkly reminded of how different her life had become.

"Tell her not to expect me tomorrow, Marianne, but I will try to come soon."

Marianne did not have the heart to press her. With a gentle squeeze to Anne's arm, Marianne told her she understood. The two women sat talking about the way Marianne was feeling when Jennings found them.

"How are you, Miss Gardiner?"

"I'm well, Mr Jennings. And yourself?"

"Very well, thank you. Did I see the Colonel walking yesterday?"

"You might have. He didn't get home until evening."

"I've wondered several times," Jennings admitted, "what he does when you come to church. Has he ever attended with you?"

"Not since he's been ill. If he's home when I leave, he asks me to pray for him, but he never wishes to accompany me."

"Was Marianne inviting you to lunch just now?" Jennings asked, thinking it might be just what she needed.

"No, she was delivering a message from your sister."

"Well, with that mission accomplished, why don't you join us for lunch, Miss Gardiner? The children are all home."

Anne's eyes reflected longing, but she still began to shake her head.

Marianne answered to rescue her.

"Anne is staying a little closer to home these days, Jennings, but she'll be out and about soon."

Anne smiled a thank-you in her direction and wished them a fine day as they took their leave a few moments later.

She watched them walk up the aisle of the church, catching sight of Mr Weston again, still in conference with several men, and wondering for the first time if she was handling her situation well. Making her way toward the side door, she determined to speak to Pastor Hurst and Judith that very week, hoping they could shed some light on her complicated position.

❧ ❧

Brown Manor

"A message just arrived from London, sir," Mansfield told Weston the moment he arrived home. "It wasn't five minutes ago."

Weston took the paper from Mansfield's hand, his heart sinking with dread as his eyes scanned the words.

"My mother is ill," Weston said quietly. "I must be away directly."

"Certainly, sir. I'll ready everything."

Giving orders as he dressed for the trip, Weston thought nothing of changing all of his plans for the week. His mother meant the world to him. Right now little else mattered.

Chapter Six

London

"I've never been so weak," Lenore Weston whispered to her son, many days after he arrived to find her very unwell.

"I'm only glad you're here at all," he commented from the chair at her bedside. "I've never seen anyone so ill."

"I still have a headache."

"The doctor said that would last a few days longer."

Lenore's eyes began to close, so she forced them open. "You didn't come all this way to watch me sleep."

Weston laughed softly.

"Go to sleep, Mother. I'll be here."

"You mustn't stay on, Robert," she urged him, even though her heart wanted him to remain. "Go back to Brown Manor and continue with your work on the conservatory."

"Shhh," he hushed her, with no plans to do as he was told. "Brown Manor and everything else in Collingbourne are doing just fine without me."

Lenore sighed.

"You'll be here?"

"I'll be here," he assured her, leaning forward to kiss her pale cheek and smiling when she closed her eyes to let sleep overtake her.

Collingbourne

It's occurred to me that the whole town knowing that it was Robert Weston who was involved wouldn't solve a thing,

Anne. And in light of that, I don't know what you could do differently. The ones who know you and love you understand. We'll comfort ourselves with the fact that these things usually blow over. We will just hope this time that will be the case sooner rather than later.

Pastor's words to Anne rang in her ears a full three weeks after he said them, but they were of little comfort. Each time she went to town it seemed to be worse. She was always welcomed at her regular shops—they were owned by kind people—but many of the townsfolk had become distinctly cold in her presence.

She had stopped going into Gray's tearoom, no matter how famished she felt, and she avoided the apothecary shop altogether. That proprietor's wife all but glared at her when she dared to show her face. While these businesses were not a part of her regular routine, being made to feel uncomfortable anywhere in town was altogether new to her.

She loved Collingbourne, and for that reason her heart was heavy with its rejection of her. These days she gained the necessities on her list and departed from town as soon as she was able, but the situation as it stood lay heavy on her heart. Since her father's illness, she had been considered something of a curiosity, a way of life she was used to. In more recent years—since her father's inability to manage their estate had caused them to lose their home and lands—their lack of income had forced her into situations that were not fitting of her station, but even those townspeople of the most snobbish nature had seemed to understand.

Anne couldn't help but wonder if things might have gone easier on her had she told all, but she was not going to satisfy the gossipmongers in town for any reason.

A feeling of dread had begun to settle all around her, and Anne fought it. Years ago, when her father had still been comatose, a friend had urged her to ask God for His very best. Her advice had been, *Never expect to only survive,*

Anne. God wants you to thrive. The words had been life-changing. Anne had patterned her prayer life and time in the Word with that very thought in mind, and she believed God had blessed her puny efforts. Not until now, when she felt like an outcast in her own hometown, did Anne's heart begin to falter.

Making her way home, her small list filled and the basket hanging on her arm, Anne asked God to help her remember all His goodness. She asked Him to examine her own heart for pride or anything that would hinder her fellowship with Him. And she also asked God to help her critics have compassion toward her. Anne couldn't think of anything else that might restore her good standing in the community.

≈ ≈

"Welcome back to Collingbourne, Mr Weston," Pastor Hurst greeted Weston at the end of the sermon on the last Sunday of the month; he hadn't seen the man for several weeks. "How is your mother?"

"Much improved, thank you."

"Your man got word to us, and we've been praying."

"Thank you. I'm happy to report she is on her feet, and though she is still rather weak, she is gaining strength every day."

"Excellent."

The word was no more out of Pastor Hurst's mouth when Weston glanced over the other man's shoulder and spotted Anne Gardiner. She was on her way out through the side door, so it was a view of her back, but he was certain it was she.

"Was that Miss Gardiner just leaving?"

"It probably was," Pastor Hurst said with a glance in that direction. "I believe she and Judith were visiting."

"How is she?"

"Getting along," Pastor Hurst said, his voice sobering a bit.

"I'm glad to hear it," Weston said, not catching the tone or Pastor's troubled gaze.

"Do you have plans for lunch, Mr Weston?" Pastor suddenly offered, realizing he didn't know this young man very well. "Can you join my family?"

"I'd be happy to dine with you, Pastor. Thank you very much."

"Good, good. I'll just close up and we'll head over to the manse."

Weston stood quietly as Pastor Hurst shut the front doors and then followed him out the side door, near the front of the church, and across the grass to a sprawling stone house. The men entered through the kitchen door, their voices traveling ahead of them.

~ ~

The Manse

Having planned to stay only a moment, Anne stood in the kitchen with Judith, discussing a recipe Anne had shared with her. Judith was repeating the ingredients back to her when Anne suddenly gripped her friend's arm.

"That's Mr Weston's voice!" Anne whispered.

"No!"

"Yes, it is."

"Frederick wouldn't bring him this way."

"It's he, I'm sure. I must go!"

"But why, Anne?" Judith said to her friend's rapidly disappearing back.

"Judith," her husband called as he entered the room, Mr Weston at his heels.

"Oh, Frederick, I must see if I can catch—" The sight of Weston stopped the words in her mouth. "Hello, Mr Weston. Please forgive our informality."

"Not at all, Mrs Hurst. I hope my presence won't inconvenience you."

"Not in the least."

"What were you saying, dear?" the unsuspecting pastor questioned his wife. He received only an odd look from her.

"Where are you going?" Margaret, the eight-year-old, was heard to ask rather loudly from the direction of the dining room.

"Where is who going?" Pastor Hurst now asked, still not understanding his wife's demeanor.

Judith didn't reply.

"Anne?" Margaret was now calling, and Weston suddenly found himself all ears, something the Hursts did not miss.

"Is Miss Gardiner here?" he asked.

"Actually," Judith answered as tactfully as possible, "she was just leaving."

"Did you need to speak with her, Mr Weston?" Pastor asked, his face giving nothing away.

"As a matter of fact I had hoped to talk with her, but if she's busy, it can wait."

"I'm sure she has time," the pastor replied expansively, drawing a look of disbelief from his wife. "Come along this way," he directed. "We'll catch her before she goes."

This wouldn't have been possible if Anne had not stopped to quietly explain to Margaret that she had to get home, but as it was, she was just arriving at the front door. She had the portal partially open when the pastor called her name.

"Anne, can you wait a moment?"

"Certainly," she managed gracefully, even when she saw that her pastor had brought his visitor along.

"Can you remain for lunch?"

"Thank you so much, Pastor, but I must get home," Anne said with a smile that encompassed both men.

"Well, then, I'll let Mr Weston speak with you as he wished to do."

Anne watched as the pastor moved away with Margaret. Surprised by this action, she realized that she herself was being studied. She forced her eyes to meet those of Mr Weston.

"Frederick," his wife said to him in whispering tones the moment he stepped into the dining room. Margaret had been asked to check on her brother. "What are you about? She didn't want to see him!"

"I suspected as much."

"Then why did you push the point?"

"Because here it's private. If their first meeting were in town or even at church, it would be much more awkward than if it occurred in our foyer."

Judith nodded with understanding, glad that there was nothing more to it, but then she glanced back into her husband's face and reconsidered that thought.

"There's more, isn't there?"

The pastor looked at the woman he cherished with all of his heart, knowing he could tell her anything, but also knowing that his impressions on this subject were new and needed more time.

"Yes, there is more, but I'm still thinking on it."

Judith nodded. Thoughts of pushing the point never even entered her mind. She knew Frederick would discuss the matter with her when he was ready.

For the moment, however, Anne was still in a tight spot. Judith went to check on Phoebe and lunch preparations, praying for Anne all the while.

ॐ ॐ

"Hello, Miss Gardiner."

"Hello, Mr Weston."

The two bowed in acknowledgment before Weston looked up and stared at her again.

When he remained quiet, Anne found his manner very confusing but still offered, "We heard about your mother. How is she feeling?"

"She is much improved, thank you," he answered, feeling as if he'd been thrown a lifeline. Every word he'd planned to say had flown from his head. They were slow in returning. "Your father, Miss Gardiner—how is he?"

"He's very well, thank you."

"Has it worked for you to be home?"

Anne's mind cleared with understanding.

"Yes, it's fine. I hope you have not been overly concerned, Mr Weston. Father hasn't remembered any of the events surrounding your visit."

But you remember every detail, Weston couldn't help but think. *And you're embarrassed in my presence as though you did something wrong.* None of these thoughts could be expressed. However, the owner of Brown Manor felt almost desperate to keep this woman talking.

"Do you think that if your father saw me again, he would remember me?"

"That's hard to say," Anne said with a small smile. "As you might guess, he's most unpredictable."

Weston smiled back at her, a smile full of gleaming white teeth. Anne found herself distracted and suddenly awkward.

"I really must go," Anne said, her hand reaching for the door again.

"Let me get the door," the gentleman offered, even walking Anne to the front yard.

"Goodbye," she said as she began to move on her way.

Weston didn't answer. He was busy looking for her carriage when he realized she didn't have one.

"You're walking, Miss Gardiner?" he called after her, moving to cover the distance between them.

"Yes, it's not far," Anne explained, turning slightly but continuing toward the road.

"My coach and man are right at the church. I'll just go along and find him. He can give you a ride."

"There's no need, Mr Weston, thank you anyway," Anne said over her shoulder, still in motion.

"I insist, Miss Gardiner. Please wait here."

"*No!*"

She had stopped, faced him, and spoke more firmly than she intended. His shocked face caused her own cheeks to flame with color. With a calming breath she went on more quietly.

"Your kindness is not unnoticed, Mr Weston, but you've been in the area some weeks now and your coach will be more recognizable. Thank you, but I really must decline. Goodbye, Mr Weston."

Weston said a quiet goodbye as he watched her hurry along the road. Everything within him rebelled at the idea that she would not accept his offer, but he felt helpless to act. He also knew that he was missing something.

He returned to the house, determined to question Pastor Hurst about what had just occurred, only to find the family waiting for him. And not just Pastor and his wife. Around them were four children, all very polite and kind as they were introduced, but clearly they were going to put a damper on Weston's plans for table conversation.

ॡ ॷ

Brown Manor

Weston walked through the front door of his own home a few hours after lunch. Everything was in its usual state of neatness, and on this day the cleanliness led his mind to Anne. He called her Miss Gardiner when he spoke to her or referred to her, but in his mind she was Anne. And why did she stay in his thoughts? Years before he knew of her existence, she lived as she did with no help or thought from him, but now that he knew of her, he couldn't get her from his mind.

And still something was missing.

He'd had a great time around the Hursts' dining table. The food and fellowship had been very fine, but never had he been alone with only the adults.

Weston shook his head to try to clear his thoughts. He decided that a ride was in order, and he called for his horse to be readied in 30 minutes time. Thinking he needed to get out and take in some air, he never realized that the man who could answer all his questions lived directly under his roof.

ॡ ॷ

Tipton

"Your surprise plan worked," Palmer said to his wife as he brought Anne to the bedroom on Monday morning and left the women to visit in privacy.

Anne went to hug her friend, who, still taking it very slowly with a week-old baby, was very glad to see her.

"Will you ever forgive me?"

"I don't know," Anne pretended to consider it as she took a seat next to Lydia's bed, shaking her head slightly over her friend's sneak attack.

The Palmer coach had suddenly arrived at Levens Crossing, the coachman bearing a note asking Anne to come. Anne was taken so unawares that she climbed into the carriage without hesitation. When she arrived at Tipton, it was to find everyone in delightful spirits; they had all been in on the plan and praying that she would come. Anne had taken time with all the children before Palmer had offered to take her to see Lydia.

"Where is your little Oliver?" Anne now asked, looking about for a basket or cradle.

"He's with Fanny, our mother's help, and should be back any moment," Lydia answered.

Anne smiled at her friend.

"You look wonderful."

"I feel very good. He was so long overdue that I had some moments of discouragement."

"But he's here now."

"Yes, and I'm dying for you to see him. But before he comes, Anne, how are you?"

"I'm well, thank you. The basket of breads was lovely, Lydia. I can't tell you how much I appreciated it."

"It was our pleasure. You've been on my mind so much, and I can't help but wonder if you have someone you're going to for counsel. Have Judith and Pastor been available?"

"Yes. I do go to them, and they've been very helpful. Thank you for checking on me."

"Well, now that we've broken the ice, you must keep coming to Tipton. Often."

Anne's look became decidedly strained at this idea. Lydia would have to have been blind to miss it.

"Anne," Lydia said sincerely, reaching out to take her hand. "I care not what others say. I know you are a woman of honor and a friend. Please come as often as you can."

Anne nodded, not able to ignore this plea. She was in the habit of putting others before herself and realized that Lydia was now trying to do that for her. Even with a certain measure of fear that her friends would suffer, she could not refuse such a gesture.

"Thank you, Lydia," Anne said simply, gaining a warm smile from her friend.

And only just in time. Moments later there was a knock at the door before Fanny entered with the very new Oliver Palmer.

ର୍ତ୍ତ ରୁ

Thornton Hall

"What are you doing?" Jennings asked quietly from behind his expectant wife, startling a small squeak out of her as she turned from the bookshelf.

"You scared me!"

"You deserve to be more than scared. You were about to climb on that chair, weren't you?"

Marianne Jennings worked at looking very innocent, but she'd been caught red-handed and there was no way out of it.

"What book did you want?" Jennings asked, working not to smile at the face he loved.

Marianne gave him the title and then watched as he plucked it from the shelf, his height making the chair of no use. Jennings handed the book to her but didn't let go. Marianne's eyes met his.

"You're supposed to be resting."

"I was going to sit and read the book," she told him sweetly. "What could be more restful than that?"

"Before or after your middle put you off balance and you fell from the chair?"

Before Marianne could frame a reply, Thomas, the oldest of the Jennings children, appeared in the door. He stared at the adults and smiled.

"Do I miss my guess, or is Marianne in trouble?"

Both Jennings and Marianne laughed.

"I hate being so easily read," Jennings commented, relinquishing his hold on the book and placing the chair she'd moved back into place.

"What did you do?" Thomas asked the woman who was married to his guardian, his tone light, his mouth ready to smile.

"I was going to climb up and get a book."

All Thomas' humor fled.

"You were going to stand on the chair?" the young man asked in disbelief.

Jennings laughed at his wife's look of surprise before turning to Thomas.

"I've been called a hen for weeks now, Thomas. Thank you for seeing things my way."

"You could have fallen," Thomas told her in no uncertain terms.

"Who could have fallen?" James, now making his appearance, asked.

The situation was no more spelled out for him when Penny, the youngest of the children, entered the room. She listened quietly to the explanation of what had gone on before going to sit close to Marianne, her presence meant to commiserate.

"Well, at least one of you has compassion for me," Marianne accused the males in the room, a smile lurking in her eyes.

"Is that why you sat by Marianne, Penny?" Jennings asked. "Do you feel sorry for her?"

Penny nodded very solemnly. "It's hard to be short."

No one in the room expected this, but it gained Penny a hug from Marianne and caused Jennings and the boys to laugh.

Just the year before, the children had been orphaned. Their closest relative was William Jennings, unmarried but still willing to take them in. The transition had not been without bumps, but in less than a year's time, he had taken in his cousin's three children and married Marianne Walker. Now Marianne was expecting their first baby. And since the school term had ended, she found she had four sets of eyes lingering on her on a regular basis.

"Are you feeling well, Marianne?" James asked when the room grew quiet, his little heart sweet and sensitive to Marianne's plight.

"I am, yes. Thank you, James."

"It takes a very long time, doesn't it?" he commented.

"Some days longer than others," Marianne told him with a smile.

"Days when I'm being hen-ish?" Jennings teased his wife.

"Yes," she told him, a laugh escaping. "Especially on those days."

The couple exchanged an amused glance, and seeing it, the children exchanged some looks of their own. There had been a plot on their part, many months past, to see these two married, but in the end Jennings and Marianne had needed no help. Theirs was a love match—there was no mistaking that.

"All right, children," Jennings said as he stood. "Let us head out for a walk through the park. That will give Marianne a chance to rest."

The children went without argument, but not before watching Jennings head to Marianne's seat. He bent low and kissed her gently on the mouth, whispering something softly to her before straightening.

Such displays did not embarrass them. For too many months their lives had been topsy-turvy and unsettling. Such sights only gave them peace of mind.

Chapter Seven

Collingbourne

On this trip into town Mansfield and Weston went together. Weston knew what he wanted for the large drawing room, his bedroom, and the small salon, but he had told Mansfield to handle things in the kitchen as he liked, as well as the rooms below stairs.

"I'm going to start in Vintcent's office to make sure the workers are still coming on Monday. From there I'm headed to see that furniture maker—I can't recall his name."

"Pelham?" Mansfield supplied.

"Yes, that's it. Then I'm to Benwick's. If you don't arrive at Benwick's before I'm through, I'll be at Gray's having tea."

"Very well, sir. I shall endeavor not to keep you waiting."

"Don't worry about it. We might as well make the best of this trip. Once the conservatory is underway, I may want to be home more."

Putting their plan into effect, Weston proceeded to the architect's and received good news from Vintcent. The workers would begin on Monday morning, Vintcent himself overseeing the process.

The furniture shop did not take long either. Weston liked blue, and Pelham had his fabrics sorted by color. In little time five sofas, seven chairs, and six side tables of various woods had been ordered. It would be some months before delivery, something that would have been faster in London, but he wanted to support the local trade, and shipping costs would have been high.

Weston was at Benwick's 90 minutes later, hoping that man would have the lamps he had in mind. Benwick was busy when he walked into the store, so Weston contented himself with a slow browse through the aisles, something he found very enjoyable.

"I don't believe we have met."

Weston looked down to see that he was being addressed. A small, somewhat round woman with more airs than a duchess stood looking up at him.

"I believe you must be right," Weston said graciously, although he was still deciding if he was comfortable with the lady.

"You may tell me who you are," she now commanded.

Weston had all he could do not to laugh.

"My name is Mr Weston."

"Then you must live at Brown Manor."

"I do indeed."

"Do you know Anne Gardiner?"

"I don't believe I caught your name," Weston replied, dodging the question, his voice cooling.

"I am Mrs Musgrove. I live at Dorfold Park. You've heard of it, I'm certain."

"I have, yes. It's a beautiful home."

"Indeed, it is. Do you know Anne Gardiner?" she now persisted.

"I certainly do. She and I attend the same church."

Mrs Musgrove's stance became rigid.

"That is certainly proof that exposing someone to religion does not mean it will take."

Weston's eyes grew stone cold, but he said nothing. Mrs Musgrove began to speak again, but Weston cut her off with as much grace as he could muster.

"I believe Benwick is free now, and I must see him. Good day, Mrs Musgrove."

That lady huffed a little when he bowed and moved on his way, but that didn't stop her from noticing that he was a fine-looking man, fairly tall and dark. It was too bad her own Augusta was getting a bit long in the tooth, or she might think of introducing them.

◈ ◈

"Lamps?" Benwick repeated. "Right this way, sir."

From there, Weston's shopping went downhill. He picked out five different lamps, but with almost no idea what he was getting. Never dreaming that Anne's name would come up in such a way, he had been put completely out of step. Finishing up at Benwick's, he asked that everything be delivered and crossed the street to the tearoom, hoping against reason that Mansfield was waiting for him.

His heart knew nothing but relief to find the coach coming up the street. The moment he climbed inside, Mansfield observed that something was amiss, but naturally he kept quiet. Weston kept quiet as well, but only until they'd cleared the streets of town.

"Is there talk in town concerning Miss Gardiner?" Weston asked directly.

"There is, sir," Mansfield told him, his voice more neutral than his feelings.

"What is being said?"

"It would seem that after your wedding incident, her father traveled into town and announced that his daughter had been married. Your name was never mentioned, but when Anne arrived in town many days later with no husband, she was not welcomed."

Weston's gaze went to the window. Why had this not occurred to him before? Things began to flash in his mind like a slow-moving dream. He remembered the way Anne had not wanted to be seen on the side of the road during their picnic. And the last time he was in Benwick's, there had been two women gossiping in the next aisle. He'd heard part of their conversation about a woman who was not telling where she'd been.

"She's protecting me," he said aloud, but to himself.

"I believe you must be right, sir."

Weston looked over at his man. He'd almost forgotten he was there.

"I'll need my horse as soon as we arrive."

"Yes, sir."

Mansfield didn't ask a single question. He would be told when and if there was a need, but there was no doubt in his mind that this ride would not be for fresh air. Mr Weston would be looking for answers.

☙ ❧

The Manse

"I've only just learned about Anne's situation in town" were nearly the first words from Weston's mouth.

Pastor Hurst, who had been home eating lunch, had seen Weston into the salon and twice asked him to sit down, but Weston didn't seem to hear him.

"It seems that you and Mrs Hurst have contact with Anne. Has it been difficult for her?" Weston asked.

"Yes," the pastor felt he had to admit.

Weston finally took a seat on the sofa, everything about him showing that this news was beyond painful to him.

"What can I do?"

"Nothing, Mr Weston. You had no choice in the matter, and neither did Anne."

"But that doesn't change the situation."

"No, it doesn't, but the people who know Anne—the people who count, I might add—know she is innocent. As for someone making it public that Anne was at Brown

Manor or that you were the man the Colonel set upon that day, I can't see where that would help Anne in the least. I'm not sure Anne would tell the details even if she felt it would help, but at any rate, I've advised her not to. For now we are praying that this will quiet down very soon. I don't know if there is anything else we can do."

"Did I spoil things for Anne?" Weston needed to know. "Was she engaged or promised?"

"No, she's quite alone."

The words—said with no hidden meaning—had a devastating effect on his heart. Weston rose to his feet and moved to the window. For several minutes he stood looking out. Pastor Hurst knew there were many things he could say, but he first wanted to glean a full picture of why this young man had come.

He also found it more than a little curious that Mr Weston, new to their midst, had referred to Anne by her first name during the entire conversation.

"I only wish there was something I could do."

"Well," Pastor Hurst said, a small twinkle in his eye, "you could marry her."

Weston looked neither shocked or amused.

"I was joking, Mr Weston."

"I assumed as much, but in truth I did think that Anne's getting married would solve the problem. I don't suppose there are many prospects."

"I'm afraid not."

Weston again felt a pang in his heart. It was unlike anything he'd ever experienced before, and he found it very odd.

"What advice would you give me?" Weston asked to take his mind from his emotions. "When I talked to Anne last Sunday, she was not happy to see me. She was gracious but also very embarrassed, and I don't wish for that. If you think it best to avoid her, I'll do that. Whatever will put her most at ease."

Pastor Hurst thought for a moment. He had not expected to see Weston before Sunday and in truth had not given much thought about the incident from the previous week. He'd told his wife he was still working it out, but time had been taken with other matters.

"May I think on that and get back to you, Mr Weston?"

"Of course." Weston stood. "I barged in here, and you've probably left your meal to listen to me rant. Thank you for your time."

"Not at all. In fact, if you haven't eaten, why not join me?"

"Are you certain?" Weston asked, his heart pleased because he genuinely liked the man.

"Come along," Pastor Hurst said lightly, leading the way from the room.

Weston found himself included in the most natural way, enjoying it even more when Mrs Hurst joined them. Being thankful for the first time in this situation concerning Anne, he thought, *If Anne has friends like these, she's in very good hands.*

❧ ❧

"You look very far away."

Judith Hurst jumped, a hand going to her heart before turning to her husband. It was later the same day. They were in the garden, and supper would be ready in less than an hour.

"Oh, Frederick, you startled me."

"I'm sorry."

He moved close to kiss her and then took the flower basket from her hand. Both her hands were free now to snip the blossoms and add them to the growing pile.

"What were you thinking about?"

"Mr Weston."

"He's certainly a surprise, isn't he?"

"Yes. I can't think why he hasn't married."

Pastor's brows rose. His wife was not known for her matchmaking schemes. But she didn't notice his response. Her head still bent, she methodically snipped the flowers one by one, adding them to the basket in her quiet way.

"Do you have anyone in mind for him?"

"Only Anne."

The pastor all but dropped the basket.

"Judith."

"Um?" she said absently, her eyes on the rosebushes.

"Look at me."

Judith obeyed, blinking when she saw her husband's astounded face.

"What is it, Frederick?"

"That's what I'm hoping you'll tell me. I've never heard you talk this way."

"No, I guess you haven't," she agreed sedately. "But I can't help but think about Anne finding someone to love and cherish her. I know God can do things we never think of, but I would be made of stone if I didn't wonder whether Mr Weston has noticed our Anne."

"Why would you be made of stone?"

"Because there have been so many days I wished someone would rescue her, and now Mr Weston comes into our midst. He's charming, kind, and I can tell by the questions he's asked you about Scripture that he's digging deeply and taking his faith seriously." Judith let out a little sigh. "If he would only love and marry Anne, he'd be just about perfect."

Pastor had nothing to say. He was thoroughly stunned with his wife's admission. And at the same time he agreed with her. He hadn't given hours of thought to the matter, but wasn't his own heart wondering the same thing just last week when he left Weston and Anne alone in the foyer?

"What does that look mean, dear?" Judith asked into his confused thoughts; she had stopped all movements and turned to face him.

"It just means that I have a lot of praying to do."

"Meaning?"

"Meaning that I've been trying to work this out so I could pray sensibly, when in truth I've been trying to work it out so I could tell God what to do. I need to pray for Anne and Mr Weston, not as a couple, but as God's children, remembering that He has a great plan for each of them."

Judith thought about this a moment and then asked, "So would you advise me *not* to pray that Mr Weston notices Anne?"

Pastor Hurst smiled.

"May I think about that and get back to you?"

Judith's smile matched his own. She laid the small shears in the basket with the flowers, tucked her arm into her husband's, and turned them so they could walk toward the house. His lack of answer for her might not help Anne at the moment, but as her husband had just said, it wasn't their job to help, it was their job to wait on God.

☙ ❧

Levens Crossing

Anne watched her father stride across the field on Saturday afternoon. She had told him she was making supper, but he had been a man with a mission. Sword belted into place and hat low on his brow, he exited through the back door and was gone. Anne had no idea where he was going or when he would return.

She watched his progress slow a bit and muttered to herself, "Heaven knows how muddy that field might be."

The words were barely out of her mouth when she heard horses on the road. She would have thought nothing of this, but the clopping of their hooves told her they had stopped out front. Anne circled the house slowly and found Palmer, Frank, Walt, and Mr Weston in her yard.

"Hello, Anne," Palmer greeted, swinging down from the saddle. "We're on our way to Tipton and thought we'd stop and say hello."

"I'm so glad you did." Anne smiled and met everyone's eyes briefly. "You just missed Father. He's off on an adventure."

"Miss Anne," Walt chimed in, "I think you have a hole starting in your roof."

"You're probably right, Walt," she agreed, turning her back to the group so she could inspect the spot to which he pointed. Palmer had come to stand on one side of her, and Weston had gone to her other.

"One of my coachmen is very handy," Weston said, gazing at the roof. "He could have that patched in less than an hour."

"Oh, thank you, Mr Weston, but I'm sure we can manage."

"But why should you?" Palmer shocked her by asking, his voice making the matter sound simple.

Anne looked to him.

"If Weston's man can see to it, Anne, his fixing it would be a fine idea."

Anne looked up at Palmer for a moment and then turned slowly back to Weston. She felt embarrassed in his presence but still met his eyes.

"Thank you, Mr Weston. I hope I didn't sound ungrateful."

"Not at all, Miss Gardiner," he replied, his eyes meeting hers, his voice quiet and kind. "There won't be time this afternoon, but I'll have Bert come on Monday."

"Thank you," she offered again, this time not able to look away for a moment.

"We'd best be off," Palmer said.

"Before you leave, Palmer, will you tell me how Lydia is doing?" Anne felt rescued when she was able to turn and ask.

"Very well. She'll be there tomorrow."

"At church?"

"That's what she says."

Anne laughed. "Tell her I think she's mad, but I can't wait to see her."

"I'll give her the message."

The men departed after that, Anne waving them on their way. She stood watching the horses and riders as they moved out of sight, and for that reason, caught the fact that Mr Weston turned often in his saddle to look back at her. Anne found it curious but refused to give way to fantasies. With a stern word to herself, she went inside to finish making supper.

ဢ ဢ

Tipton

"How did Anne seem?" Lydia asked over supper, her eyes on her two sons.

"She's getting a hole in her roof," Walt told her. "And Mr Weston has a man who can fix it."

"How nice, Mr Weston. I'm sure Anne and the Colonel will appreciate that."

"If the Colonel notices," Frank put in, his tone lacking criticism.

"That's certainly true," his father agreed. "The last time I saw the Colonel, he spoke to me about my father in a most lucid manner. The time before that, he didn't know me at all."

"And Anne has said that it's not unusual for him to prepare a meal for them," Lydia inserted, "and even lay the table. He likes Anne to fix tea, but the Colonel is surprisingly competent in the kitchen."

"I like his sword," Emma said softly, drawing a smile from her father.

"Forgive us, Mr Weston." Lydia noticed that he had grown quiet. "You probably don't know about Anne's father."

"Actually, I do. He's a fascinating chap."

"Indeed. I'm sure all small towns can boast a character, but I don't know how many of them are armed for battle."

"Did he see active service?" Weston asked.

"Yes," Palmer answered. "He served in Burma and saw plenty of action, even sustained a few injuries."

"But that's not why he's ill today," Lydia filled in, unaware that Anne had already given him these details. "He ran a high fever some years ago now. Everyone was certain he would die. When he came out of it, he was never the same."

"Miss Gardiner has no siblings, no other family?" Weston asked before he remembered that Pastor had told him this.

"No. Her mother died when she was 14—a gentle and lovely woman. She's the reason Anne is such a lady."

"She is that," Weston said quietly, his eyes on the meat he was cutting.

Lydia couldn't help but notice the comment. She looked at her guest and then glanced at her husband. Their eyes met for just a moment, but much was communicated.

❧ ❧

"He smiled!" Lizzy Palmer said with excitement.

"I saw that," Anne said, eyes on the baby in her arms.

"I've got to tell Mama that Oliver smiled!"

Lizzy darted off, but Emma stayed close, leaning against Anne to have a look at her brother.

"Is he a good baby?" Anne asked Emma.

"Yes. He doesn't cry very much at all. We hope that Marianne has a boy too, so they can play together."

"That would be fun, but don't forget that you're a girl and you like to play with your brothers."

"Not as much as I do with Penny and Lizzy." Emma's reply was a fervent one and her eyes had grown large.

Anne smiled at her, and after Emma smiled back, she transferred her gaze back to the baby.

"He's so sweet," the eight-year-old said in a sweet voice of her own.

"Yes, he is," Anne agreed, glancing over at Emma. "Isn't it fun when babies finally arrive and you can meet them?"

"Yes, and Mama's not so tired now."

"I can see that," Anne said after she looked over at the group of women visiting in the center aisle of the church, completely unaware that she was the topic of conversation.

❧ ❧

"Anne's birthday is next week," Judith told Marianne and Lydia.

"Which day?" Marianne asked.

"Sunday."

"Let's have a party," Lydia suggested.

"Yes, let's do that."

"We can have it at the manse. Whom should we invite?"

The women grew a bit quiet. Lydia peeked around her sister-in-law to see the back of Anne's head as she bent over to see the baby, and she was struck with one thought: *vulnerable*.

"Let's keep it small."

"I think that's a good idea. How about our three families and the two new families—so we can get to know them?"

"The Allens and the Shepherds?"

"Yes."

"Good idea."

The matter settled, the women separated and went on their way. Marianne found Jennings outside talking with several other men. Palmer invited them to lunch and even offered to take their brood in the carriage. Because they were alone, Marianne told her husband of the birthday plans as soon as they were underway.

"Are we inviting Weston?" Jennings asked immediately.

Marianne turned to gawk at him.

"Why did you ask that?"

Jennings shrugged. "Surely it hasn't escaped your notice, Mari, that Weston's falling for Anne would be very convenient."

Marianne's hand came to her mouth. This was so unlike her spouse that she wanted to laugh, but she could see that he was sincere.

Jennings glanced over and caught her look, causing a smile to tug at the corners of his handsome mouth.

"You're on the verge of laughter."

"It's out of shock, I assure you."

Jennings didn't comment; he only smiled and captured his wife's hand in his larger one and held it in his lap.

Marianne did nothing to disturb the silence for the remainder of the trip, but she was still in shock when she arrived at Tipton. She was mulling on the exchange, or rather trying to, when her sister-in-law approached.

"Palmer thinks we should invite Mr Weston to Anne's party. What do you think?"

Marianne's mouth swung open.

"Jennings said the same thing."

The women stared at each other, unsure of what to do.

"I think this might be something that Judith and Pastor need to decide," Marianne said at last.

Lydia looked relieved. "You're right. I'll send a note to Judith, and then we'll leave the decision with them."

Glad to have the matter settled—at least for the moment—both women went in search of the family.

Chapter Eight

Anne heard the knock at the door on Monday morning, but her mind was far away as she walked through the house to see who might be calling. She was snapped back to her Saturday conversation with Mr Weston when she found a coachman on her step. He bowed, handed her a letter, and stood expectantly. She read:

> *Dear Miss Gardiner,*
>
> *This is Bert. He has been commissioned by me to attend to your roof. I'm certain you will find his work most satisfactory, but if for any reason you are displeased, send word to me and I will rectify the situation.*
>
> *I sincerely hope this finds you and your father well. Please let me know if I can be of further service.*
>
> *R. Weston*

Anne read the missive over twice before looking into the kind eyes of the servant before her.

"Shall I go to work, miss?"

"Yes, please," Anne couldn't help but respond to the cheerfulness in his voice.

"Very good, miss. If you'll just show me the spot."

"Of course."

Anne led the way outdoors, stopping at the corner of the house and pointing to the spot on the roof, the one that seemed to be growing each day.

"I see it there," Bert spoke with confidence. "Shouldn't be any problem at all."

With that he went to work, and Anne got out of his way. She went indoors but found she no longer wanted to linger over her cup of tea. She read the letter twice more, studying the neat, bold hand, and for just a moment allowed herself to think on the man himself.

It was simply too bad that she had met Mr Weston under such trying circumstances and that her own situation was so unenviable because he was one of the most amiable men she'd encountered in a long while.

Anne caught sight of a jagged nail on her left hand just then, her heart sinking low at the sight of it. She was a gentleman's daughter, but that was a well-hidden fact these days.

Before she could start to inspect her dress or fuss over her rough skin, Anne began to wash the breakfast dishes. There was no point in crying for things that could not be.

Not to mention, Anne said to herself, *you're not getting any younger, and eyes made puffy from crying will only add to that point.*

✍ ✍

"Did you get my note?" Pastor asked Weston the moment he saw him on Sunday.

"I did, thank you."

"Are you going to be able to join us?"

"Certainly, I wouldn't miss it. I did pick up a small gift, but I wasn't sure what you had planned."

"Let me check with Judith to be certain, but I believe we have a gift for Anne as well."

Weston nodded and Pastor went on his way, the service scheduled to begin in less then ten minutes.

Weston took a seat and tried to read his Bible to prepare his heart for the morning, but he was distracted. His eyes strayed around the room several times and often to the door. He wasn't certain, but it didn't appear as though Anne were present. He wondered if Pastor knew that. A small frisson of fear spiraled through him when he thought about Anne at home. He knew her father was often about, but that man did tend to wander. What if Anne needed something and no one was there...

Only by the greatest force of will did Weston remain in his seat. At the very least he wanted to find Pastor Hurst and ask him where Anne could be. Working to remember that Anne had gotten along well enough before he had entered the scene and praying for calmness, Weston readied himself to listen to the service when it began. Nevertheless, it did his heart a world of good to see Anne slip into church about halfway through the service.

❧ ❧

"Happy birthday, Anne." Judith greeted her friend and gave her a warm hug the moment the sermon ended and she found her near a back pew.

"Thank you, Judith."

"I didn't see you at first and worried that something would keep you away from lunch at the manse."

Anne smiled. "Father remembered my birthday and wanted to talk, so I was late."

Judith's mouth opened and Anne laughed.

"Isn't it amazing?"

"Yes! Did you invite him to lunch?"

"I did, but he didn't answer."

"What a nice birthday surprise, Anne," Judith went on warmly. "I'm so pleased for you."

"It was very nice, and the most exciting part about it was that I've been reading in 2 Kings where the widow's oil fills all the jars. I was so struck by Elisha's words to the widow when he told her to gather the jars. He said, 'borrow not a few.'"

"Why were you struck by that?" Judith said, momentarily forgetting it was her job to get Anne to the manse.

"It just reminded me of expectations. I often come to God expecting only a thimbleful of blessing. The widow didn't really know what Elisha was about, so his telling her she needed many jars was appropriate. On the other hand, I know what a big God I have, but I wouldn't expect to need many jars. I would assume God had very little for me when He might have much.

"And then this morning when Father gave me birthday greetings, I realized I haven't been trusting in the big God I have. I don't ask God for much. I don't believe the way I should."

Judith put her hand on the younger woman's arm. "How blessed you are, Anne, to see this. How wonderful God is to show us where we lack. I'm so pleased for you. I'll be praying that this is only the beginning. I'll be praying that you keep seeing how big our God is and recognizing all the ways He demonstrates it."

It was a sweet moment, one between special friends that certainly would have ended in another hug, but Anne's stomach rumbled just then. She giggled when Judith laughed.

"I just realized that Father and I talked right past breakfast."

"In that case," Judith stood with a mission, "I think it's time to get you some lunch."

Anne stood to join her. She was not going to argue with that.

≈ ≈

"They're coming!" Pastor Hurst said in excitement as he shot back into the dining room.

"Which direction?" Margaret Hurst asked.

"The kitchen."

The group moved as one to the side of the room that would keep them out of sight the longest. Just two minutes later, their voices coming ahead of them, Judith and Anne appeared in the doorway and the group shouted birthday greetings.

As was expected, Anne was shocked speechless. Gifts were pressed into her hands, hugs were given, and all Anne could do was stare at their faces.

"You're giving me a party?" she said at last, and the friends, some new and some old, laughed at her.

Lunch was underway just moments later. Allens, Shepherds, Palmers, Jenningses, and Hursts were sprinkled all around the table. Anne found herself between Weston and Lydia, and across from Jennings, Marianne, and Emma Palmer. For a moment Anne listened to Jennings and Weston discuss the work on the conservatory at Brown Manor, but when there was a break, Anne turned to the man on her right.

"Your man came on Monday, Mr Weston, and repaired the roof. Thank you so much."

"You're welcome. How did it turn out?" he asked, even though he'd ridden past it very slowly in order to inspect the job.

"It's perfect. I don't think it will ever leak again."

"I'm glad to hear that, but should you find yourself with more drips, do let me know."

"Thank you."

Weston realized that she hadn't agreed, only thanked him, and for a moment he held her eyes with his own.

"You'll inform me?"

Unable to look away but not wanting to commit, Anne took in his expectantly raised brows and nodded.

Weston smiled at her, and Anne felt her face heat. The dishes were being passed and she had an excuse not to look at anyone while she served herself from the platter, but she couldn't help but wonder if this might not prove to be a very long afternoon.

෩ ෨

Brown Manor

"I'm leaving for London in the morning," Weston told Mansfield when he arrived home.

"Very well, sir."

"Keep things going on the conservatory, but if something is delayed, don't worry about it. I'll be home within the week."

"Yes, sir."

Mansfield had no questions and soon left his employer in peace, something Weston welcomed. He'd had a delightful time at the manse, not just with the five families that were there, but with Anne as well—most especially Anne. She had been somewhat shy whenever she realized he was near, but there were plenty of opportunities to observe her interacting with the others and to see for himself that she was quite genuinely loving and sweet.

Not that this surprised Weston. It did, however, make him thoughtful. He felt a need to visit with his mother and decided to stay with his decision to visit her that week, but Anne lingered on his mind for the remainder of the day and even as he journeyed to London.

෩ ෨

Levens Crossing

Anne sat alone in the kitchen, looking at the gifts she'd received, her heart melting in pleasure all over again. She couldn't remember when she'd had such a special birthday. Each and every person had taken time to speak with her and wish her a happy day.

Anne reached for the lovely handkerchiefs Mr Weston had given her. He had been as kind as everyone else, but Anne couldn't help but notice his gaze had been rather watchful.

Anne was not a person to daydream, but in truth she did find Mr Weston most interesting. She didn't indulge in any type of fantasy where he was concerned, but he lingered in the back of her mind until her father came looking for something to eat.

❧ ❧

London

"Did I ever tell you that Henrietta came to see me at Brown Manor?"

Lenore Weston, who had been arranging flowers in a vase in the drawing room, stopped and turned her head to study her only child where he sat on the sofa, legs stretched out in front of him, relaxed as a lazy cat.

"I don't believe you did."

Weston had nothing more to say, and Lenore deserted her flowers. Something was on her son's mind, and she hoped to learn what it was.

"Did she stay long?"

"No, very briefly. It was most uncomfortable."

"Do you wish she had?"

"Lingered? No."

Silence fell again. Lenore was intent on Weston, but Weston's mind was clearly elsewhere.

"Do you wish to find love again, Robert?"

Weston smiled as he looked at her.

"I think it might be overrated."

Lenore felt a deep pain around her heart on this announcement but didn't give herself away.

"I saw Anne on Sunday," Robert volunteered.

"How is she?"

"I think well. It was her birthday."

"Was there a party?"

"Yes. I was invited."

"So the two of you are getting close?"

Robert laughed. "Not exactly."

"What does that mean?"

"She's still quite shy in my presence."

"I can understand that. She's probably still embarrassed."

"Probably."

Lenore let the silence linger this time, determined that Weston would be the first to speak. When he did, Lenore was glad she was sitting down. Without a sound she listened to his words, not disagreeing, but finding she needed some moments to adjust.

"Come back with me," Weston finally invited. "You're overdue for your visit to Brown Manor as it is."

"You're certainly right about that," Lenore agreed, suddenly wanting to visit very much.

"So you'll come?"

"Yes."

Weston looked pleased.

"Have you spoken to Pastor Hurst about your plans?"

"Not yet. I'll do that soon."

Lenore nodded and then smiled at him.

"What's that smile for?"

"I just realized how much I like you, Robert Weston, and that makes me smile."

Weston laughed at her discovery and leaned over to kiss her cheek.

"Let's hope I'm as well liked in Collingbourne, shall we?"

"We shall!" Lenore agreed, and the two of them talked of nothing special but covered many topics for the rest of the afternoon.

 ❧ ❧

Tipton

Lydia smiled down at her youngest child. Three-week-old Oliver didn't notice. His brow was lowered with some inner concentration his mother found adorable. She lifted him close to her face for a kiss, thinking he was the loveliest miracle she'd ever seen.

A knock at the door brought her attention around as Judith put her head in long enough to make an announcement.

"Miss Gardiner is here."

"I'll be right there, Judith."

Knowing that Anne would wish to see the baby, Lydia took Oliver with her and met Anne in the salon.

"How are you?" Anne said, reaching for the baby and snuggling him close.

"I'm doing well. A bit sore suddenly, but nothing abnormal."

"And how is this little man? He's so rosy and pink."

Lydia laughed. "Palmer accused me of secretly wanting a girl, and now we've been blessed with a child who's pretty enough to be one."

"Did you want a girl?" Anne asked astutely.

"Part of me did, for Lizzy's sake, but she's so delighted with Oliver that I can see it didn't matter."

Anne rocked the baby for a moment while Lydia studied her.

"Did you enjoy your birthday?"

"Very much. I'm still getting over the surprise of it all."

"Were you terribly embarrassed over Mr Weston's appearance?"

"At first," Anne admitted. "I felt somewhat conscious of him the entire time, but he's so gracious and kind that it wasn't all bad."

"Maybe it's the fact that he's gracious and kind that draws you to him."

Anne nodded. "He's quite the gentleman."

Lydia was tempted to question her more but held off. Much as she wished to know Anne's true feelings concerning Mr Weston, Lydia knew it was not her place to ask.

"How is the Colonel?" the older woman asked instead, changing the subject.

"Much the same."

"How do you keep from growing discouraged, Anne?"

"Some days I don't, but on days when I'm thinking well of the situation, I keep reminding myself that God is in control and that He loves my father and me very much.

"Please don't misunderstand me, Lydia. Life is not easy, but we never go without. I don't have a parent I can confide in, but I have many people who are available for me. Mine is an easy situation to pity, but pity is not necessary. I think that it's easy to look at someone else's situation—a more painful situation—and somehow comfort ourselves in that. But should we be looking any further than eternity?"

"I'm not sure I know what you mean," Lydia had to admit.

"My father isn't well, but I have eternal life," Anne explained. "I have to walk most places even when I'm tired or hot, but I have eternal life. We don't live in a beautiful home any longer, and we've lost our estate, but I have eternal life. If I view my situation by just looking at my own life, I do better than if I start comparing it to someone else's in order to find comfort or something to be thankful for."

Lydia thanked her for the reminder. She had asked about her father, thinking it might do Anne some good to talk about him, and it turned out she had been the one to hear something she needed. Often busy with five children, Lydia was at times tempted to feel sorry for herself. Not many days ago she had done just as Anne cautioned against, reminding herself that things could be worse. It was far better to find joy and peace in all that God had already given her.

The women had a nice, long visit, and that was fine with Lydia, but as soon as Anne left, she knew she had some confessing and soul-searching to do. She found some solitude and took care of it as fast as she could.

☙ ❧

Brown Manor

"Robert!" his mother exclaimed for the fifth time, her eyes huge with delight as she took in her son's home for the first time. It had been years since Lenore had been inside Brown Manor, but her joy stemmed from more than that. Her son had made it a home. It was warm and welcoming, and she couldn't have been happier as he gave her a tour.

Weston was very pleased by his mother's reaction. He was delighted with the outcome as well, but it was doubly rewarding to have his mother's approval.

"Come outside with me now," he invited. "I want to check on the conservatory work, and we might as well do that before we clean up from the trip."

To please her son, Lenore complied. She was dusty and a bit tired, but her first glimpse of the gardens was worth the exertion.

"Oh, Robert, the colors! They're amazing."

"Aren't they, though? I can't take any credit. The gardens were in fine shape when I arrived. We've had only to spruce them up a bit."

Lenore took in the numerous cobblestone and gravel pathways that crisscrossed their way toward what would obviously be the new conservatory. Lining every path and covering every spare inch of earth were flowers, bushes, shrubs, and plants of every conceivable color, type, and variety. The paths would take the strolling couple through the occasional archway, and each trellis dripped with climbing roses or clematis.

"There's a kitchen garden around the side there," Weston pointed as he began to explain the conservatory plans. "I have planned high glass on three sides, and the building itself will be 60 by 100 feet."

Lenore listened intently, picking the occasional flower and working to take it all in. She was proud of her son—he had grown into a fine young man—but she hadn't seen him take charge in this way. It pleased her but also gave her pause.

"Shall we go in?" Weston suggested, taking in his mother's quiet face.

Lenore stopped and turned to him.

"It's lovely, Robert. I'm so pleased for you."

Weston smiled. For a moment he couldn't read her thoughts, but the eyes she turned to him were the ones he knew: kind, warm, and supportive.

The twosome made their way indoors and relaxed for the remainder of the day. The trip from London had been tiring, and both wanted to be fresh for church in the morning.

❧ ❧

The Manse

"I've disturbed your lunch again, haven't I, sir?"

"Not at all, Weston," Pastor Hurst said kindly to the younger man. "Come right in. Did you have a good visit with your mother?"

"Yes."

"Is she still here?"

"She left Saturday. She had appointments and could only stay a week."

"Well, how nice for you that she could come. We certainly enjoyed meeting her."

Weston had no reply to this. Pastor had seen him to a chair and taken one himself but now gave him a few moments to initiate conversation.

"I've come seeking your advice today," Weston began.

"All right."

"What do you think of my asking Anne Gardiner to be my wife?"

The room was quiet for several heartbeats.

"May I ask you some questions?"

"Certainly."

"Are you in love with Anne?"

"No, sir, I'm not, but I do care about her."

"When did this begin?"

"It's been coming for some weeks now, but my mind really began to move in this direction during her birthday party."

"Did something happen?"

"Nothing and everything."

"What does that mean?"

"I don't know exactly, Pastor, except to say that she's so unspoiled and sweet. I've never known anyone like her. I gave her the handkerchiefs, if you recall. They were nothing special or fancy, but she handled them with such delight and thanked me with great sincerity. I haven't been able to stop thinking of her."

"So you feel sorry for her."

Weston laughed. "Not in the least. She doesn't invite those types of feelings from anyone, but there is something very vulnerable about her, and I find myself nearly irresistibly drawn."

There was something more here—Pastor sensed it—but he couldn't put his finger on it.

"It bothers me that she's being shunned in town," Weston continued, his face pained as he looked across at the other man. "I believe that a marriage can be built on mutual respect and caring, and that's what we would have. If we were to marry, I think her position in town would be restored to her. As my wife, I guess I'm hoping that her reputation would suffer no further."

"And do you seek a real marriage—a marriage in every sense of the word?"

"Yes. It will certainly take some time to fully know each other, but I believe you would recommend Anne as a fine wife, and I'm hoping you'll be able to recommend me to Anne."

"You understand she comes with nothing, no income of any kind?"

"That is the least of my worries."

"What are you most worried about?"

"That you won't approve of me for Anne, and that Anne will go on having to pay for my actions on that day. Or that she'll refuse me and never be comfortable in my presence."

There's more than just caring going on here, but he doesn't even know it. He's half in love with her and hasn't a clue.

"In truth, Mr Weston," Pastor's thoughts scrambled before he found what he wanted to say, "I would be happy to give my consent. I know Anne very well, and I've come to know you over the summer. I find it hard to believe that your love for Jesus Christ and the Word is feigned. However, exactly how Anne will respond to this is yet to be known. I would never push her to do something she does not care to do, not even a little."

Weston nodded in complete agreement.

"But if you're quite sincere about this, I would be happy to broach the subject with her."

Weston came forward in his seat.

"You would talk to her for me, Pastor? At least to begin with?"

"Yes. I don't mind telling you that Anne's welfare is often in my prayers. Having you marry and take care of her would certainly ease her situation."

Weston nodded, but the interview had cost him. He felt very spent just then and out of words.

"Give me a few days, Weston, and I'll see to the matter."

"I thank you, sir."

Pastor Hurst looked him in the eye.

"If Anne agrees to become your wife, I think you will be thankful, Weston. Anne Gardiner is very special. She's sweet, godly, and kind. The man who wins her affections will be blessed among men."

It was not what Weston expected to hear, but it did his heart good. He thanked the pastor several more times before leaving, his heart also thanking God that the doors were still open. What the next few days and weeks would bring, he would have to wait to see.

Chapter Nine

"Mother?" Jane Hurst caught that lady's hand before she could leave the room.

"You're stalling, Jane," Judith said, fighting a smile.

Jane grinned up at her.

"Now, dear, Margaret is already asleep. You do the same."

"But I did have a question."

"All right. Ask quickly, and don't question my answer."

"Can Mary Clements come to visit tomorrow...maybe spend the day? We spoke of it on Sunday."

"It will probably work out, but I'll give you my final answer over breakfast."

"Thank you." Jane smiled up at her, and Judith leaned to kiss her once more. A swift check on the boys caused one more delay when five-year-old John complained of being cold, but at last all blankets were in place, everyone was kissed, and she was headed downstairs to find her husband. That that man had something on his mind all through dinner and the evening had been more than clear to her, but they had not been alone so she could question him. Asking didn't mean she would get an answer, but tonight she was going to try.

"Judith, is that you?"

"Yes, dear," she answered, following her husband's voice at the bottom of the stairs and turning into the small salon to find him.

"Please come in. I wish to tell you something."

Judith was not going to argue with that. She was most eager to hear. Nothing, however, could have prepared her for her husband's news. Judith sat in stunned silence upon hearing Weston's request for Anne's hand. She seemed incapable of speaking or moving.

"I've shocked you," Pastor said at last.

"Yes."

"Is this the way Anne will react?" he asked.

"Much worse, I'm afraid."

"And what will her answer be?"

Judith thought on this but honestly did not know.

"I think she could be talked into it, but I wouldn't want to be the one to do that."

Pastor was already shaking his head.

"No. I've told Weston I won't push her. I told him I would introduce the matter, but I won't push Anne."

"What if she doesn't know what to do and asks your advice?"

"I'll tell her to marry the man."

Judith had to think on this a little more. She cared a great deal for Mr Weston, and she adored Anne, but her heart couldn't help but ask the question *What woman didn't wish to marry for love?* Nevertheless...

"What can I do to help?" Judith now asked.

"Invite Anne over so we can both talk with her. Let me know what time works out for both of you."

"All right. Soon?"

"Yes. There's not going to be a lot of flowery courtship, but Anne should have a chance to think on her answer as soon as possible."

It all sounded very neat and tidy, like some sort of business transaction, but both Hursts were very mindful of the hearts and emotions involved in this venture. They talked only a few minutes more on the subject before they knelt together to pray.

≈ ∽

Thornton Hall

"Are the walls getting a bit close?" Anne asked of Marianne on her visit. The women had enjoyed tea and now were content to sit back and talk.

"At times. I'm tired, and that makes it easier to be confined, but Jennings," Marianne's voice went up a notch, "and the children tend to hover a bit."

"I heard that," a deep voice said good-naturedly as he passed the doorway.

The women exchanged a smile.

"I can see you're simply miserable having an attentive husband," Anne gently teased her expectant friend.

Marianne was laughing when the baby delivered a small kick. She didn't say anything to Anne, but it was something she never grew weary of.

At moments like this Marianne asked herself what life must be like for Anne Gardiner. She had no one to take care of her and no prospect of a suitor. Marianne had been looked after her entire life. She wasn't sure she would know how to survive in Anne's world. At the same time, she recognized Anne's strength in the Lord because of her adversity.

"Well, I'd best be off," Anne said, effectively cutting into Marianne's busy thoughts. "Pastor and Judith have asked me to lunch at the manse."

"Let me call the coach for you, Anne."

"Oh, Mari, I don't mind the walk."

But Mrs Jennings wouldn't hear of it. It was a good distance to the church, and Anne had already walked to Thornton Hall. Marianne was not about to let her walk back. And as she was going by coach, they had more time. The two of them visited a bit longer before Anne took her leave.

She was heavy on Marianne's mind even after she left, and Marianne wondered why.

"You look pensive," Jennings commented when he found his wife alone on the drive.

"I was thinking about Anne."

"Is she all right?"

Marianne turned to face her spouse.

"She was when she left, but for some odd reason I think something rather momentous might be looming."

Jennings' brows rose, but he didn't comment. He wasn't exactly sure what his wife meant. Beyond that she looked as though she needed to be alone with her thoughts.

Jennings put a gentle arm around her to lead her back inside but didn't question her further.

◈ ◈

The Manse

"I fear she'll think we've plotted against her."

"All right. How else do you suggest we do this?"

Pastor and Judith stared at each other.

"Judith?" her husband pressed, and Judith looked helpless in her frustration.

"Frederick," she said at last, her voice still telling of her worry. "If we tell her as soon as she arrives, she won't be able to eat a thing. If we wait, I won't be able to pretend that nothing is going on, and she'll wonder at my odd behavior during lunch."

Pastor nodded, his mind working on it. His wife had a very good point. This subject was sure to have an effect on his behavior as well.

"I'm certain there will be nothing brief about our conversation," Pastor suddenly realized. "We'll tell Anne as soon as she arrives—over lunch even—and we'll encourage her to eat when she's ready."

"All right."

Pastor Hurst looked down at his wife's face, seeing for the first time how painful this could be for all of them. Prior to this he had only thought of Anne and Weston. His wife's strained face was a reminder of how shortsighted he'd been.

"Miss Gardiner is here," the housekeeper announced from the doorway.

"Thank you, Phoebe. We'll be right along."

Giving his wife a last look and even taking time to smile into her eyes, Pastor Hurst took her hand and led her toward the door.

Anne was being hugged and greeted by the couple just moments later, her eyes alight with pleasure at seeing them.

"How are you?" Judith asked.

"I'm well. I was just over to see Marianne Jennings. She's feeling rather confined these days, but we had a lovely visit."

You would have walked all that way to see her, Judith couldn't help but think. *And then Marianne would have ordered a carriage to bring you back here. Please, Father God,* Judith suddenly begged, *please take care of Anne. If marrying Weston is the way to do that, please help her to see.*

"Lunch is on," Judith said, trying to cover her riotous thoughts. "Shall we go in?"

"That sounds lovely."

In the spacious, wood-paneled dining room, Pastor took the end of the wide table, his wife on his right side and Anne on his left. He asked Phoebe to leave the dishes so they could serve themselves, and when everyone had bowls of soup, conversation began.

"We have news, Anne," Pastor began.

Anne swallowed the soup in her mouth and looked up. "Have you?"

"Yes. Someone has asked for your hand in marriage."

Anne blinked, her spoon frozen over the bowl.

"Are you all right, Anne?" Judith asked.

"Is it someone I know?" she asked after a moment of silence, suddenly looking terribly young and vulnerable.

"Yes," Pastor said, knowing the moment was at hand. "It is Mr Weston."

The spoon landed back in the soup bowl an instant later, splashing some of the liquid onto Anne's hand. She didn't appear to notice.

"Why?" was the only word she could manage.

"A number of reasons. He admires you and cares for you. He is also aware of the changes that have occurred in your life since the 'marriage,' and knows that your becoming his wife would rectify that."

"So he pities me." Anne's voice was flat and resigned.

"Not in the least!" Pastor said briskly. "I asked him that very thing, and he laughed at the idea." The man studied her for a moment. "He also feels it's best to act swiftly. He's very mindful of your reputation and feels it's suffered enough."

Suddenly flustered, Anne looked down and reached for her napkin. After cleaning her hand, she pushed her soup bowl away. Judith's eyes went to her spouse, begging him to somehow rescue them all.

"Does he not understand that I come with nothing?" she asked, her voice showing her shock. "Does he not understand the full extent of my circumstances?"

"Yes, he does."

"Then he's a fool, and I couldn't marry a fool!"

For some reason the statement, along with Anne's outraged face, caused Judith to chuckle. When a small giggle slipped out, the other occupants of the table both looked at her in surprise.

"I'm sorry," she said, still fighting a smile. "It's just so funny."

"What is?"

"Anne's outrage that Weston's a fool for wanting to marry her. I've been thinking that if he *doesn't* notice her, he's a fool."

"Why, Judith?" Anne asked. "Why do you feel that way?"

"Because you're a godly, lovely, and sweet woman, and he would be blind not to fall for you."

Anne looked to her pastor.

"Are you saying he's in love with me?"

"No, I'm not. But as I said, he does care, and he believes that you can have a marriage built on mutual respect and caring."

"A real marriage?" Anne clarified.

"Yes."

Anne fell quiet. Not looking at her hosts, she sat and prayed, asking God for wisdom but also knowing whom else she must ask: the person she had often gone to in the past.

"Pastor Hurst?" she called his name and looked into his eyes.

"Yes, Anne."

"Do you feel I should accept this offer?"

"Yes, Anne, I do."

"And you did say he wanted a real marriage, not one in name only?"

"Yes."

"Judith, may I see you alone?"

"Of course, dear."

"I'll go," Pastor offered when the women made to rise.

They thanked him and sat looking at each other even after he exited. For some odd reason, Judith wanted to cry, but she held herself in check.

"Judith, will Mr Weston want intimacy right away?"

"I don't know, Anne, but if he does, it would be best to follow his lead."

"Why is that?"

"Waiting for such things can put a strain on both of you. It sounds horrific when you don't know one another well, but that's an aspect of marriage that should not be in limbo. Unless both parties agree to abstain, doing so is just too stressful. Does that make sense?"

"Yes, I understand. It's the way we're created. It's just a bit hard to imagine when we're not in love."

"Do you not think, Anne," Judith asked quietly, "that you might come to love him?"

"That's just it, Judith, I probably will. It's not knowing whether he'll ever return my love that frightens me."

"Do you not think he'll fall for you as well?"

"Why would he?"

Judith smiled, a huge, knowing smile that caused Anne to laugh.

"It's all very well for you to laugh at me, Judith Hurst, when you're not faced with the prospect of marrying a stranger!"

Judith reached for her hand, her face still wreathed in soft smiles.

"Please don't think we're being lighthearted about this, Anne. We know how serious it is, but Frederick has become quite close to Mr Weston, and I do trust his advice on the matter. If your heart tells you otherwise, you must listen, but if you're not sure what to do, do not be afraid to heed my husband's counsel."

Anne fell quiet again, but this time the silence was brief.

"Must I decide now, Judith? Would it be all right to ask Mr Weston some questions?"

"Certainly. I believe Frederick was going to advise that very thing. He feels the two of you should meet and share your thoughts on the matter. You both need to be certain of this."

Judith made sure Anne's questions for her were covered and then went in search of her husband. When he came back to the table, Anne informed him she would like to meet with and discuss the matter with Mr Weston.

Outwardly quite calm, Pastor Hurst agreed, telling Anne he would see to the matter, but inside he was feeling as though he could weep with thankfulness.

ᔕ ᔐ

Levens Crossing

Anne studied her father quite openly at dinner that evening. He ate, but his mind was many miles away—she could read it in his eyes—therefore he had no hint of her scrutiny.

When she took time to think about it, she realized they got on very well. There was always the worry of money running short, but odd as the situation had become, it was survivable. Whenever Anne's mind did stop long enough to think along these lines, she would ask herself what went on inside of the man she called Father. She also asked questions about a fever so elevated and lengthy that it affected a man's mind forever. The illness had been a long and frightening time for her, but nowhere near as long as the time since. She could count on one hand the occasions he'd looked at her with true recognition. At times she ached for the father whose eyes had been filled with love for her and her mother, but she had learned early on that it did no good to pine.

Tonight she missed her mother too. Losing her had been a severe blow. Anne had only been 14. At a time when a young lady needs her mother, Anne's had been gone. Her mother's sister had been around for a while, but she could not get over the loss. Only months after her sister's death, Aunt Caroline had announced she was going away. She didn't say where she was headed or when she would return, but her lack of contact over the months and then years confirmed one thing. She would not be coming back.

But all was not lost. Anne had had her father. His smile wasn't quite as bright, and he didn't laugh as easily, but they had fared well together. Then, less than two years after her mother's death, her father grew ill. Life did not recover its normalcy after that. Anne found herself merely surviving.

Having her father remain but not as the same man had left Anne in a sea of worry and doubt. She had had no choice but to turn to God's Word, as she'd seen her mother do countless times. Only then did she find solace and a way to cope with all that life had placed before her.

And now a new issue had surfaced, certainly not one born of tragedy, but one that left a lingering question: What was to be done about Mr Weston's suggestion? Would she suddenly know what to do once they'd met face-to-face at the end of the week to discuss the matter?

Anne shook her head and spooned preserves onto the bread in her hand. It didn't seem likely. She didn't want to leave Mr Weston in doubt for an unreasonable time, but Anne seriously questioned if she would know that swiftly.

You could just take Pastor's advice, she thought to herself and then mulled that option over for a time.

"Is there tea, dear?" her father suddenly questioned her, and she found his eyes on her.

"Yes, Father. I'll get you some."

"Is that a new dress?"

"No, I've had this one for a time," Anne told him, not wanting to think about how many times she'd made it over and repaired it.

"Well, it's very nice on you."

"Thank you."

"Does your husband like it?"

Anne froze. She had just filled his teacup but now stood quite still.

"My husband?"

"Yes, Mr Weston. Does he like it?"

Oh, mercy! was Anne's only thought as she worked to frame a reply, but she need not have worried. A moment later her father's face turned away again. A glance at his eyes told Anne he had returned to that faraway place.

Anne went back to her meal with shaking hands. She was genuinely hungry—something she hadn't been during lunch—and did eat, but an odd sensation had begun to spiral inside of her. It lingered until she retired for the night.

∾ ∿

The Manse

"Are you nervous?" Judith asked quietly.

"Dreadfully," Anne admitted, feeling a bit ill.

"He'll be here soon."

"Was I early or is he late?"

"You were early," Judith told her and then smiled. "Nerves must have made you cover the distance in half the time."

Even Anne smiled a little over this and then noticed her friend's own worried brow.

"Where are the children today?" she asked to distract them both.

"Shopping in town. They've been asking to do just that for several weeks, and today seemed to be the right time."

Anne nodded, noticing Judith still looked tense.

"Thank you for everything you've done, Judith."

The older woman looked at her in surprise.

"What have we done, Anne?"

"Tried to see me happy and cared for."

It was too much for the pastor's wife. Tears rushed to her eyes, and she moved swiftly to Anne's side. She took Anne's cool hands in her own and gripped them firmly.

"At times I think I would do anything to see you fall in love and be loved in return, Anne, and someday you might be, but my deepest heart's desire is that you be cared for. I hope you understand how much I've prayed for that. We can only do so much. It never seems enough. So when Mr Weston came along, I naturally began to dream about the security he could give you. I've wanted it for you so desperately, but not at the expense of your happiness, Anne. If you have any doubts, you must say no. Tell me you understand, for I know I've been rattling on."

Anne put her arms about the older woman.

"Thank you, Judith. I understand completely. It will be all right," she reassured her. "Either way, everything will be fine."

Judith looked into Anne's eyes, seeing wisdom born of experience, but also a weariness. On top of that, the hands she'd been gripping were work-roughened. If Judith let her mind roam, she would be in tears all over again.

A knock at the door brought both women's heads around. It was Pastor Hurst.

"He's here. Are you ready, Anne?"

"Yes."

The pastor smiled at her and waited for his wife to hug her one more time. The couple exited together, and a moment later the door opened and Mr Weston walked in.

Chapter Ten

"How are you, Miss Gardiner?" were the first words from Weston's mouth, his eyes not missing the tense way she stood before the long davenport.

"I'm well, Mr Weston. How are you?"

"Very well, thank you. Until I received Pastor's note, I wasn't certain if we would meet or not. He must have told you of my proposal."

"He did, and I was hoping we could speak of it."

"As do I. Are there any questions I can answer for you?"

"Yes." Anne heard the breathlessness in her voice and tried to calm the frantic beating of her heart. "Would you mind telling me, Mr Weston, how you came to Christ?"

"Not at all. I was a lad," Weston began before he realized they were both still standing. "Maybe we should sit down."

"Oh! Of course. I'm sorry."

Weston smiled as she took a seat on the davenport, and he then took the chair opposite. He began his story in a quiet voice, and Anne found herself captivated.

"It wasn't complicated or dramatic, unless you take into account the very work Christ did on the cross. Then that changes everything. That was dramatic and full of conflict, but because I was only five, I wasn't able to understand the full measure of what God did for me. However, when my father spoke to me about how my sin would stay with me forever if I didn't let God remove it, I became fearful.

"We had gone riding on a well-used path in town. Failing to concentrate once too often, I lost my seat. Unfortunately,

I landed in horse droppings. I couldn't believe how badly the smell lingered on my skin and clothing, and my father used that as an example of sin before we have forgiveness. I was so taken by it that I knew I must do something. I repented that day and asked Christ to be Lord of my life. I didn't begin to study and take the Word seriously for several more years, but I believe with all my heart that that was the moment my name was written in the Lamb's Book of Life."

"Thank you for telling me," Anne said sincerely.

"Will you return the favor, Miss Gardiner? I would love to hear your story of salvation."

Anne was certainly glad to oblige. Her own account began with her mother.

"My mother often read the Bible in the evenings to my father and me. My father rarely commented about what was read, so whenever I had questions, I would go to my mother. I can't remember a time that she didn't open her Bible and have an answer for me. I was so impressed with her knowledge of Scripture that I wanted to read God's Word for myself.

"I told her of my plan, but she shocked me by saying that Scripture was personal. I was rather stunned, but she went on to say that God's Word is for His children and that unless I was God's child, I shouldn't expect to know and understand all the words. I naturally wanted to know why I wasn't His child, and she explained that it doesn't just happen. She said that when I was old enough to understand what sin was, then I had a choice to make.

"I told her I knew that sin was committing a wrong against God, and our conversation progressed from there. She explained to me in detail about Christ's death, burial, and resurrection. I wasn't able to take it all in, but like you, I knew I wanted the forgiveness that came with His death.

"That's the day that lingers in my mind. That's the day God has used to keep me going when I lost my mother and then watched my father lose everything. I know that's the day eternity was settled for me."

Weston smiled as she finished, thinking about her as a child and wondering if she was always this sweet.

"Thank you for telling me. It's always amazing to me how the Lord works in different hearts."

Anne nodded, feeling a little embarrassed. She had more questions for this man, but right now she was too shy to ask.

"What else can I tell you?" Weston asked when Anne remained quiet.

"Oh, well, I don't wish to be intrusive."

"I appreciate that, but I have no qualms about sharing. If we're going to be married, I think having things out in the open is the only way it's going to work."

"I'm sure you're right. I have never considered marriage before, and I'm not quite sure how to go about it."

"Even if you were sure, our situation is unusual. We might have to do things differently."

"In light of that very thing, Mr Weston," Anne volunteered as her tongue began to relax, "I guess I would like to ask you why you offered. Pastor told me what you said, but perhaps I could hear it from you."

"Certainly. I'm very aware of how the situation between us has changed your life. I've been able to go about my business, but you've suffered greatly for my taking you to Brown Manor. The thing I need to make more than clear to you, Miss Gardiner, is that no matter how much you might have suffered, if you had not been a woman that my own pastor could recommend as a wife, I would not have offered for your hand.

"I have things that I want to share with the woman who becomes my wife—many things—but most importantly her faith in Christ and her commitment to Him. Nothing would have induced me to propose had your faith not been established. I would have still regretted my course of action, but

I would not have tried to repair it, at least not in this way. The second thing I wish you to know is that I only began with those thoughts. Since then I've observed you under various circumstances, and I can see for myself what a warm, caring person you are. That we would start our marriage on unfamiliar ground is not lost on me, but we both would care about each other, and that seems to be more important."

"But do you not wish to marry for love, Mr Weston?" Anne couldn't help but ask. "Is there not a woman who has claimed your affections?"

"I was engaged more than a year ago, but that's over."

"Is the woman's name Henrietta?" Anne asked on a sudden memory.

"Yes, it is. How did you know?" Weston's face showed all the surprise he felt.

"Someone visited the last day I cleaned at Brown Manor, and you said that name."

"I'd forgotten about that. Yes, that was Henrietta."

"Things didn't work out to restore the relationship that day?" Anne asked, even knowing it was obvious.

"No. Henrietta had broken our engagement over someone else. When things didn't work out with that man and I didn't immediately welcome her back, I saw another side of her. Not until that moment did we talk—as we should have before—about salvation. Henrietta hadn't a clue as to what I was talking about. I assumed she was saved because we grew up in the same church and we both read the Bible and often discussed it, but I completely misread things. Even my mother was fooled. The time away had changed Henrietta, and when I tried to speak to her of spiritual things, I saw how wrong I had been."

Anne nodded, sure she understood. He'd been disappointed in love and naturally didn't wish to repeat that experience. By taking a wife he wasn't emotionally involved with, there was no risk.

"May I ask you a question?" Weston ventured.

"Certainly."

"If my suit is acceptable to you, will you wish me to speak with your father?"

Anne smiled at the question, thinking him most kind.

"In truth, Mr Weston, I think it might complicate matters."

"It's best that he's completely forgotten me?" Weston guessed.

"As a matter of fact, he hasn't," Anne surprised him by saying. "He mentioned you by name this very week."

Weston stared at her.

"Is that normal?"

"Not in the least. I was rather taken aback."

"So you spoke of the wedding?"

"No, he wanted to know if my husband—he even called you Mr Weston—liked the dress I was wearing at the time. He'd no more asked when his mind drifted elsewhere, but I was still very surprised."

"I can see how you would be, but if I may be so bold as to suggest that your father might see something that you do not."

"What would that be?"

"That I might take better care of you, that my situation might lend itself to better care for his daughter than he is able to give."

Anne had to process this for a moment, and when she did, only one question came to mind.

"Do you believe, Mr Weston, that it's right for me to marry you to save my name or make my life comfortable?"

"That's only where we start, Anne," he said, using her name for the first time, his tone warm. "The possibilities of where we go from there are nearly limitless."

Anne had not expected this and found she could say nothing. Clear thoughts refused to form in her head, but somewhere in a small recess of her mind she could picture herself married to this man.

❧ ❧

Brown Manor

Weston began his letter Monday morning.

> *Dear Mother,*
>
> *I have asked and the lady has answered. The banns will be read this Sunday, and then a quiet ceremony will take place in the manse on Monday, 12 August.*
>
> *Thank you for your prayers. We will visit after we've taken a few weeks to settle in, probably when the August heat has cooled. I am looking forward to seeing you and introducing you to Anne.*
>
> > *Lovingly,*
> > *Robert*

Weston read the letter over before folding it for the post. He was quite certain that his levelheaded mother would not have sentiments about attending the ceremony. She would be more concerned with the life they were going to lead. A visit to London in late August or early September would be a nice outing for Anne, as well as provide an opportunity for his mother to meet his bride.

It was true that Weston himself was being rather level-headed about the whole matter, something he found easy to do whenever he was not in Anne's presence. When that lady was about, he wasn't quite so calm.

Dismissing it as a normal reaction in light of their upcoming wedding, Weston gave it little thought. He readied the letter for Mansfield and then decided to go for a ride.

❧ ❧

A special license was acquired the very week Weston asked Anne to marry him, which meant that the banns had to be read in church only one Sunday. Pastor Hurst took care of this the moment the service ended.

Friends of the future groom, and especially the bride, were shocked by this announcement—there had been no hint—but that swiftly gave way to their pleasure.

Pastor Hurst had suspected as much. For this reason he had left the reading until the end of the hour, knowing how exciting and distracting the news would be.

As would be expected, Anne and Weston, who were sitting quietly in the rear, were thronged. Hugs and well-wishes abounded, all warm and genuine. Some of Anne's closer friends, such as Lydia, asked to see her soon, but Anne was unable to give an answer.

"When you can." Lydia left her with those words, and in time Anne found herself alone with her intended.

"Are you all right?" he asked.

"Yes, but it's all so sudden. I hope you weren't embarrassed."

Weston's brows rose. "To be marrying the lady who dwells in the heart of every member of this church? I don't know why I would be."

Anne looked at him in surprise.

"Is that really how it seems to you?"

"Certainly. Name one family that doesn't check on you and mother over you."

The words could have been said in jealousy or as an accusation, but there was none of that. Anne saw that Mr Weston's eyes were smiling and he looked very pleased.

"Maybe I'm not a charity case after all," she said quietly, knowing that her pride was smarting a bit.

"Is that the way I've made you feel?"

"No, but I just can't help but wonder—" Anne stopped, not certain she wanted to voice the words.

"You can tell me."

Anne might have done just that, but Judith and Pastor Hurst were coming back inside the church—they had been seeing folks off—and Anne decided to keep her mouth closed on the subject.

"I'd best be going," she said. "I still have things to do."

"I'll see you out," Weston offered before both of them bid the Hursts goodbye.

"Thank you."

"I do wish I could give you a ride home," Weston said as they stepped into the warmth outdoors.

"Thank you again, but I'll be fine."

"I'll come for you in the morning."

Anne looked up at him.

"Since we'll be married shortly after, I didn't think it would matter."

"I'm sure you're right."

She had agreed, but Weston heard the hesitancy in her voice.

"Would you rather I didn't?"

"I was just thinking about the fact that it might do me good to walk one more time."

Weston hated the very thought, but even more than his own feelings right now, he wanted to bow to her wishes.

"In that case, I'll meet you here."

"You don't mind?"

"The fact that you won't have to walk after tomorrow makes it tolerable."

Anne's head tipped to one side.

"Why does that bother you?"

"I don't know," he admitted honestly. "It's not so bad when you're only carrying your Bible to church, but when you're laden down with things from town and have to make that long trek back to Levens Crossing, it doesn't sit well with me."

"Thank you," she simply said.

"For what?"

"For being kind."

Weston did little more than bow in acknowledgment to this, but his heart was thinking, *Being kind to you, Anne Gardiner, might be the easiest thing I've ever done.*

The two parted, both a little in awe over the events of the last week. They both trusted their own ears and eyes, as well as the words of their pastor, but that didn't alter the fact that life would soon change forever.

❧ ❧

Thornton Hall

"Are you trying to put me into labor?" Marianne teased Jennings when he arrived home with the news.

"It's true, Mari. They're to be married at the manse tomorrow morning."

Marianne's mouth swung open.

"But how? When?"

"I didn't get the minute details, but it seems that Weston approached the Hursts about offering for Anne, and Pastor supported the idea. The very day she came to visit here and went on to the manse was the day the Hursts spoke to her. At some point Weston asked and Anne accepted."

"Oh, my," Marianne managed before the youngest of the children found them, repeating Jennings' news all over again.

"What shall I wear to the wedding?" Penny asked after the story spilled out.

"We're not going, dear," her guardian told her, and she looked to Jennings in surprise.

"But we love Anne," she argued.

"Yes, we do, but the ceremony is private."

"Who will be there?"

"I believe only Pastor and Mrs Hurst."

The little girl looked confused and crestfallen over this.

"We'll have them to dinner after the baby comes, Penny," Marianne suggested. "You can wear a special dress then."

The little girl was forced to be content with that, Marianne reassuring her with a few more words, but she was glad when Penny said she wanted to check on lunch, and Marianne could be alone with her husband again.

"How did Anne seem?"

"Overwhelmed and shy, but also somewhat pleased."

The words did not comfort Marianne overly much. Part of her heart understood what a wonderful step this was for Anne—she would be cared for—but marriage was a serious issue, a permanent one. Would she and Mr Weston be happy together?

Marianne's gaze dropped to her well-expanded waist. Were she in any other condition she would have gone to Anne on the spot. She was left with only one option: to pray and trust God to take care of her, something she would need to work at for the better part of the day.

෨ ෩

Levens Crossing

"I couldn't wait" were Lydia's words when Anne opened the door to find her there. Church had been over for many hours, but Anne was still on Lydia's mind.

"Come in, Lydia," Anne invited with a smile, not all that surprised to see her.

"Are we alone?"

"Yes. Father is gallivanting. He actually remembered Mr Weston this week, and it's made him a bit more agitated. He's glad I'm finally going to live with him."

Lydia looked surprised by this and then noticed the trunk in the living room.

"Tell me you didn't carry this down on your own."

"No," Anne said on a laugh, "Father did. He just didn't wait for me to finish. I've been dashing up and down the stairs all day."

Lydia laughed at the idea and then offered to help. The women visited as they folded Anne's wardrobe. Anne told her how it all came about and the reason they were moving swiftly.

"And you're all right with this?"

"Since neither one of us is marrying for love, yes. I wouldn't be in a hurry except that Mr Weston is right. My reputation will be rescued all the sooner if we don't tarry."

"Are you certain you know enough about one another?"

"We actually know a good deal about each other. For four days straight we met at the manse and spoke. It didn't start out that way. I thought we would meet one time and one of us would see we were wrong, but we had more questions and kept coming back to continue our dialog. When we met the fourth day, he asked and I accepted."

"And you're sure?"

"Yes. We've always known that a man of some means would be the answer to most of Father's and my problems, Liddy. I just didn't know a believer who would have me. Now Mr Weston has come along. He doesn't seem the least put out that we're not in love, so I'm leading with my head and not my heart. I'm going through with this."

Once the packing was complete, Lydia left to tell her sister-in-law just what Anne had said. She went directly to Thornton Hall, realizing that Jennings would have taken the word home and Marianne would be wondering.

Knowing that the judgment of the people involved could be trusted, she prayed and asked God to bless this marriage and everyone who would be affected.

❧ ❧

Anne left her home with plenty of time to spare on Monday morning. She rather felt as if she was giving something up this day. She knew she was gaining much, but not until just then did she realize how much she cherished her freedom to walk where she pleased. Oh, there were times when it was arduous, but most of the time she enjoyed it. It gave her time to think and pray.

Today she did a lot of both. Nearly strolling on the road to the church, Anne prayed especially for her father. He always fared very well when she was away, but this time she was not coming back.

Please take care of him, heavenly Father. He needs You so. Help him to be well and somehow mindful of You. Help him not to be plagued with fears. Help him to find comfort in You.

Anne heard a carriage approaching and moved carefully off the road. She was getting ready to turn and wave when it slowed to a stop. Weston emerged in short order, a smile on his face.

"At this rate, you're going to be late for your own wedding."

"Is it late?" Anne asked, at first not seeing the teasing glint in his eyes.

"No, I'm early." He smiled charmingly, and Anne smiled in return. "Are you certain you won't take a ride?"

Anne could not resist him.

"I believe I will ride the rest of the way. Thank you, Mr Weston."

Once in the coach she was very aware of the man across from her but did her best not to let her thoughts roam.

They were at the church almost before she could settle in. Pastor and Judith were inside waiting, their smiles giving Anne just enough confidence to proceed.

It was all very neat and swift. In a surprisingly short time, she was Mrs Robert Weston. Judith and Pastor both hugged her warmly and then asked if the new couple would come to the manse for a late breakfast. Anne looked to her spouse, who agreed without hesitation.

"The children are home," Judith warned. "The girls are dying to see you, Anne."

"I'm so glad. To visit so many times last week and take no time for them must have seemed uncaring."

"You can make up for it today," Weston told her.

"You're not in a hurry to leave?"

"No. Take all the time you like."

That time came over breakfast. Anne sat next to Margaret and John and listened to their activities of the week.

"Emma came to play with me." This came from Margaret.

"What did you do?"

"We had our dolls out and had tea."

"Very fun," Anne said sincerely. "What about you, John? What were you doing at the time?"

"Jeffrey took me to the pond. We searched for minnows."

"How many did you find?"

John looked to his older brother.

"Many," Jeffrey said with a smile.

"Many," John turned to tell Anne.

Anne laughed as the stories continued. She had missed visiting with these children and hoped that by the time the meal ended, her reputation of always taking time for them would be restored.

"Thank you for everything," Anne told her hosts when the time came to depart.

"You are so welcome. Don't stay away long," Pastor Hurst urged them.

He hugged Anne once more and shook Weston's hand. The whole family walked them to the carriage and watched as the horse trotted away on the half-circle drive.

Husband and wife exchanged a look of hope and excitement. Together they offered a sincere prayer that God would bless this new couple and that they would follow after Him with every portion of their hearts.

Chapter Eleven

The carriage pulled smoothly away from the manse before picking up speed, Anne waving out the window before settling back for the ride. Weston had chosen the seat across from her and waved at their hosts as well. When their eyes met, Anne felt her face flush and willed it to stop.

In an effort to cool her heated cheeks, she glanced back out the window and continued to keep her eyes averted. It was for this very reason that she knew the exact moment they sped directly past Levens Crossing. Without thinking she spoke.

"Where are we going?"

"To Brown Manor," Weston answered simply.

"My trunk!"

"Would have been picked up and delivered to the manor already."

"Oh!" She took a moment to contain herself. "All right. I guess we're off to Brown Manor then."

Her voice did not encourage him.

"You don't care for Brown Manor?" he ventured, trying to think if this had come up during any of their conversations. He was certain he would have remembered.

"Oh, Mr Weston, it's a lovely home, quite possibly the most lovely in the area. It's just such a large home to clean."

Having completely forgotten the incident, Weston felt his heart plummet. Her face, so sweet and tired as she had appeared to him that day, swam in his mind. A moment later he acted impulsively and joined her on her seat. He turned to Anne and picked up her hand.

"It's not going to be like that anymore. You're Mrs Weston now. We have a large staff to see to your every need."

"Of course, you have servants," she echoed back to him in almost a whisper, her face heating again. "How foolish of me."

Weston studied her a moment.

"I don't believe there's anything foolish about you."

If Anne did not believe her blush could deepen, she was wrong. The warmth of his voice and eyes, not to mention the hand holding hers, sent fresh color to her face.

"I suddenly seem to be very embarrassed in your presence, Mr Weston. I don't know what's come over me."

Weston's gaze searched her eyes for a moment, but he didn't speak. Releasing her hand but not moving back across the carriage, they finished the ride in silence.

᠀ ᠀

Brown Manor

Anne could not have spoken if she tried. The manor was so altered from the last time she'd seen it that she was struck dumb. Gone were the sparsely furnished rooms and empty walls. Tapestries hung everywhere, and fine artwork could be viewed even from the entryway. Beautiful furniture in every wood, shape, and size was scattered throughout, and Anne had seen an ornate clock in every room.

"I collect them," Weston told Anne when he found her studying one in the main hall. "It's almost at the top of the hour. Keep watching that one, and you'll see it move."

Anne did as she was told, her mouth opening a little when the tall pendulum clock began to strike and a small woodsman went into action. He began chopping the tree that sat in the middle of the numbers. Anne smiled when it fell and then all went back into place to wait for the next hour.

"Oh, my," was all she could say.

"I thought it rather fun."

"Indeed."

"There is a small clock in your room. If the ticking or chimes bother you, we can move it."

"I'm sure it will be fine."

Almost soundlessly Mansfield appeared. Obeying orders given to him by Weston before he'd left for the church to see to his wife's needs, the servant bowed to Anne and spoke with reverent tones.

"Welcome, Mrs Weston."

"Thank you, Mansfield."

"If you'll come with me, I would be happy to show you to your room."

"Certainly."

Anne started that way, but Weston caught her hand.

"I had a tour all planned before remembering how well you know the house. No room is off-limits to you. Come and go as you please. If you have questions, see Mansfield or myself."

"Thank you."

"We'll have a late lunch today. Does 1:30 suit?"

"Yes, very well."

"I'll see you then."

Anne was only happy that she didn't blush. Mansfield had waited for her, and she now moved in his wake. She remembered the rooms to which he took her, but as with the rest of the house, they looked vastly different.

"This is your room, Mrs Weston, and through here is Mr Weston's."

Mansfield opened the door and Anne peeked inside. She then turned back to the servant, who shut the adjoining door.

"I believe Mr Weston wanted to leave this room to your decorating discretion, so things are a bit sparse. He also did not want me to find a personal maid for you, certain that you would wish to have a say in that choice. If you have need of anything, just ask for me, Cook, or Sally. When you are ready to interview maids, I can assist you."

"Thank you, Mansfield."

"Will there be anything else?"

"No, thank you. On second thought, where does Mr Weston have lunch?"

"In the small dining room. Do you remember it?"

Anne smiled.

"Distinctly."

Mansfield bowed and went on his way, just covering his own smile. He knew very well the reason given as to why his master had taken this lady for a wife, but that was not all he knew.

He'll fall in love with her, Mansfield speculated as he went below stairs to the kitchen. *I'd be willing to wager my job that he'll realize he loves her in less than six months.*

ה ה

"Did you have a chance to see the gardens when you were here before?" Weston asked his bride over lunch.

"Only from the windows."

"You'll have to go out. We're building a conservatory."

"Are we?" Anne asked, hoping she didn't sound as ignorant as she felt.

"Yes. If you'd like to see it, I'd be happy to take you, or at least point you in the right direction."

"Thank you. Maybe after lunch you could show me?"

"Fine."

Silence fell for a time at that point, but it was not a tense quiet. Anne was sitting in quiet contemplation over the delicious food and the fact that she would not be needed to wash the dishes. Her eyes caught sight of her rough hands, and she wondered how long it would take for their softness to return.

"Are you all right?" Weston asked. He had been closely watching her.

"I am, yes. I was only thinking of how different life is going to be. Every time something occurs to me, I'm surprised all over again."

"What was it this time?"

"The dishes. I don't believe your staff will want me in the kitchen."

"It's your staff as well, and you can go anywhere you like."

Weston had worked to keep his voice light, but he too was having some reactions to Anne's new surroundings. There was one major difference, however. Anne was feeling wonder; he was frustrated. He knew it was wrong. God had taken care of Anne before he had come along, but having her finally attaining what he felt she'd deserved for years was proving to be quite a test.

"I fear it will take some time for me to adjust," Anne offered, thinking she needed to apologize.

"Ignore my tone." Weston was quick on the uptake. "At times I find myself unhappy with your past circumstances, and if I sounded sharp, please excuse me."

Anne nodded. This was not new to her. She had seen every type of reaction to the way she lived her life from people over the years.

"It doesn't make you angry, does it, Anne?"

"The way I was living? No. There was a period in my life when I did a lot of feeling sorry for myself, and at times I mourn the loss of lighter days, but I know this is the plan God had for me, so I work to be thankful."

Maybe you can enjoy light, fun times now, was the thought that ran through Weston's mind, but he didn't voice it.

"Are you ready to see the garden?" Weston asked. He was no longer hungry, and Anne seemed finished with her meal as well.

"Yes, if you're certain you have time."

Weston didn't answer. He only stood and went over to pull out Anne's chair.

"We'll go out the side door, I think, and start in the walled-in garden, the kitchen garden."

"You have a walled-in kitchen garden?" Anne asked with such delight that Weston came to a complete halt. Anne naturally stopped as well and stood looking up at him.

"*You* have a walled-in kitchen garden," he said quietly, marveling again at how much he wanted to give this woman. "I can't say that I'm overly thoughtful about what is grown out there, so if a kitchen garden is your pleasure, we have one started for you."

Anne stared up at him for a moment.

"I'm looking forward to meeting your mother, Mr Weston."

"Why is that?"

"I would enjoy talking with a woman who raised a son to be so kind and thoughtful."

"You're my wife, Anne," he said simply. "I shouldn't be anything else."

But we're not in love, and I didn't expect this.

Anne's thoughts didn't show on her face, however. She nodded and even smiled a little before the two ventured out-of-doors.

❧ ❧

The Manse

"Something is troubling you," Pastor observed to Judith as she sat at her dressing table, seemingly in no hurry to finish with her hair and come to bed.

Judith turned on the bench to look at her husband, who was in the process of fluffing the pillow at his head.

"Yes, there is."

"Can you tell me?"

"I'm regretting my advice to Anne about following Weston's lead."

"I'm not sure I know what you're talking about."

Judith briefly told her husband of her conversation with Anne regarding intimacy.

"Maybe they have spoken of it," Pastor said simply. "They did spend several days in conversation, Judith. Weston told me some of the topics they covered and how many things they agreed on. The private side of marriage could have easily been one subject."

Judith did not know why, but she doubted this had been the case. Naturally Anne was very innocent, and Weston gave every indication of taking such matters seriously, but by nature men were more interested in such things. Did Anne really know what to expect?

It was a question for which Judith would not receive an answer. She knew she needed to let the matter drop, something she was not willing to do. Her husband long asleep, Judith lay and worried on the matter for hours.

       ᴥ ᴥ

Brown Manor

How the day had moved so swiftly Anne could only guess. Lunch was past, the tour of the gardens was over, dinner was eaten and enjoyed, and husband and wife now sat in one of the small salons, Anne with some correspondence and Weston with the newspaper.

Had an observer not known better, he would have guessed them to be an old married couple, but Anne knew differently. As the shadows of the day lengthened, that night's expectations had come to rest stronger and stronger on her mind. If she let her mind wander even a little, she felt fear creeping in like a thief.

At the moment, she had all she could do to concentrate on the letter in her hand.

"I'm headed up now, Anne."

Anne looked up swiftly to see that her husband had come to his feet.

"Join me when you're ready."

Anne nodded, her face presenting a calm visage, but when she rose to climb the stairs just minutes after Weston, her legs were trembling so violently she wondered if they would buckle. By the time she reached her room, she was nearly sick with nerves but made herself undress and climb into her best nightgown. It had been new several years ago but was now past its prime.

Her robe was in even worse shape, but she refused to go through that door without it. Anne tied the sash at her waist and made herself move for the adjoining door, not even remembering to take down her hair. The feel of the cool door handle made her feel chilled all over, and fear made her light-headed.

I can't do this, she said to herself, even as she opened the door, stepped inside, and closed it. Her own heart pounded so that she could hardly push the words out, but she made herself speak.

"Mr Weston?"

"Yes?"

He was still dressed and standing on the other side of the bed, but now he moved toward her. Anne stood, her breath coming hard for a moment, trying to force more words out.

"Yes, Anne?" he repeated, standing in front of her.

"I'm not sure I can do this."

Even in the pale lantern light he could see that she shook violently.

"It's all right, Anne."

"I'm sorry."

"No, don't be."

His words didn't help. She shook until her teeth chattered.

Hearing that and overcome by compassion, Weston put his arms around her, his heart wrenching when he felt how truly frightened she was.

"It's all right, Anne," he continued to say softly. "Don't worry about anything."

"I'm so sorry."

"We'll just wait," he said, moving to look into her face. "We don't need to do this now. We'll pick another time."

"When?"

"We'll decide together, when it's not so frightening."

Anne looked up at him.

"You're going to be sorry you married me, aren't you?"

To her surprise he laughed.

"No, I'm not. I'm very thankful for the wife God has given me."

On impulse he pressed a kiss to her brow.

"Go on to bed, sleep well, and I'll see you at breakfast."

The trembling had eased, but Anne still felt so cold inside. She looked up at him and saw only warmth and caring in his gaze.

"Goodnight," she said in return as she reached for the handle.

Weston stood very still after she'd left, relief radiating to every nerve in his body. Thinking that it was the right thing to do and that Anne would expect as much so she would know of his sincerity in this marriage, he had felt intimacy was required of him. To know that Anne needed to wait was nothing short of a rescue.

Help us, Father. Help us to know when. We're both a little lost in all of this, but we know that You have a plan. Thank You for my wife. Thank You for her sweetness. Help us to have a life together, one that glorifies You.

Weston went to bed and prayed himself to sleep. He thought about checking on Anne—she had been so upset—but he didn't want to startle her or wake her if she was already asleep.

He need not have worried. Anne was awake for about the same amount of time, doing just as her husband was doing, praying for their marriage.

☙ ❧

Anne had not found her way to every room in the manor the day before. In fact, she hadn't tried. Awakening early on her first morning as mistress of Brown Manor, Anne dressed, read her Bible, and decided to walk around the quiet house. She hoped that the wonder on her face would wear off before anyone could notice. Her responses to some of her husband's possessions were rather gauche, but in truth she was in awe of her new home and surroundings. She had been quite sincere when she'd told Mr Weston that Brown Manor might very well be the loveliest home in the area.

"Oh, my," Anne stood quietly and stared into the contents of the china cabinets in the large dining room. She couldn't ever remember seeing china so lovely and perfect. The set she now looked at was cobalt blue and gold, so delicate and fine that Anne desperately wanted a closer look.

She carefully opened the glass-fronted door, her face breaking into smiles of delight to be so close and see that the plates, platter, cups, and saucers were all as lovely as they first appeared.

The cup directly in front of her was turned a bit, not giving her a full view of the handle. Anne was reaching to turn it when Weston entered and spoke.

"There you are!"

Anne was so startled that her hand crashed into the cup, making it clatter loudly on the saucer.

"Oh, no!" she exclaimed, swiftly drawing back and turning her head, afraid to look. "Please tell me it didn't break. I don't know how I would ever replace it."

"You wouldn't," he said as he approached and lifted the unbroken cup into his hand. "It's just a teacup, Anne."

"Mr Weston!" Anne's voice revealed her shock as she turned to face him. "This is the most beautiful china cup I've ever seen."

Weston's mouth quirked into a smile.

"In that case you'll be happy to know that there are at least 30 more in the cupboard."

Anne glanced to where he pointed and saw that there were indeed many more, but she was still relieved not to have broken the first one. Taking it from Weston's hand, Anne carefully placed it back on the saucer and shut the door.

"More cups or not, I think I'll just keep well away from them."

"Don't do that," Weston told her. "They're here to enjoy."

"No one can do that very well if I break them."

"And that wouldn't have been an issue if I hadn't startled you. Surely you've handled china before."

"I have, yes."

Weston suddenly looked at her.

"Do you have your mother's china at Levens Crossing, and do you wish to have it brought here to Brown Manor?"

"It had to be sold."

There was no mistaking the look on his face.

"I beg you, please do not be angry," Anne boldly ordered her husband for the first time.

Weston blinked in surprise at her firm tone, and Anne briefly put a hand on his arm.

"I could see in your eyes that my answer frustrated you. I can't live my first weeks or possibly months here having you grow angry every time you're reminded of how difficult my circumstances were. It would be very tiring as I would be forced to start monitoring everything I said."

"You are quite right. I can't promise that it won't happen again, but I will make an effort."

"Thank you."

Their eyes met for several moments before Anne felt shy and looked away. Seeing that he needed to stop standing and staring at her, Weston spoke instead.

"Ready for breakfast?"

"Yes, please."

"How did you sleep?" he asked as they exited the room together.

"Very well."

"The bed will be all right?"

Anne couldn't stop the smile that came to her mouth, but she only quietly said, "Yes."

"What did I miss? You're very pleased about something."

"Telling you about my bed feels a bit odd in this new situation, but it was such a surprise."

"Why was that?"

They had reached the small dining room and now took seats. Food began to appear, and Anne thought the matter had been dropped, but as soon as the prayer was said and she had filled her plate, she glanced up to find Weston's eyes on her, his brows raised.

"I'm dying to know about this bed," he told her, a smile lurking in his eyes.

Anne laughed.

"It's nothing, really. I was just so warm and comfortable. I didn't expect that."

"I take it you don't wish for your bed from home?"

Anne only smiled and took a sip of her coffee. Weston realized then and there how much he could enjoy Anne's discovery of everything at Brown Manor. It was sure to be a reminder of where she'd been, but more than that, he could enjoy her delight and share in it with her.

Anne was cutting a piece of bacon when Weston was ready to speak again.

"I've a trip planned for us."

Mrs Weston looked up.

"We're going to London in a few weeks."

"Oh, how nice," Anne said. But she was already mentally working on her wardrobe. Her clothing wasn't very suitable.

"It should be cooler by then, and my mother would like us to visit."

"I'm looking forward to meeting her."

"She's looking forward to meeting you. She remembers seeing you when she was here."

And she didn't object to your marrying a small, country mouse? Where the thought had come from Anne could not say, but she did her best to push it aside. Such ideas would only make her seem defensive. *But aren't you a little defensive, Anne?* she now asked herself. *Don't you feel a little like a charity case?*

Anne didn't like the direction of these thoughts either. It might be true that she had been needy, but no one had forced Mr Weston to ask for her hand, and she had not expected anything of him, let alone an offer of marriage.

It's time for you to figure out how you can contribute to this marriage, Anne. You can't do that if all you're going to do is question how it came to be.

That little talk behind her, Anne asked God to strengthen her for the days ahead. She asked for wisdom as well. Getting to know a man you were already married to was going to take a great deal of thought. Anne knew she would use all the wisdom God could impart to her.

Chapter Twelve

On only the second morning that Weston woke with a new wife in the house, he knew he was going to have to make some changes. He could not spend each day hovering near Anne to make sure she was all right. He wanted to take care of her, but staying close and watching her face for signs of need was not going to work. He had a large estate to run, land to manage, and several farmers who answered to him. He was even looking into the purchase of more land, not to mention the continued work on the conservatory. He trusted the builders, but such things could not be left unchecked.

For these reasons and several more, he told Anne he would be in his study if she needed him and proceeded to retire to that room the moment they finished breakfast. At first it looked as if it would be a fruitless venture. His mind was so preoccupied with his new wife in his house that he couldn't even concentrate, but in time the move paid off. Weston made himself stay at his desk, his account books around him, until at last he was lost in the business at hand.

Anne worried her lower lip, not certain where to begin. Her second day at Brown Manor had passed as swiftly as the first, and now she woke to her second morning, her father very much on her mind. Checking on him had not been a hard decision to make. She felt she must. How best to get back to Levens Crossing, however, was a whole new issue.

She hated to bother her husband, who had retired to his study to work, but ordering a carriage on her own was simply out of the question.

What if Mr Weston doesn't want a carriage out? What if he decided he wanted a certain carriage, and then found out I have it?

These questions plagued Anne until she realized there was only one person who could answer them. Desperately hoping it was not a mistake, Anne knocked on the study door.

"Come in," Weston called from his chair.

Anne carefully opened the door.

"Mr Weston?"

"Come in, Anne," he bade, coming to his feet.

"I'm sorry to bother you."

"Not at all. What can I do for you?"

"I feel a need to check on my father, but I didn't know if I should ask for a carriage. I can walk, but then I'll be gone longer, and I didn't know if you wanted me to be away so long."

Weston had come around the desk and moved until he was standing in front of her.

"You may order a carriage anytime you wish, and, as for being away, as long as I know where you are, you may be gone as long as you like. I shall do the same for you should I need to leave."

"Thank you."

"When are you leaving?"

"I was hoping to go right away. Is that all right?"

By way of an answer, Weston used the bellpull. Mansfield was at the door less than a minute later.

"Yes, sir," he said with a slight bow.

Weston, however, said nothing. He looked to Anne and waited.

It took a moment for Anne to realize that Mansfield had turned his attention to her.

"Oh!" She squeaked a bit and turned red even before she began. "May I have a carriage to take me to Levens Crossing, Mansfield?"

"Certainly, Mrs Weston. Right away?"

"Please."

Weston smiled at Anne when Mansfield took his leave.

"I'll see you out."

They had begun to walk that way when Weston asked, "Will you be long?"

"I may stay and do a little baking, so I might be."

"Don't hesitate to stay as long as you wish, Anne, but before the carriage comes around, let us find Cook or Sally and have her prepare a basket from the kitchen."

Anne was turning to protest, but she caught her husband's eyes. They were steely with resolve, and the words died in her throat.

"Your father is family now," he said quietly but firmly. "We'll take care of him together."

"Thank you."

"No thanks are necessary."

Anne looked uncertain over this, and Weston reached out and touched her cheek. Her eyes softened at the gesture, and Weston smiled at her.

"It's a good match we've made, Mrs Weston," he said as he turned Anne and started her down the hall once again. "Just give us time, and we'll figure it out."

Twenty minutes later, having just watched a large basket filled with baked goods and meat pies being loaded ahead of her, Anne stepped into the carriage in a near state of shock. She waved to her husband as the conveyance pulled away, and then she sat back against the squabs to try and talk to the Lord.

I don't know what to think. I never dreamed. You've been so good. He's so kind.

Those muddled thoughts having raced through her head, Anne sat still and tried to take it all in. She felt like laughing and crying all at the same time. For years she had kept her emotions in check, and now it felt as though they might tumble out of control.

Anne forced herself not to dwell on all that just occurred. If she cried when she saw her father, he would wish to know why, and right now she couldn't explain it. Her mind as settled as she could manage, Anne began a mental list of what she wanted to get done at Levens Crossing so she wouldn't be gone all day.

≈ ✷

Collingbourne

The *girls* were on an outing. About midmorning a carriage from Tipton carrying Lydia, Emma, and Lizzy Palmer, as well as Penny Jennings, arrived in town. The mission was a simple one, to divert Penny's thoughts from Marianne's condition.

That little girl had begun to hover a bit, her small face showing more concern with each passing day. That Marianne was feeling more tired and taking things very slowly only confirmed in Penny's young mind that something terrible was going to happen to her mother.

That babies arrived safely every day was not a fact she could grasp. Her own mother had died having her, and Penny was now fearing the worst.

"I think we'll start at Benwick's," Lydia told her young group. "How does that sound?"

"Will we go to tea?" Emma was distracted by the thought.

"Certainly. Won't that be fun?"

The girls agreed that it would be, and little coaxing was needed to persuade them that this outing was going to be a wonderful diversion.

"All right," Lydia began, once in the shop. "Emma and Lizzy, you may stay together and shop on your own for a time. Penny and I need to pick out a gift."

"What gift?" Emma asked without thinking, drawing a look from her mother.

"Go on," she urged them, and the youngest Palmer females—holding hands—started through the aisles.

"Now, Penny." Lydia hunkered down to be on the little girl's level. "You're going to do a great favor for Marianne today. You're going to help me pick a lovely wedding gift for Anne and Mr Weston that will be from your whole family. How does that sound?"

"I'm picking it out?"

"Yes. I'll help you."

This was met with a wide smile that Lydia returned.

The two began in the housewares aisle, and Penny didn't need much time at all.

"Oh, Aunt Lydia," Penny breathed, her eyes on a crystal compote. "This is so pretty."

"Yes, it is," Lydia agreed, half wishing she'd spotted it. "I think you may have found just the gift."

Looking remarkably pleased, Penny went to the front counter with Lydia and stood by while Lydia charged it to her brother's account and asked that it be delivered to Brown Manor.

"It's not going to Thornton Hall?"

"No, dear, it's best that it go directly to the Westons."

"But then Marianne won't see it."

"I know, love, but you can tell her all about it, and some-time when you visit Anne, you can explain to her that you'd like Marianne to see it. I know Anne will understand."

Some of her pleasure in the moment slipping away, Penny nodded in understanding before joining the Palmer girls. Together the three youngest shoppers browsed through the shop while Lydia looked for a wedding gift of her own.

The rug she found was exactly what she would choose for Anne, and she hoped that Weston would like it as well. Not even attempting to carry it to the front, she simply told Benwick which one she wanted and asked that it also be delivered to Brown Manor.

By the time the foursome finished their shopping and added some odd and ends, they were ready for tea indeed. In high spirits they crossed over to Gray's. One look at Penny's face told Lydia this outing to town was doing the trick.

❧ ❧

Levens Crossing

"Well, Anne," the Colonel uttered in surprise as he entered the back door of the house to find Anne in the kitchen. "I didn't know you were home."

"I thought I'd stop and bring you some lunch," she answered as she heated one of the pies.

"It smells good."

"Sit down," she invited him, kissing his cheek once he did.

"How nice to see you," he began lucidly, but when Anne began to question him as to how he'd been, his mind rambled a bit.

"I've been looking at that home at the west side. I think someone is living in there."

"Which home is it?" Anne asked, hoping she could keep up.

"The new one."

Anne didn't know of a new home anywhere in the area, but then her father got out more often than she did.

"Did you see someone about?"

"He wasn't wearing regimentals."

Anne gave up all pretext of conversation. She saw to it that her father had a large slice of shepherd's pie and a nice loaf of bread at his elbow before going on with her work. She aired the living room and her father's bedroom a bit before doing the dishes and dusting the kitchen and living room.

The thought occurred to her in the midst of this work that it might be longer than she planned before she enjoyed soft skin, but the small sacrifice was worth it to know her father was all right.

ᔑ ᔐ

Brown Manor

"Mrs Weston has returned," Mansfield informed his employer, watching as he immediately set his work aside and went to meet her.

"How did it go?" Weston asked, taking Anne's hand as she emerged from the carriage.

"Very well, thank you."

"Your father is all right?"

"Yes, he's been wandering a bit, but he seemed fine."

"Good. Some things arrived while you were away." Weston offered his arm as they went inside. "I didn't open them."

Anne looked up at her husband, her mind at sea

"What sort of things?" she ventured.

"Without opening them I couldn't be specific, but I believe they might be wedding gifts."

Anne's mouth dropped open in an amusing way, and Weston laughed.

"Is it really so surprising?"

They had come to the small salon, and Anne now saw the packages for herself.

"It shouldn't be, but for some reason it is."

Weston continued to smile at her reaction.

"Shall we see what's come?"

"All right."

But Weston wouldn't open a thing. Three packages had arrived, and he was happy to watch his wife open them, handing her one after another.

"It's from Pastor and Judith." Anne read the card and then brought forth a lovely pair of candlesticks.

The next gift was from the Crofts, who had sent book-ends. The last box contained long-stemmed goblets from Dr and Mrs Smith.

Anne, looking as stunned as she felt, said, "Everything is so lovely. I'll have to get notes off soon."

"How are you for stationery?"

"A bit low, I think."

"Well, when you next head into town and need spending money, it's in my study. I'll show you exactly where."

Anne looked dreadfully uncomfortable with this, and Weston waited to see what was on her mind.

"How much will I know to take?" she ventured after a moment's thought.

"Whatever you need."

"How much is that?"

Weston smiled.

"I've no fears of you bankrupting us, Anne. If you have a large purchase coming up and wish to check with me, that's fine, but I'm not going to lord it over you and check your every purchase."

"I didn't think that you would."

Weston's brow suddenly furrowed.

"What did you and your father do for money?"

"Oh, various things. We might sell something, or I might do a small job that gave us a little bit. Sometimes someone from the church would help us."

"It sounds like it could have been humbling."

"Indeed," Anne admitted. "I found that pride can be an ugly thing, and we have more pride than we like to think."

"At the same time," Weston reasoned, "we don't own anything. We have what we have only because God bestows it upon us."

"I could have used your voice of reason many years ago. It took me quite a long time to figure that out. It felt so awful to be without and to think of myself as a charity work, but as you said, everything is from God's hand, which means we're all works of charity—His charity."

"That's nicely put, Anne."

Feeling shy of a sudden, Anne studied her fingernails. Weston followed her gaze. A moment later, he reached over and picked up her right hand. He studied two broken nails before relinquishing her hand and meeting her eyes.

"Let me guess. You cleaned while at Levens Crossing."

"I did dust a bit," Anne admitted, hearing that his tone was light.

"Hmm. I can see I'm going to have to keep an eye on you. I think the next time you visit, I'll just send along a maid."

"Then what will I do?"

"You'll just visit with your father."

"What if he wants to know about the maid?"

Weston's brows rose and his mouth quirked. "Do you honestly think he'll notice?"

A laugh escaped Anne before she could stop it. She put a hand to her mouth, an action that only widened Weston's smile.

"I like your laugh, Anne Weston."

"And I like how committed you are to seeing after my needs, even though I don't always know what to do about it."

"That was wonderfully honest."

Anne nodded. "I'm working on that. It's not easy."

"No, but wouldn't it be a shame if months from now we're still strangers?"

"Yes, it would, so in light of that, I'll ask you how your day has gone and if you accomplished your work in the study?"

"My day has gone well, thank you, and as for my work in the study, I'm looking into purchasing some land so I'm scouring my accounts to make sure I've kept everything in order."

"Is the land nearby?"

"Yes. It's a parcel over near Escomb Dale. It's not openly on the market, but Mr Vintcent, the architect who designed the conservatory, heard of something and mentioned it. When I checked into it, I was quoted a rather irresistible price. I have until the end of the week to give my answer."

"Who owns it right now?"

"It's part of an estate owned by the Brodhead family. Evidently Brodhead hates the area and would love to be rid of it."

"I've heard of him all my life but never met him."

"He never lived here. He prefers Bath or London, so I'm told."

It occurred to both husband and wife at that moment that they were talking like old friends. Their eyes met and both smiled.

What a lovely thing, Anne thought when the two eventually parted, Anne to clean up for lunch and Weston to check on the conservatory. *I like him. He makes it very easy to like him.*

∽ ∾

Thornton Hall

Marianne woke slowly, her body feeling heavy and fatigued. She lay still and listened to the clock strike nine times, nearly shaking her head at how late it was. She had gone to bed almost ten hours ago and slept hard all night.

The sound of footsteps brought her eyes completely open, and she smiled to see Jennings headed her way.

"Good morning."

His deep voice always caused her to smile.

"How are you?" he asked.

"Tired. And tired of being tired."

The handsome man who sat on the bed stared down at his wife, his mouth just beginning to smile.

"If you had said yes to me the first or second time I'd proposed, you probably would have been pregnant sooner and already had the baby. You have no one to blame but yourself."

Marianne laughed. The way he'd proposed, or rather the tenacity in the process, was a long-standing joke between them.

"Shall I ring for tea?" he asked after he'd leaned to kiss her.

"No, I think I'll start with a cool bath. It's been so warm, I feel a bit cooked."

Jennings noticed that her face was flushed and her skin had been warm to his touch. And if the sun streaming through the windows was any indication, it was going to be another hot day.

An hour later Marianne, bathed, dressed, and finally ready for breakfast, was on her way downstairs when the first pain hit. Her back had been aching that morning for the first time, but she hadn't expected this. She sat down on the stairs and gasped a little at the intensity of the contraction. Even when it eased she kept her place and was glad when Thomas wandered by.

"Marianne, are you all right?"

"I am, Thomas, but I've decided to go back upstairs. Will you walk with me?"

Thomas offered a hand when she came to her feet and did as she asked. They visited companionably in her bedroom as another pain didn't come for more than 15 minutes.

Had Marianne not been concentrating on the contraction of her abdomen, she might have laughed. Seeing her condition, Thomas ran as though his jacket were on fire, shouting for Jennings and generally informing the entire household that the baby was on its way.

❧ ❧

Tipton

Both Palmer and Lydia met the three Jennings children when they arrived by coach, the children's sober faces telling the story.

"When did contractions begin?" Palmer asked Thomas.

"About an hour ago." Thomas briefly told his story of finding her on the stairs and finished with, "Jennings felt it best that we cleared out."

"They'll keep us informed," Palmer assured him before lifting a dejected Penny into his arms. Lydia came close to speak to her.

"Margaret Hurst is here playing with the girls. The four of you will have a wonderful time."

"I didn't want to leave," she said, the first tears coming.

"I know you didn't, but Jennings knows best, Penny, and God can hear your prayers from Tipton. Marianne needs you to be praying right now."

"I could have held her hand. I could have gotten her a drink."

"And she would have appreciated that, but Jennings wants to make sure you're all right too. That's why he sent you here to us."

James had hung back a bit, his own 12-year-old heart uncertain about all that was happening.

"How will we know?"

"They'll send word," Palmer informed him. "And if things go on a bit, Lydia can pop over and check on the progress."

The children smiled at Lydia—she felt like another mother to them—before going into the house. When they left, Palmer and Lydia stood hugging on the drive. Oliver's birth was very fresh in their minds, and they both knew very well what a special time this was.

"I'm so excited for them, Palmer."

"As am I. I hope it's a girl."

Lydia laughed.

"There was a time when you didn't care, Palmer. What's come over you lately?"

"I'm growing opinionated in my old age."

Lydia enjoyed this. She was still laughing when they started back inside.

Chapter Thirteen

Brown Manor

"Have you seen Mrs Weston?" Mr Weston asked of Mansfield on Friday just before lunch.

"I believe she took a basket to the garden, sir."

"All right. That's where I'll be."

"Did you wish me to speak to Mrs Weston about the menu, sir?"

"I'll do it. Are we ready for the weekend?"

"Cook can plan the menu as she always does on Fridays, but she would prefer Mrs Weston's input."

"Of course. I'll see to it right now."

It didn't prove as easy as it sounded. The gardens at the manor were extensive. When Weston didn't find Anne in the kitchen garden, he wandered to the back and found her some distance away, to the south of the new construction site, a lone figure cutting blossoms and placing them in a basket. She was in a dress he hadn't noticed before, but it was one that had seen better days. For a moment he absently wondered when would be the best time to tell her they were going to shop while in London. For most women this would be good news, but Weston was loath to do anything that might make Anne feel indebted to him.

Anne heard his approach and looked up, holding her basket in front of her.

"I've been found," she said before he could speak.

"Were you hiding?"

"In this old dress, yes, I was."

171

Weston couldn't claim not to have noticed, but there was no point in admitting as much.

"What have you found?" he asked instead, concentrating on the contents of the basket.

Anne's sigh was heartfelt. "Some of the loveliest flowers I've ever seen. These gardens are spectacular."

"You're not too warm?"

"Not yet."

"More gifts arrived just before I came looking for you."

"Did you open them?"

"No, I wanted to wait for you."

"But you didn't open any yesterday. You let me do it all."

"I thought women enjoyed opening gifts."

"We do, but you got married also."

Weston only smiled about this, and Anne gave him a pointed look.

"What's that look for?" he asked, his voice and eyes full of teasing.

"One would think you might be having second thoughts," she teased him, unnecessarily arranging flowers in the basket, her eyes down to keep from laughing. "One might suspect that gifts arriving reminds you that you're now tied to a wife."

"I shall go this instant and open every one."

He said this so swiftly and comically that Anne laughed.

"Let me take the basket for you."

"Thank you."

When they started toward the house, Weston broached the subject of the menu.

"Thanks to Mansfield, Sally, and Cook, I've been eating like a king, but they're used to my taste. Cook would much prefer to have your input, and if it suits you, she does the menu on Friday."

"Oh, of course. I'd be happy to speak with her, although I certainly have no complaints about the food."

They ventured back to the house in companionable silence, but as soon as they were inside, Weston invited Anne to open gifts.

"Would you mind terribly if I cleaned up a bit?"

"No. Do you want lunch before we do gifts?"

"Opening them before lunch would be nice."

It struck her as she answered that he was excited about these presents. He didn't need to be the one to open them, but he was pleased.

"I'll be back in about 20 minutes," Anne offered. "Will that do?"

"Yes. I'll tell Mansfield we'll lunch directly after."

While the two were apart, Anne made good use of her time, washing up, changing her dress, and doing her hair. Her room was left in something of a clutter when she finished, but she didn't wish to be late.

Weston wouldn't have noticed. He had gone back to the book he was reading and was quite absorbed when Anne arrived. Anne took a chair and watched him for a moment. She didn't think her footsteps had been that silent on the floor, but he didn't seem to notice her presence.

Anne didn't mind. It was nice to sit quietly and watch her husband's bent head. He had dark, wavy hair that Anne found herself admiring. His handsome face wasn't hard to look at either. It passed through her mind to wonder what he thought of her own looks, but he looked up before she could process the idea.

"Have you been there long?"

"Not overly."

Weston's eyes studied her, working to gauge if she was only being polite.

"It's good that you're finding out early," he said without explanation.

"Finding out what?"

"When I'm reading something, I tend to become rather lost."

Anne smiled. There was certainly little comparison, but she was so used to living with a man who was often *completely* lost that it gave her the most irresistible urge to laugh.

"What did I say?"

"Nothing," Anne said, not able to wipe the smile from her face, and in turn, not being very convincing.

Weston's gaze narrowed with teasing. His voice deepened as he said, "I'll have to figure out a way to make you talk."

Anne couldn't stop the laughter that bubbled out of her.

"That's just the right note to start on," Weston said as he went toward a long cylinder wrapped in plain brown paper, "I think this must be a rug. Shall I do the honors?"

"Please," Anne replied, still wanting to laugh.

A few moments later the paper was torn back so Weston could roll out the rug at Anne's feet. Her eyes widened with pleasure, and her mouth rounded a bit. It was beautiful—a work of art.

"Who sent this?" she asked quietly after finding her voice.

"The Palmer family, and I think it would go very well in your room."

"Oh, no, Mr Weston, that's not right!"

"On the contrary, it would be perfect. I'll have Mansfield see to it today."

Anne was ready to argue, but the rug was being rerolled, and as soon as the task was complete, Weston went for another gift. He placed it in Anne's lap and took a seat to watch her.

Anne, still uncomfortable over the rug, opened the package slowly, hoping this was something they could share. Anne nearly sighed when she saw a crystal compote.

"Isn't it lovely?" Anne breathed, lifting the bowl out to be viewed and spotting the card.

"What does it say?"

"Best wishes and our prayers, Jennings, Marianne, and family. The note at the bottom says Penny picked it out."

"It's very nice."

Anne looked at her spouse, a sparkle in her eyes.

"I think it might go well in your room."

Weston was still chuckling as he went for the third gift. It was from the Shepherds, and when Anne opened it she found more candlesticks. She glanced at them and then looked more carefully. At last she turned a beaming face to her husband.

"These were my mother's."

"The candlesticks?"

"Yes."

"Some you had to sell?"

"Yes, Benwick gave me a fair price, but I never saw them in the shop because he doesn't usually deal in secondhand wares."

"That's marvelous."

"Isn't it? I'm so pleased. I wonder if Mrs Shepherd had any idea."

Weston didn't answer. He was getting an idea of his own, but not one he was willing to speak of at the moment.

It was still on his mind when Mansfield sought them out and told them lunch was served.

∂∞ ∞

Thornton Hall

Lydia waited several hours. Not surprised that there was no news, she also realized that Penny had come to check with her a little more often. In an effort to rescue the little girl, Lydia had told her she would go to Thornton Hall and check on Marianne's progress. She had called for the carriage and now made her way quietly up the wide staircase at her brother's home.

Things were still as she climbed. Not until she reached the upstairs landing did she hear the soft footsteps of Mrs Walker—Marianne's mother—as she paced in the hall. As soon as Mrs Walker spotted Lydia, she came and hugged her.

It was while the women embraced that they heard a tiny infant's cry. For a moment their eyes met in shock before Mrs Walker broke down. Wordlessly Lydia held her and let the older woman cry, fully understanding the need.

When they heard a nurse bustle from the bedroom, Jennings at her heels, both women turned and waited.

Jennings beamed at them. "A girl. A perfect little girl."

"And Mari?" her mother asked.

"Doing fine."

Mrs Walker all but sagged with relief. Lydia saw her to a downstairs salon and ordered tea, but she didn't linger. Much as she wanted to go upstairs and see Marianne and this new little person, right now she was needed at Tipton. She had to tell three children that they had a baby sister.

❧ ❧

Brown Manor

Anne looked through her sewing basket a third time before sitting back with a sigh. She had a jacket that needed mending, but the dark blue thread she'd used last time was gone. She hated the very thought of asking Mr Weston for anything, but right now she felt she had no choice.

She was on her way downstairs to find him when a clock chimed in the hall. She stood and listened to the soft sounds it made and was given a chance to notice her reflection in the hall mirror.

How will I ever wear this dress to London?

Anne stood in discouragement for a moment but then realized she just might have time to do something about it. She continued toward her husband's study, hoping he wasn't too busy. He called for her to enter the moment she knocked.

"Are you terribly busy, Mr Weston?"

"No, please come in. Sit down."

"Oh, I won't stay long," Anne said, almost immediately seeing she would not have the courage to say everything that was on her mind. "I just wanted to let you know I'll be going into Collingbourne in the morning."

"Oh, fine. Be sure and let Mansfield know of your needs."

"I will, thank you."

Anne was back out the door in record time, telling herself she was going to have to be more careful about disturbing him. He'd had papers all over his desk and obviously been ensconced with work.

For a moment Anne stood with her back to the closed portal, trying to figure out how she would explain her actions when she didn't go to town the next day.

"Maybe I could spend the day in the gardens," she whispered softly to herself. "Or possibly I'll think of something else to sell."

Anne finally walked away, her steps slow as she realized that selling something would bring embarrassment to her well-established husband.

Mansfield, who had come upon her but not been seen, stood watching her move out of sight. His eyes went to the study door for a moment, his mind quickly making some deductions. A moment later he was not at all surprised to enter the study and find his employer buried in his books.

❧ ❧

Thornton Hall

"What will you call her?" James asked of Marianne when the children visited her and the new baby for the first time.

"This is Catherine Anne," Marianne told them. "Do you like it?"

Agreeing that they did, the boys smiled and even laughed a little at the wrinkly red person in Marianne's arms, but Penny did not utter a word through this entire interchange. Jennings and Marianne exchanged several looks, but not until the boys went on their way did Jennings speak directly to Penny.

"Are you all right?"

"Yes."

"Is something on your mind?"

Penny looked up at him but didn't answer.

"You can tell me."

"Emma said sometimes babies die." Tears had come to Penny's eyes on this announcement.

"What caused you to talk about that?"

"I don't know. It wasn't today, but I remember her saying it."

Marianne offered the baby to Jennings so she could motion Penny to come close.

"I want to hold you, Penny," she said, needing this little girl so much at the moment.

"Are you afraid that Catherine will die?" Penny asked.

"No, but I hate it that you're afraid, and I want to hold you."

Jennings put Catherine in a cradle across the room and joined Penny and his wife on the bed. "I need to tell you something, Penny," he began. "Many people don't believe that our God is a God of great purpose. They believe He haphazardly flings His power across the universe, but that's not so. No matter how painful it would be to lose Catherine, God does not do things without a plan. We don't always understand His reason, but we can trust that God knows what's best for us."

"Papa died."

"Yes, he did."

"I miss him, but I have you and Marianne."

"That's right. And you need to remember that even though we don't know the exact reason why your father died, God has taken care of you, Thomas, and James."

"Can I pray that Catherine won't die?"

"What do you think?"

Penny looked to Marianne, but she only smiled down at her. Penny looked back to Jennings.

"I think yes, but I have to remember the part about God's will."

Jennings reached for his youngest ward, feeling, as Marianne had, the need to hold her.

"I love you, Penny."

"I love you too."

Penny had tipped her head back to look into his face. Jennings pressed a kiss to her soft, pale cheek.

"I'm certainly going to be praying that our little Catherine is with us for a very long time. Do you know why?"

"Why?"

"Because you're going to be a wonderful big sister."

Penny's sigh could be heard all over the room.

The three of them sat and talked until Catherine needed some attention. By the time Penny went in search of her brothers, Catherine's dying was the last thing on her mind.

～ ～

Brown Manor

"Will there be anything else, sir?"

Weston looked up in surprise, not recalling when Mansfield had ever disturbed him to ask such a thing. The faithful servant always delivered the tea, laid it out, and quietly went on his way.

"No, I'm fine," Weston answered, finding his voice.

"Very well, sir. I understand Mrs Weston is going to be selling something?"

Weston's accounts melted from his mind.

"What have you heard?"

Mansfield described the brief scene some ten minutes past, his voice impersonal but his eyes not missing a thing. As he'd expected, Weston was very interested in this news.

"Thank you, Mansfield."

That man only bowed before moving toward the door, but he was well satisfied. He was looking forward to telling Cook yet again that he'd been correct: This was going to be a fine match.

ов ел

"What will you shop for tomorrow?" Weston asked at dinner that evening.

"I need some thread," Anne told him, her mind still preoccupied with the whole matter, not to mention her own cowardice.

"Anything else?"

"No." This time she answered thoughtlessly.

"All the way to Collingbourne for thread?"

Anne looked up from her plate, her facing growing pale before she blushed furiously.

"How foolish of me," she said, her voice becoming breathless. "Of course I won't go. It's only thread. I'll wait for another time. I'm sorry to have been so thoughtless."

"Anne, I didn't mean it that way," Weston replied, his voice as patient as he felt.

"Even so, you're correct. Going all the way to town for thread is a waste."

Weston didn't know how he was going to gain the information he sought without being completely honest.

"I assure you, Anne, there was no rebuke intended. I just thought there might be something else on your list that you were reluctant to discuss with me."

Anne stared at him for a moment in misery before it all came spilling out.

"I thought I could talk to you, but my pride has gotten in the way. You've never told me where I'm to retrieve my spending money, and my clothing is so awful—several things need mending—and I'm so terribly afraid of embarrassing you in London." She sounded on the verge of tears and simply ended with, "I'm sorry."

"We're shopping for clothes when we get to London, Anne—both you and I. That has been the plan all along, and because I'd not told you, it is I who should be apologizing to you. And as for the money, I'll show you directly after dinner."

Anne bit her lip. She was not easily given to tears but did feel like crying. With a brief word of thanks, she bowed her head back over her plate.

"Are you ever foolish, Anne?" Weston suddenly asked.

Anne looked up at him. "I fear I am quite often."

"Well, I've been foolish enough to think that because we've discussed a few things, there will be no bumps in the path. That's rubbish, of course. We've only just started on this marriage, and it takes years to know another person and grow comfortable with her or him."

The occupants of the room were quiet for a moment, but Anne had mentally agreed with Weston and knew she must voice it.

"You didn't sound foolish at all just now."

Weston's mouth quirked.

"Well, stick around, Anne. I'm bound to fall short of the mark before long."

Anne smiled at him before going back to her meal.

They didn't have a lot of conversation as they finished, but Weston was good on his word. Directly after dinner, he took Anne to the study and showed her everything she needed to know.

ᔕ ᔕ

Anne had nearly torn the wardrobe apart. Her husband had told her that they would be shopping once they gained London, but she might not have her clothing right away. There was still the matter of getting to that city. Anne told herself if she had to remake and mend every dress, she would be presentable.

It was early on Saturday morning, earlier than she should have been awake, but she was eager to have her list complete. Something told her that if her husband could see her dashing about and making lists, he would tell her she could return to town or send a servant anytime she wished, but he had already been so kind, and she never wished to take advantage.

No, it was best to get everything on this one trip, come home, and get to work. Her goal was to be presentable, and she was not going to waste any time.

Busy with this determination, Anne dragged a box toward herself, not seeing she had dislodged another. It hit the floor with a thud, stopping Anne in her tracks.

You're going to wake the entire household! she chided herself. Moving a bit more slowly so as not to make noise, she continued to rummage and look for anything that might help in her mission.

❧ ❧

The thumping noise disturbed Weston so that he woke slowly. He was turned on the side that allowed him a view of the door that led to his wife's room. It wasn't at all unusual to think of her when he first woke, but today he remembered she was headed to town. The reason he married her came flooding back. There was no bitterness, no regret, only a deep concern not to see her hurt any more.

And can you be certain her heart won't be bruised if she heads to town without you?

It was a question that didn't take a moment to answer. Seeing that it was still early, Weston didn't rush, but he did have a plan. When his wife left for Collingbourne, he would be with her.

Chapter Fourteen

"Good morning," Weston greeted Anne when he got to the dining room table a few hours later.

"Good morning," she greeted him back, but Weston could tell she was distracted.

"What time are we leaving for town?"

Anne blinked but recovered and asked, "Are you going also, Mr Weston?"

"I thought I might."

"Oh, well—" This stopped Anne a bit. "What time is good for you?"

"I'm perfectly happy to follow your agenda. Whenever you wish to leave will suit me."

Anne nodded but didn't answer. She didn't know why this made her uncomfortable, unless... Her thoughts trailed off and her face grew red at the thought of her husband witnessing her treatment in town. She was married to a gentleman now, and that was supposed to bring respectability, but it was hard to think of how it had been and not dread repeating the ordeal. Would her marriage really alter her status in Collingbourne?

"Are you all right?" Weston asked, his eyes on her.

"Yes. I did want to offer, however," Anne replied, swiftly improvising, "to add anything to my list that you might need. I might be able to save you a trip."

"Thank you. I appreciate that, but I'm not going to shop. I'm going to make certain my wife is treated with kindness."

Anne searched his eyes before asking, "Are you serious?"

"Quite."

Anne's mouth opened a little. She was so stunned she had run out of words.

Mansfield came in just then. A housemaid trailed him to check on the toast rack and teapot. The manservant had some mail for Weston, a normal routine, but this morning he also handed a letter to Anne. She felt rather relieved.

Weston looked at his own post for a time, but he wasn't ready to let Anne off the hook just yet. His breakfast complete and his full teacup close at hand, he sat back and looked at her again.

"Was there a reason you didn't want me to go?"

Anne looked up, knowing she could pretend not to understand but not wanting to live under that kind of deceit.

"There is a reason, but I don't know if it's based on my pride or my desire to protect you."

"Protect me from what?"

"The townsfolk. Not all of them have been very kind. The marriage is supposed to repair that, but if it doesn't, I don't want to subject you to them."

Weston's head tilted to one side before he said, "It's been a while since someone tried to protect me. That's very kind of you, Anne, but you mustn't worry about me. I will be fine. I am accustomed to respect here in Collingbourne, and I don't expect that to change. You, on the other hand, are a different story. We will not frequent establishments whose owners do not know how to be kind to you. There is no reason why we should. I could ask you to report to me who has been unjust, but I'm willing to give the proprietors a second chance. If I go with you, I'll be able to assess the situation and discuss it with you."

Anne never dreamed he'd given it that much thought. She was still rather speechless when she realized her food was growing cold and so was her tea. Almost at the same time she knew she was no longer hungry.

"I believe I will freshen up a bit."

"All right. Do you want to give me a time when we're leaving?"

Anne thought about it. "Thirty minutes?"

"Fine. I'll order the coach."

"Thank you."

Wishing she had a nice dress for her first trip to town as Mrs Weston, Anne exited to her room to do her best.

∾ ∾

"Did I see Mansfield hand you a letter at breakfast?" Weston asked when they were settled in the carriage and on the way to town.

"Yes, he did."

"From anyone I know?"

"I don't believe so. It was from Lucy Digby, wishing me well on my marriage."

"Digby," Weston tested the name. "I don't believe I know them."

"Lucy was a Benwick. Billy Digby used to come and do small jobs for Benwick. The two fell in love. It might not have been Benwick's first choice for his daughter, and he probably lost business over it, but she's happy."

"And the two of you are friends?"

Anne glanced at his face to see what he was thinking, but he looked interested, not condemning.

"We had been friends all along, but we became closer friends once my situation changed. Prior to that, Lucy was protective of me because of my position."

"But then she relaxed with you," Weston guessed.

"Yes," Anne answered as she realized things had altered again. "She had a baby earlier this summer, and I went to help her." She stopped just short of admitting all her thoughts.

"So she and Billy are parents."

"Twice. Meg is two and Liz is the baby."

"Shall we stop and see them today, or will that make someone uncomfortable?"

Anne angled her whole body to see her husband better. Weston watched her, waiting to find out what he'd said to garner this reaction. He was not to find out—at least not without some work. Anne turned back to the front, her eyes forward.

"Anne?"

"Yes?"

"What happened just now?"

"Nothing."

Weston smiled at her profile. She was really quite lovely, and he was learning that when she didn't wish to speak of something, her cheeks grew pink.

With a gentle hand he cupped her far cheek and brought her eyes to his.

"What did I say?"

"I don't know what to do with you!" she blurted, her eyes large and confused.

"*What* did I say?"

"You're willing to visit Lucy. I didn't expect that."

Weston studied her eyes a moment. His hand had dropped away, but Anne was still looking at him.

"To a certain extent we have to be careful, Anne, but there's no reason to shun those who have shown kindness—especially to you—regardless of their station. If you normally visit Lucy when you're in Collingbourne, my presence shouldn't alter that."

Anne nodded.

"So what do you think? Shall we visit Lucy or not?"

"I don't know. Unless she's expecting me, I usually just see how my time goes."

Weston studied her some more.

"You're looking worried, and there's no need."

"No, I guess there isn't, but for some reason I am."

"Well, don't be on my account. I'm just along to keep track of you. Nothing more."

Anne didn't know if this was a comfort or not. She was confused about several things and wasn't certain how to respond. However, Weston let the matter drop, and in a short time they were in town.

"Are we starting at Benwick's?"

"Yes. I think most of my list can be covered there."

"All right, but don't hesitate to change stores or leave something for next time. If I said anything this morning that makes you think I disapprove of how you shop, I'm sorry. Proceed as you wish."

Anne looked at him and nodded, still trying to take it in. She might have attempted to express her feelings, but the coach was stopping.

Once inside, Anne began with stationery. She needed to get thank-you letters off for the gifts that had arrived and continued to arrive. It was a lovely confirmation to have friends supporting them, but often her marriage still felt unreal and amazing to Anne. She hoped that if she put her thoughts down on paper in the form of a thank-you note, the union would begin to seem more genuine.

For the moment, however, she forced herself to push all such thoughts from her head and concentrate on her list. After stationery she went directly to fabrics and sewing needs, determined to set her wardrobe to rights. She was very successful. Benwick had every color of thread she needed. But not until she was done did she realize she hadn't seen her husband in some time. She began a tour of the store and spotted him in the section where Benwick kept larger items: rugs, furniture, and such.

"Did you find something?" Anne asked after she'd approached and stood next to him.

"Yes," he answered, his eyes still on a large mirror that leaned against the wall. "Do you like this mirror?"

Anne followed his gaze.

"It's lovely."

"Good. I want it for your bedroom."

"My room? You just put a rug in there."

"Oh, that's right. What was I thinking? You've had your quota of furnishings for the month."

Anne put a hand to her mouth to keep from laughing, no easy task with Weston's mischievous eyes now looking down on her.

"I only meant," she began, but halted, wanting to laugh at his innocent expression.

"You only meant what?"

"My room is fine," she said at last, not able to come up with any other retort.

"Your room is very bare, and we're going to rectify that. Now, if you don't care for the mirror, you must say so, but if you like it, it would do quite well on the wall across from your bed."

Anne stared off for a moment and then met her husband's gaze.

"That wall is rather bare, isn't it?"

Weston smiled at her.

"What did I say?" Anne asked when she witnessed his look.

Weston didn't answer. He gave her hand a quick squeeze and said he would speak to Benwick about the mirror.

"How does tea sound?" Weston offered when they were back in the carriage.

"It sounds wonderful," Anne said before remembering. "Gray's?"

"All right." Her voice had become quiet, but Weston didn't notice.

"How much more shopping do you have?"

"Not much. In fact, if you'd rather have tea at Brown Manor, I can be done now."

"No, I'm looking forward to Gray's." Weston looked at Anne the moment he said this and asked, "Unless you'd rather not."

"No, it's all right."

Weston needed no other information. The strain in his wife's face told the whole story. Nevertheless, he was not going to be put off by a few gossiping attendants in the tearoom. Anne was Mrs Weston now, and they would need to remember that.

They were seated at a comfortable table not ten minutes later, a solicitous young woman hovering nearby for their order. Anne was very tense, but Weston did the honors: tea, sandwiches, and cakes. The table was quiet while they waited, but almost as soon as the tea arrived, conversation began.

"We will see how this goes today, Anne. If you are not treated with respect, we will not return."

"It seems all right so far."

"Better than the last time for you?"

"Yes."

Weston squeezed her hand and changed the subject.

"Do you think we'll visit Lucy today?" Weston asked.

"I don't know if today would be the best day."

Weston knew he would feel better after tea, but before the sandwiches and cakes arrived he realized he was a bit tired.

"Would it bother you if we made it another time?"

"Not at all."

"I find I'm a little tired just now, and that's not the way I want to first meet your friends."

Anne was on the verge of telling Weston how kind that was when she remembered that he had been nothing but kind from nearly the moment they'd met.

"I am looking forward to meeting your mother," Anne said instead.

"Where did that come from?"

"I *do* want to meet the woman who raised you."

Weston's eyes twinkled.

"Maybe I developed my charm after I left my mother's care."

The waitress took that moment to come with their food, and Anne had to put her napkin to her mouth to keep from laughing.

"I think you might be incorrigible," she teased when they were alone.

"I haven't been called that since I was a child."

"What had you done?"

"Answered back, probably. My tongue got me into the most trouble as a child."

"What would your mother do?"

"My father would handle me most of the time."

Anne looked surprised.

"I was under the impression he died when you were quite young."

"I was 15, halfway to 16."

"A young man. How painful for you."

"It was. We were very tightly knit. My mother's attempts to give me siblings all ended in heartache, so the three of us were rather close."

"And what of today? Are you as close to your mother?"

"Yes, very. She even came to visit so she could see you."

This news stopped Anne.

"I don't remember meeting her."

"You didn't. I pointed you out from across the church."

The relief on Anne's face was unmistakable.

"Why is that a comfort?"

"I'm just glad she knows what I look like."

"Why is that?"

Anne picked at her scone, wishing she'd kept silent. Weston touched her hand, his fingers light and gentle. Anne met his eyes.

"You can tell me."

"I'm only glad to know that she's seen me. When we meet, she won't be expecting me to be fancy or beautiful."

"I don't care for fancy women, and who told you you're not beautiful?"

Anne could only stare at him. At last she admitted, "I keep wanting to feel sorry for you, since you felt pressured to marry me, but it's not working."

Weston smiled into her eyes.

"No one forced me to do anything."

Anne couldn't take her eyes from his, and Weston didn't try. The two sat staring at each other for several moments.

"Well, now." A distinct voice came from behind them as footsteps approached their table. "I'd heard that this marriage was one of convenience, but you two seem quite taken with one another."

His eyes sending a message to Anne, Weston forced a smile to his face, stood, and turned.

"Hello, Mrs Musgrove."

"Mr Weston," she intoned regally before turning her gaze to Anne, who had also come to her feet.

"Well, Anne," she said grudgingly, "you're looking well."

"Thank you, Mrs Musgrove. Are you shopping today?"

"Yes, I'm going to Bath this winter and need a new wardrobe. Will you be in Bath this winter, Mr Weston?"

"Mrs Weston and I have no firm plans at this time."

His vague answer and reserved tone finally got through to the older woman. She had been looking Anne over as though she were a piece of meat and now met Weston's solemn gaze.

Opinionated as ever, Mrs Musgrove declared, "Well, you don't know what you'll be missing!" This said, she turned and went on her way.

The Westons bid her good day, but she didn't turn or acknowledge them. It was with a certain amount of relief that they took their seats and went back to tea.

"Has she always been like that?"

"I'm afraid so. She owns the largest estate in the area and feels we ought to pay her a certain amount of homage."

"No family?"

"Only a daughter, and she doesn't get out much."

"Will her daughter accompany her to Bath, do you think?"

"I imagine. She rather does anything she's told."

Weston's look became thoughtful as he reached for his tea. Anne thought she saw compassion in his gaze and found herself thankful for his tender heart.

They finished their tea in a leisurely manner—everyone at Gray's making them most welcome—and with Weston's urging, Anne made two more stops. By the time they arrived back at Brown Manor, Anne was a little short on time to sew, but by bedtime she had repaired a dress for Sunday morning that she hadn't been able to wear in months.

◆ ◆

"I have a sister," Penny said very softly to Anne when the service was over the next morning. "Her name is Catherine Anne."

"I think that's wonderful. Have you held her?"

Penny nodded. "She only cried a little."

"You must have been very gentle."

Penny looked shy and pleased all at the same time.

"Do you know what arrived for Mr Weston and me this week?" Anne asked.

Penny glanced at Weston who sat on the other side of Anne. He smiled at her before she looked back at the lady herself.

"Was it a gift?"

"Yes, and the note said you picked it out for us."

"It was a bowl," Penny told her unnecessarily, relieved she could finally speak of it.

"A beautiful compote."

"Yes," Weston agreed with his wife. "You'll have to come and visit us at Brown Manor, Penny, sometime after we return from London, so we can put it to use."

"You're going to London?"

"Yes, we are."

"When?"

Anne looked to her spouse, realizing she didn't know that answer.

"Monday, next week."

"What will you do?" the little girl asked.

"We'll visit with Mr Weston's mother and do a bit of shopping. Doesn't that sound nice?"

Penny was still agreeing with Anne when Jennings approached. Both Anne and Weston came to their feet.

"Congratulations!" Weston offered as the men shook hands.

"Thank you."

"How is Mari?" Anne wished to know.

"She's very well."

"Up to visitors?"

"Absolutely. Come soon."

"They're going to London," Penny put in when Jennings glanced down at her.

"That sounds nice. Are you going with them?"

Penny looked shocked.

"I can't leave when Marianne needs help with baby Catherine!"

The adults were still laughing at her when the boys joined them.

"How is life with a baby in the house?" Anne posed the question with a smile.

"It's fine," Thomas said in his kind way.

"A bit noisier," James added in his usual honest, matter-of-fact way.

The group visited a little longer, hearing some of the details and more impressions from the children. When they said their goodbyes and went in separate directions, Anne noticed that Weston was a bit quiet. She didn't question him, but if she'd been bold enough, his answer might have surprised her.

Robert Weston was still thinking on Catherine Jennings. And not just Catherine, but babies in general.

Chapter Fifteen

Anne woke slowly—her neck stiff—with no idea where she might be. She put her hand out to push off her pillow and encountered soft fabric over a firm surface. Finding it too difficult to raise her head, she simply tilted it backward and found her husband's face very close, his eyes looking into hers, as he sat on the carriage seat beside her.

"I'm sorry," she said quietly when she realized she was lying against his chest.

"Don't be. I slept as well."

His arm still supporting her, Anne felt too lethargic to move.

"I should move, but I find myself rather drained."

"You probably need more sleep."

"Possibly," she agreed, even as she found the strength to sit up. "But my neck is a bit stiff."

Weston didn't answer. His side felt bereft of her presence, and he had the most irresistible urge to draw her back to him.

Trying to clear the webs from her mind, Anne only turned to look at Weston when he reached up and touched her cheek.

"My shirtfront left you with a few creases," he said after a gentle caress.

"Oh." Anne's hand came up as she groaned. "I must be a mess. Are we close to London?"

"Very."

Anne closed her eyes. "Your mother will take one look at me and wonder what you've gone and done."

"My mother will take one look at you and ask where you've been all my life."

Anne gave him a skeptical glance as she worked to smooth her hair. Weston unashamedly watched her.

"You're staring, Mr Weston," Anne said without looking at him. This was the second long day in the carriage, and both had become quite relaxed in one another's company.

"Is that a problem?"

"It all depends on what you're thinking."

His thoughts had suddenly turned rather intimate, wondering if she always looked this good right after she woke up, but he didn't think now was the time to voice his musings. He didn't, however, avert his gaze. Anne gave him a direct look, but all he did was smile.

"I believe I'm seeing your incorrigible side again."

"You might be."

"Might?" Anne laughed before asking, "How are the creases on my face?"

"Fading quickly."

"I can only hope you're telling the truth."

Weston put on the most innocent face he could muster, which made Anne laugh.

"Will we stay long?" Anne now asked, realizing she didn't know.

"That depends. If we're having a good time and not missing Collingbourne too much, we'll probably stay two weeks. If we want to return before then, we shall do that."

"Will your mother have plans for us?"

"Most likely not. She tries to keep her own schedule even when I visit, and we can accompany her whenever we like. We might go to dinner one evening, and of course we'll go shopping."

Anne's eyes went immediately to her dress. She was in the midst of adjusting her sleeves and checking her neckline when Weston caught her hand. Anne watched as he held her eyes but lifted her hand to his lips and kissed the back.

"You look lovely," he said softly. "You always look lovely."

Anne wanted to believe him but feared he was only being kind. Telling herself she was far too concerned with her looks, she simply thanked him and, when he released her hand, sat back for the remainder of the journey.

❧ ❧

Berwick

"You're looking strained again," Louisa Cavendish said to Lenore Weston, who had wandered to the window yet again. A neighbor and dear friend of Lenore's, Louisa missed very little.

"It's only just occurred to me," Lenore said, turning from the window.

"What has?"

"Robert had no real desire to marry, and now he's taken a wife. I trust Robert's judgment, but what if he's made a horrible mistake? What if she's all wrong for him? What if she's a—" Lenore stopped, but her friend would not let her off so easily.

"Another Henrietta?"

Looking defeated, Lenore came and sat across from her friend.

"First of all," Louisa began before Lenore could say a word, "we know Anne shares our faith, and with what Robert recently learned, we know Henrietta did not. Secondly—"

A knock on the door halted their conversation. Betsy, Lenore's housekeeper, opened the door enough to announce, "The carriage has arrived, my lady."

"Thank you, Betsy."

The door shut, and Louisa stood and began to walk across the room.

"I'll just slip out the back and see you later."

"But you never finished what you were saying."

Louisa stopped and looked at her friend. "I don't need to. Robert and Anne will be here in a moment, and you'll see for yourself that your son is exactly the man you and James raised him to be."

She didn't wait for Lenore to reply but went on her way, leaving the new mother-in-law on her own. Not a minute passed before the door opened and Robert ushered his bride into the large salon.

"Robert," his mother said, smiling when she saw how well he looked. "And, Anne, I'm so glad you're here."

"It's so nice to meet you, Mrs Weston."

"Lenore," she corrected warmly, even as she went directly to Anne and drew her in for an embrace. There was no missing the way the younger woman trembled.

"Oh, Anne, I was so nervous before you arrived that I asked my neighbor to come and sit with me. She only just left."

Weston laughed even as Anne admitted her own case of nerves. The women ended up laughing with him.

"Come," Lenore invited. "Betsy is bringing tea."

The three settled onto comfortable sofas, Weston and Lenore with a sigh and Anne still with a measure of uncertainty.

"How was the trip?"

"Not as long as usual," Weston said, his eyes on Anne. "It's nice to have company."

Anne smiled at him, and Lenore felt pleasure spiral through her as she witnessed their warmth and comfort with each other.

"And your father, Anne? How is he?"

"Well when I left him."

"Will he be all right with you gone?"

"The Hursts will check on him, and he usually manages very well on his own."

"Has he visited you at Brown Manor?"

"I haven't invited him," Anne admitted. "He's not overly fond of carriage rides, and Brown Manor is a long walk from Levens Crossing."

"Anne, I want you to know that Robert has told me how things haven't always been easy for you."

Growing more relaxed by the moment, Anne didn't try to stop her smile.

"Mr Weston is at times overly sensitive."

Weston shouted with laughter over this, and although Lenore looked surprised, she laughed as well.

"Someone must tell me the joke I've missed."

"I'm the joke," Weston filled in. "Every time my poor wife refers to anything from her past, I begin snorting like a bull. She's told me she'll never survive unless I stop."

Lenore looked as though she would comment on this, but the door opened and Betsy and two other maids entered with a splendid tea.

"I didn't even let you freshen up," Lenore apologized, "but I thought you must be utterly parched after all those hours in the coach."

"Thank you, Mother. This is just right."

"Where did you stay last night?"

Weston answered the question while Anne was busy with her tea, but in an instant she was back in time to the night before.

"Well, it seems we have a large room," Weston told her as they climbed the stairs at the Newbury Inn, "but only one."

"All right," Anne said quietly, not wishing to show the alarm she felt. It had been a good day of travel together— they were growing more comfortable all the time—but

sharing a room was a little more intimate than Anne bargained for.

"I'll just take the settee," Weston announced when they were upstairs, the door closed and their bags delivered.

"That makes no sense at all," Anne replied, having to look up to say this to him. "I'll be much more comfortable there."

"I'm trying to take care of you, and you won't let me."

"I thank you for trying, but on this occasion, I assure you, the settee will be fine."

Weston looked as though he could argue some more, but Anne smiled at him, and lately that had been his undoing.

They had already eaten, and both were tired and hoping for an early start, so they took turns behind the dressing screen as they readied for bed. By the time Anne emerged, Weston had used pillows and blankets to make the settee most comfortable. It wasn't a wide piece of furniture, but Anne knew she would do fine.

In the middle of the night, however, when she fell hip first against the floor, she had second thoughts.

"Anne, Anne." Weston's arms surrounded her even as he tenderly called her name. "Are you all right?"

"I think so."

"Come up here." He lifted her easily and bore her to the bed. "Come and be comfortable on the bed."

"No, Mr Weston, I'll be all right." Anne tried to deny him, even as her hip began to throb, but Weston would have none of it. And in truth, the bed felt wonderful: soft and inviting. Anne's head sank against the pillow with great ease. She wasn't even concerned that Weston lay so close. He touched her hair and face, talking quietly to her. She was sleepy but trying to attend.

"Did you hit your head?"

"No, my hip."

"You'll have a bruise. Did you hit anything else?"

"I don't think so."

Weston smoothed her hair from her face and kissed her brow.

"Go back to sleep."

"I'll move to the settee," she said softly and with little conviction.

"No," he whispered. "You're fine right here."

Anne wanted to argue, but she didn't have the energy. Drifting into sleep and somewhat cognizant that he was close by, Anne couldn't manage the strength to do anything about it.

In the morning Anne woke to an empty room. Examination of the bed covers indicated that her husband had been at her side for the rest of the night, but rather than being alarmed, Anne was comforted by the thought. She was dressed when Weston joined her again, a maid bearing a tray of food at his heels.

"How is your hip?" he asked as soon as they were alone, his eyes watchful.

"A bit sore."

"You should have started on the bed," Weston told her, his eyes still holding hers.

"I didn't think I moved much in my sleep. I must be wrong."

Weston shook his head. "You don't move much at all."

Anne's questions were instantly answered. They had finished the night together, Weston evidently very aware of the fact. For a moment Anne looked up at him, wondering if she saw something foreign in his gaze.

"You'd best eat," he urged her quietly, but Anne thought his eyes might be saying something else.

"Anne—" Lenore set her tea aside and turned to her daughter-in-law.

Anne didn't hear her.

"Anne—" Her husband attempted to break into her thoughts this time, and after a moment, she looked up at him.

"Mother wants to know what you thought of the accommodations at the Newbury Inn."

She thought she caught the slightest spark of intensity in his gaze and found herself blushing.

"They were very nice." Anne forced her eyes away from the man across from her and to her hostess. "Everyone was most kind, even though they were rather busy."

"Was it full?"

"Yes."

"I'm glad you were able to get rooms."

Anne looked to her husband, but he made no effort to correct his mother. She nearly started when she thought one of Mr Weston's lids dropped in a subtle wink. She might have continued to watch him, but Lenore was offering her the plate of sandwiches.

The threesome visited a while longer before Lenore suggested that Robert and Anne might wish to rest for a time. Anne found this idea most inviting and was following Betsy from the room when Weston hung back and whispered to his mother.

"Did you get my letter?"

"Yes, it's all taken care of."

As though no words had been exchanged, Weston followed on his wife's heels, mentally making plans for how they would spend the evening.

෨ ෨

"This door right here leads to Mr Weston's room," Betsy informed Anne, who worked at not gawking at the beauty surrounding her. "All your bags have been unpacked and settled in the dressing room. And this is Jenny," Betsy finally added. "She'll take care of everything for you while you're here."

Jenny, a small young woman who was probably close to Anne's age, bowed and waited for Anne's pleasure.

"Thank you," Anne said to both women.

Betsy made her way to the door, but Jenny slipped into the dressing room and emerged with a robe.

"Did you wish to lie down, Mrs Weston?"

"I believe I will," Anne told her, thinking that a nap sounded lovely.

Jenny had Anne completely settled and had exited when Anne heard a soft knock on the adjoining door. She turned her head in time to see it open. Weston, missing his jacket and tie, peeked in and then entered when he saw his wife awake.

"Are you comfortable?" he asked from the side of the bed.

"Yes. This room is lovely."

"How is your hip?"

"It will be all right."

Weston smiled. "You didn't answer my question."

Anne smiled back at him.

"What did you think of my mother?"

"Oh, Mr Weston!" Anne became animated. "She's so kind and sweet. The two of you must be very close."

"We are, yes. She liked you too."

"I'm glad."

"Do you know what I would like?"

"No, what?"

"I would like you to drop the 'Mr' from my name."

Anne looked completely taken aback.

"I've surprised you."

"You have, yes. What made you think of that?"

"It's become so automatic for you that even last night when you were half asleep and you'd fallen from the settee, you told Mr Weston you would be all right."

"Did I?"

"Yes."

"And why exactly is that a problem?"

Weston had taken a seat on the edge of the bed. He now leaned close, a hand on either side of his wife.

"We spent the rest of the night in the same bed, Anne."

Anne's eyes grew very large before she whispered, "Did we do more than sleep?"

"No." Weston's voice was also soft. "But your calling me Mr Weston feels formal and stilted, and I think we're closer than that now."

Anne searched his eyes even as he searched hers.

"Yes, we are," she agreed. "I don't know how easy a habit it will be to break, but I shall try."

Weston leaned and kissed her cheek.

"Why don't you sleep for a time? I'll show you the house when you get up."

"All right. Thank you."

Weston had risen to his feet when Anne called to him, just remembering to drop the formal part of his name.

"Weston?"

"Yes."

"Any regrets yet?"

His brows rose. "About marrying you?"

"Yes."

Weston's shoulders began to shake, and Anne watched as he chuckled all the way to the door. His response kept her in a confused muddle until she drifted off to sleep.

❧ ❧

"What caused you to ask me that question earlier?" Weston asked. The house tour had begun, just the two of them working from room to room.

"I was tired."

"What happens when you're tired?"

"I grow uncertain and doubt myself."

Weston held the door of the gallery, and Anne went in ahead of him. The subject did not resurface, and Anne was only too happy to let the matter drop. She didn't usually let her tongue ramble, but when she did, she often had cause for regret.

"This is my father," Weston pronounced as he stood before a large portrait. Anne stood with him, looking up at an older version of her husband.

"He was so handsome."

"I've been told we look alike."

His tone drew Anne's eyes up to his. She tried not to laugh or even smile at his outrageous statement, but it was impossible.

Anne was still laughing when Weston said, "And now you're going to tell me I'm incorrigible."

"Well, it's quite true."

"How long is your hair?"

Anne, who had been moving for a closer look at the late Mr Weston, turned, her eyes and face mirroring her astonishment.

"How long is my hair?"

"Yes. You had it down last night at the Newbury Inn, but I forgot to look."

Anne was still gawking at him when they were joined by Lenore. Louisa was with her.

"I hoped I would find you here," Lenore commented, smiling in pleasure when she saw they were near James Weston's portrait. "Anne, this is my dear friend and neighbor, Louisa Cavendish. Louisa, meet my new daughter, Anne."

The women exchanged greetings, and while Louisa engaged Anne in conversation, Lenore turned to her son.

"How did she like Jenny?"

"We haven't spoken of it. I'll wait until closer to the time to leave."

"Weston," Louisa said, turning to him. "Will you take Anne to see the Coventry Gardens?"

"Certainly. I hadn't thought of it, but it's a splendid idea. Maybe you and Mother will join us."

"Maybe we will."

"When you're finished here, Louisa and I will be in the drawing room," Lenore put in. "Why don't you join us before dinner?"

"We'll do that. Is Cavendish joining us, Louisa?"

"Yes. His brother is in town, and they'll both be along shortly."

It was all so normal and family-like that Anne stood quietly for a moment after they left. It was a lot for her to take in on short notice. She only just then thought about her dress and whether it might be appropriate but forced herself not to look down and fret about it.

"Louisa has lived next door for more years than I can count. Her sons and I were chums at school."

"How many children does she have?" Anne was glad for something to take her mind from her dress.

"Four sons, all grown. She's a grandmother several times over."

"Do they live in London?"

"Two of them do. The other two married girls from northern climes and visit during the holidays."

"Do you miss London?"

"No. Collingbourne suits me very well."

"Why is that, do you suppose?"

"Well, I spent a good deal of time there as a child, so it's a little like coming home already."

"It certainly must help that Brown Manor is so lovely."

"Yes. My grandmother let it out for years, but after her death, I learned that she wished for me to live there."

Anne studied him.

"I can't help but wonder how different your life might be right now if you hadn't come."

"I don't know." His voice became light and teasing. "I think God would have still known I needed a sweet little wife whose hair is a mystery."

Anne's hand came to her mouth although her eyes brimmed with laughter.

"Show me the rest of these pictures, Weston, before you get yourself into trouble."

With a gentle hand to her back, a smiling Weston turned his wife to the rest of the gallery, thinking that if she knew how kissable he found her when she laughed, trouble might be the last thing on her mind.

Chapter Sixteen

"How are you?" Lenore asked Robert as the two took a turn around the room after dinner that evening. Anne and their guests were visiting over cards around the table in the far corner.

"I'm well."

"You seem very happy."

"I am most content, Mother."

"She's so sweet, Robert."

The young man smiled. "She is. She's very sweet."

"And you already have feelings for her, don't you?"

"I think I must. I didn't expect to."

"You didn't expect it now or ever?"

"Not ever, I guess. Not like this. I feel so protective, and it's just been a few weeks."

"Why do you suppose it's happened this way?"

Walking slowly and tucking his mother's hand into the crook of his elbow, Robert thought for a moment.

"I think all the times we met must have been having an effect on me. Our first meeting was awful, but from that time forward, all I could see in Anne was a sweet woman in need of care. I found myself utterly delighted when she agreed to let *me* be the one to give her that care."

"You can see how grateful she is, Robert, but not in an ingratiating manner. She doesn't grovel at your feet, if you get my meaning."

"Yes, I do. She is grateful, but I've truthfully told her she's not a charity case. Already she's brought many things to my life."

"Such as?"

"Companionship, for starters. She also forces me to think of someone besides myself. It's too easy to be absorbed with myself when I live alone, the whole staff waiting on me hand and foot. When I go looking for Mansfield and find he's in conference with my wife, it's good for me to have to wait."

A smile stretched Lenore's mouth as she walked. She was so pleased and proud of him that she couldn't find the words to tell him.

Weston eventually directed them over to the card table, where the game was ending. From there the six moved to the davenports and sat listening while Louisa played the piano. Weston's eyes often drifted to where his wife sat on a chair a few feet away from his place on the sofa, but Anne's gaze was always on Louisa, her visage rather wistful.

"That was lovely, Louisa," Lenore told her friend at the finish of the first lengthy number.

"Thank you."

"Play my favorite," Edward Cavendish requested, his deep voice quietly reverberating in the room. Louisa glanced at him, looking pleased as she went back to the keys.

As the strains of a minuet floated from the instrument, Weston watched Louisa for a time. But as he was turning his gaze back to Anne, he noticed that Francis Cavendish, Edward's brother, was already watching her. Anne didn't notice either man, but Weston had suddenly become very aware of his old family friend.

Had someone accused him of being the jealous type an hour earlier, Weston would have laughed, but now he wasn't so sure. With surreptitious eye movements, and Louisa's music in the background, Weston watched Francis watching

Anne. Not at any time did Anne seem to be aware of the other man, but Weston found himself remembering that Francis was many years younger than Edward. He was too old for Anne in Weston's opinion, but clearly Francis didn't think so.

Weston nearly started at his own thoughts. It mattered not in the least if Francis was too old for Anne! Anne was spoken for, and by a man who had no intention of giving her up!

"Are you all right?" a soft voice came to Weston's ears.

He'd been frowning at the younger Cavendish, and it took a moment to realize it was Anne.

"Yes," he answered automatically, having to ignore the concern he saw in her eyes while mentally being very stern with himself over his own foolish ramblings.

As if trying to gauge for herself, Anne studied him a bit longer and then turned back to Louisa's work at the piano.

For Weston the evening began to drag. His mother's neighbors didn't stay any later than they usually did, but Weston was most eager to be alone with his thoughts. It seemed hours before he was able to do this, and when he was finally alone in his room, he knew his body needed sleep. He climbed into bed, Anne very much on his mind. But he also realized that any more cogitation on the subject would have to wait for the morning.

ᴨ ᴨ

"Thank you, Betsy," Lenore said when she was handed her first cup of tea. She always started the day with tea in her room; breakfast came later. "There was something I wanted to ask you, and it has slipped my mind."

Betsy waited a moment and then suggested, "Could it be about young Mrs Weston's clothing?"

Lenore looked relieved. It was lovely to have a faithful servant who could read her mind after all these years.

"That was it, Betsy. How did things seem to you?"

"Wanting in every way, my lady."

"Underclothing?"

"Most definitely."

"Night things?"

"Those too."

Lenore looked thoughtful for a moment, and Betsy knew she could add more.

"If I may be so bold, Mrs Weston, I found only three handkerchiefs. They looked new, but her robe is threadbare."

"The robe will go on Mrs Martin's list when she's here for our fittings tomorrow, but handkerchiefs and such can be covered today."

"It's a good plan, my lady."

Lenore nodded, her face still thoughtful before it broke into a warm smile.

"We're going to take care of her, Betsy. We're going to take care of our Anne. She'll have a wedding trousseau the likes of which she's never dreamed."

Betsy exited on that positive note to leave her mistress in peace. Trusting that Anne would be pleased with the plans, Lenore reached for her Bible. The house was still quiet, and it was her favorite time to read and pray. She began with her son and new daughter.

❧ ❧

"Good morning, Anne," Lenore greeted when Anne arrived at the breakfast table a few hours later. Lenore had only just taken a seat. "How did you sleep?"

"Very well, thank you. It's a bit late. Have I held breakfast?"

"Not at all. I can tell you live in the country. For a London resident, this isn't late at all."

Anne laughed a little as she joined Lenore, sitting to her right. Tea was offered to her, and as she added sugar, food began to arrive. Halfway through eggs, bacon, and tomatoes, her husband came down for breakfast.

"You're up early," Weston said to his mother before kissing her cheek.

"Do you think?" Lenore asked him with a teasing smile.

Weston didn't answer but went directly to Anne and kissed her cheek.

"Good morning," he greeted before taking a seat across the table. "How did you sleep?"

"Very well, thank you. And you?"

"I slept very hard. It must have been our long day yesterday."

"You did have a long day yesterday," Lenore said, just realizing this. "I think I would have had the Cavendishes another night had I been thinking straight."

"Don't worry on it, Mother. We'll have plenty of time to take our ease."

"Not today, however. Today is our first shopping day."

"Did you hear that, Anne? Mother has spoken!"

"I did hear. Where will we begin?"

"I think at Lloyd's. They have such splendid accessories."

"What types of things are you shopping for, Mrs Weston?"

"Lenore," she corrected before going on. "I'm shopping for your trousseau, Anne. Did Robert not tell you?"

Anne looked at her husband, her memory serving that they were going to shop but nothing about his mother's involvement or a trousseau.

"Have I overstepped?" Lenore asked, looking a bit concerned, her gaze going from one to the other.

"Not at all, Mother. I didn't explain to Anne." As Robert turned to do this, he found his wife's face very pale.

"I'm sorry," he immediately began. "Mother wrote and asked me what type of wedding gift would suit us. I told her the first thing that came to mind, and that was that she could take us shopping when we visited London."

"But a trousseau," Anne argued. "It's too much."

"Can you name me one thing you don't need, Anne?"

The question was asked gently, but feeling very humbled and put in her place, Anne gave a swift shake of her head and lowered her eyes to her plate.

"I just remembered I must see Cook about something," Lenore put in at that moment. "Do excuse me, will you?"

"Anne, I'm sorry," Weston wasted no time in saying. "I should never have spoken to you like that in front of my mother."

"Do you think she found me rude and ungrateful?"

"No, I think she found me forgetting my tongue and you embarrassed because of it."

Husband and wife stared across the table at each other.

"Give me your hand," Weston requested. He waited for Anne to reach across the table. "I thought as much—you're trembling."

"I hate to be such a little mouse of a thing, but at times I am overwhelmed." Anne saw compassion in her husband's gaze and felt it in his touch, so she felt emboldened to go on. "I do have needs in all areas, but I still think a trousseau is too much."

"How would you like to do this?"

"I don't know. Maybe just a little at a time in Collingbourne."

"But if you have needs now and we can afford to see to them, or if my mother is offering a gift, why not take care of them?"

Anne reclaimed her hand and shrugged helplessly, her heart unsure of what to think or do next. She wasn't feeling bad about having needs, but somehow burdening her mother-in-law when they'd only just met seemed unnecessary to her. It was one thing to have her husband know of her situation—he had married her with his eyes open—but she didn't think it fair to have it fall on Mrs Weston.

A moment more of thought and Anne saw that it was a foolish notion on her part. Of course his mother would be affected by nearly anything that touched her son, but she hadn't expected it to come out in quite this way.

"No one will buy anything today that you don't want." Weston cut into Anne's thoughts with this suggestion.

Anne looked uncertain and countered, "Why don't you decide what I should get?"

"If I do that," Weston began, a smile peeking through, "you'll have the trousseau."

Anne's hands came up in exasperation before she said, "Weston, do you not think a few dresses and something more permanent for our home would be a better wedding gift?"

"Our home is full of treasures," he reasoned. "My mother is delighted to shop for you. She loves to shop. If we give her full rein—something I fully intend to do—you'll be the best-dressed lady in all of Collingbourne." Weston put his hand up when Anne opened her mouth to speak. "I know that's not your goal in life, and I was being more facetious than anything else, but you do have needs, my mother loves to shop, and she wants to buy us a wedding gift. I find that a perfect combination."

Anne watched her husband sit back and wait. She had to admit that his argument was sound. On top of that, he wanted her to have the things she needed.

"I did say that I wanted you to decide," Anne said thoughtfully.

"True."

"And it rather sounds like you have."

Weston's eyes began to smile; his mouth was soon to follow.

"You might even have fun," he teased her.

Anne shook her head in self-derision.

"We chased your mother from her breakfast."

"She'd be willing to give up eating for the day if you'll accept this gift from her." Weston's voice was quiet and gentle. He hated to see Anne upset, and her pale face was still very clear in his mind. "Mother really is quite excited, and again, I'm sorry I didn't explain. It would have taken care of all of this."

"Do I need to apologize to your mother? I think I might."

"No, she understands you were taken by surprise, and if you recall, she turned directly to me to find out why you didn't know. She understands who's to blame."

"It's like you said before."

"What's that?"

"This getting to know each other takes years."

Weston nodded. "Yes, but I think it will be worth our effort."

Anne silently agreed. It was already worth it to her. Almost daily new things unfolded, new things about herself or her husband that were helping her learn and grow. She believed God had blessed her all the years of her life, but never had His grace been so visible.

Anne would need to remember her gracious God a few hours later when the threesome was in the thick of shopping. Lenore Weston's eye for detail, her nose for a bargain, and her delight in seeing Anne with new things would make for a day that the younger Mrs Weston would never forget.

"Look at this pair, Anne. They're just right for you."

"Oh, my," Anne breathed for the dozenth time, touching the long kid gloves and marveling at their softness.

"I think several pair," Lenore was saying, consulting her list. A clerk stood at her elbow and made notes on her own pad.

"That many?"

"Certainly, dear, you never know when someone might spill on you. My Betsy is a wonder with stains, but not even she can manage…" Lenore didn't finish. She had spotted something else and was taking Anne in that direction.

"This bonnet! The color is perfect for you. Why don't you try it on? There's a glass right here."

Once again Lenore was off to see something else, the clerk chasing after her. Anne stepped up to the counter and began to place the bonnet on her head. She had just settled it when she caught her husband's reflection behind her. Anne turned as he approached.

"What do you think?"

Weston reached up to tie the ribbons under her chin. He then took hold of the brim and adjusted it slightly. Studying his work, he smiled.

"Very nice."

"Your mother liked the color."

"As do I."

Anne looked into his eyes and wondered if they were still talking about the bonnet. She might have questioned him, but Lenore was returning.

"Anne, there's a blue spencer jacket over here that matches that hat. Do try it on. Robert," she said, turning next to him, "there's a Polish beaver top hat over here in your size. Is yours in good condition? They also have Hessian boots that I want you to try on."

Husband and wife trailed after Lenore, both wanting to laugh.

"She's a bit scattered when she shops," Weston told Anne. "It's the only time I see her this way."

"I must admit I'm surprised. She's so relaxed at home, but since we left Berwick, she's been on a mission."

The spencer jacket, a very short and fitted article of clothing with long sleeves, was a perfect fit. It did look very good with the bonnet, and Anne found herself smiling in pleasure. Lenore saw it and was all the more determined to find all she could.

Weston, who had gained plenty of items for his own wardrobe, begged his mother to cease some five hours later, proclaiming that they all needed tea. Such proprieties never occurred to Lenore when she shopped, but Weston was adamant. Wringing from them a commitment to shop at least one other day before they left, Lenore acquiesced.

To Weston and Anne's relief, they found a shop and were settled down for tea not 20 minutes later.

                        ഔ ഔ

Berwick

"We'd best turn in early," Lenore said when dinner was over that night and the three had enjoyed coffee and dessert in the drawing room. "Mrs Martin will be here at 9:00, and that will make for a long day."

Weston had remembered to tell Anne who Mrs Martin was, so this was not a complete surprise. What was unexpected was Weston's question to Anne as they climbed the stairs to seek their rest.

"Have you ever been in love, Anne?"

That lady continued to walk beside the man she married, but she turned her head to look at him.

"Do you mean romantic love?"

"Yes, exactly."

"No, I can't say that I have. I do remember having something of a schoolgirl crush on a boy when I was quite young, but that hardly constitutes love."

They had reached Anne's room now, and Weston, knowing he had passage to his own room, followed her inside.

"Why did you ask?" Anne wished to know.

"Francis Cavendish seemed quite taken with you. Did you even notice?"

Anne took a moment to catch up.

"Do you mean Louisa's brother-in-law?"

"Yes."

"Am I mistaken in thinking he's a good deal older than I am?"

"No, you're quite right, but that didn't seem to put him off."

"I'm also a married woman," Anne pointed out.

"Nevertheless, he was quite distracted by you."

Anne was utterly quiet for several moments, trying to take it in. With an effort she kept her voice calm as she spoke.

"I'm very tired right now. If I don't get some rest I'm going to overreact to this news, but in the morning I will expect you to tell me why you've shared this. What possible reason could you have?"

Weston began to open his mouth, but Anne put her hand up.

"In the morning."

"You're angry with me."

"A little, yes."

"I'm sorry. I should have waited until morning to ask you."

Anne felt terribly confused but forced herself to keep quiet beyond, "Thank you, Mr Weston. I look forward to our talking about this."

They parted company, both completely forgetting that Mrs Martin was coming rather early. It did not escape his attention that Anne had once again referred to him as Mr Weston. It would be hours before they could have their talk, and it would look nothing like what either of them had planned.

❧ ❧

The Manse

"How is the Colonel?" Judith asked the moment her husband entered.

"He's better. He has a good-sized bump on his head, but he's resting comfortably."

"Will you contact Anne?"

"Not now. They'll be home in about ten days, and her father did rouse quickly."

"How do you think he fell?"

The pastor shrugged. "A touch of apoplexy, a sudden pain—I don't know. Maybe he only stumbled. His one arm seemed a little stiff, but he was very steady when I was just there. Of course, that doesn't mean he's steady all the time."

"What if something happens to him before Anne returns?"

"There's nothing to be done about that, Judith. He's not going to live forever, and it's doubtful Anne could do anything even if she lived there."

"Much as I hate to admit it, you're probably right. Anne has always been able to see to all his needs, and it's hard to have her gone. I've prayed for both of them since you found the Colonel last night."

"I've prayed as well," Pastor Hurst said confidently. "And we can keep on praying, knowing God's hand is at work even as we speak."

≈ ≈

Berwick

"What do you think of this muslin, Anne?"

"It's very pretty. Do you like it?"

"Yes, it's perfect for day dresses."

Bolts of cloth nearly covered the large salon downstairs. Anne had been measured and now fabrics and patterns were being chosen. Weston had gone to the tailor, and Lenore was in her element dressing Anne with Mrs Martin's help.

Day gowns were chosen, evening gowns, dresses for warm weather and cold, undergarments—more than Anne thought she could use in a year—and Lenore was even heard to mutter about a trip to the cobbler.

A redingote was put on order in a dark shade of blue. The long coat had multiple capelets and was lined in silk. Lenore insisted that Anne have two matching hats for that item, as well as a fox muff. A pelisse—walking coat—was also chosen, this one in a rich brown.

"Have I overwhelmed you?" Lenore came close and whispered at one point, her eyes a little large with excitement.

"Would it do any good to say yes?"

Lenore smiled.

"Have I told you how very glad I am that Robert brought you home?"

Anne hugged the older woman, who warmly returned the embrace. It didn't last long, however. Mrs Martin had more fabric to show them, and she did not like to be kept waiting.

And on it went. For hours they matched patterns, fabric, and trim. When it looked as though she was no longer needed, Anne slipped into one of the smaller salons and lay down on the settee. Weston found her sound asleep an hour later. He gave orders to the staff to let her rest and went in search of his mother.

Chapter Seventeen

London

"Is it true?"

"Yes. He was seen shopping just today."

"Here, in London? You're certain?"

"Yes, my lady."

"Did he bring his wife?"

"A young woman is with him, yes."

Quiet filled the elegant room. The servant who had delivered the news hovered nearby, waiting for further orders. They weren't long in coming.

"Tell Cook I want dinner early."

"Yes, my lady."

"And then I'll need the carriage. I'm going out."

Berwick

Anne felt like a new person after her nap, but her dress was another matter. The frock was a mass of wrinkles, and her hair was coming down around her face. Thankfully she woke to find herself alone, and with a bit of maneuvering she managed to gain her room without encountering anyone.

Jenny was on hand to choose another dress and set her hair to rights. Weston had just found her missing from the salon and was knocking on her door as Jenny made the finishing touches.

"I thought we'd lost you," he said when she beckoned him to enter.

"I snuck up the back way."

"For any particular reason?"

Anne thanked Jenny and turned from the mirror.

"How do I look?"

"You look lovely."

"You wouldn't have said that 30 minutes ago."

"I'm not so certain of that," Weston said as he offered his arm. "Dinner is nearly on. Hungry?"

"Very. I slept through tea."

"Mother's fault, I'm afraid. When it comes to shopping, she's unpredictable at best."

"How did you fare at the tailor?"

"Very well. I trust I'll look suitable beside my newly decked-out bride."

"I think that must be the least of your worries."

Weston studied her without being obvious, noting that she was very rested and relaxed just now. He had certainly blundered through things the night before and looked forward to setting the record straight later that evening.

And it looked as though he would have his chance. Dinner was an unpretentious affair, full of talk and laughter, mostly at Lenore's expense, but then the newlyweds were to be left on their own. Lenore had been invited to Louisa's for cards.

"Do you go directly after dinner, Mother, or is it later?"

"Not directly, but soon after."

They were more than halfway through their meal when Betsy entered unexpectedly. She went to Lenore and bent slightly to speak to her.

"Mrs Rooke is here to see you."

Lenore stared up at her. Weston and Anne had heard and turned to look at the servant as well.

"Henrietta's mother?"

"Yes. She wishes to see you and Mr Weston and to meet young Mrs Weston."

Lenore took a moment to respond, and when she did she had a plan.

"Tell Mrs Rooke we will be a few minutes and make her comfortable in the salon. Then send word to Mrs Cavendish that I might be delayed and not to hesitate to begin in my absence."

"Very well, my lady."

Anne watched in surprise as Lenore went back to her meal. She took a small bite of food and a sip of water from her glass before she found Anne staring at her.

"Do try to finish, Anne. I have no idea what the evening will bring, but we may need our strength." Lenore looked to Weston. "Anne does know about Henrietta, doesn't she, Robert?"

"Yes."

"Are you worried about her mother being here?"

"No, Mother, there was never any ill will between us, but I am most curious over her visiting this way."

Lenore put her fork down.

"I am too, and I'm doing little more than pushing my food around. Shall we just go now?"

Weston looked to Anne in question.

"Certainly," she said, trying to keep the sudden pounding of her heart at bay.

Led by Lenore, the threesome entered the salon just moments later. Mrs Rooke stood, all smiles, to greet them.

"Lenore, please forgive my breech of manners, but when I learned that Weston was in town, I had to come."

"It's fine, Victoria. I must say, you look very well."

"As do you, Lenore. And Weston, how are you?"

"I'm well, Mrs Rooke. It's nice to see you. Please allow me to present my wife. Anne, this is Mrs Rooke."

"How do you do?" Anne said kindly with a respectful bow of her head.

"Oh, Weston, she's lovely. You've obviously chosen very well."

"Let us sit down," Lenore invited, stealing occasional looks at the two younger people in the room.

"I must tell you," Mrs Rooke wasted no time in saying, "I have never gotten over Henrietta's breaking off with you, Weston. She's so flighty and foolish, and I also must tell you that there's been a corner of my heart that hoped it wouldn't really be over."

Lenore and Weston watched Mrs Rooke look to Anne. The older woman was smiling, but her eyes were full of regret.

"How is Henrietta?" Weston asked, forcing his eyes away from his wife's calm face.

"She's well. She's been in Bath now for weeks, living with my sister. I'll probably go this winter to visit, if for no other reason than to tell her what a mistake she made."

"How is Elinore?" Lenore asked, referring to Henrietta's older sister.

"She just had another baby!" Mrs Rooke was clearly delighted to announce. This line of questioning worked for a time, but it wasn't long before Mrs Rooke was staring at Weston again.

"I told her you were the best catch in all of London, but she let that Andre turn her head."

"Would you like tea, Victoria?" Lenore offered, praying that the social commentary wouldn't go on much longer.

"No, I really must be off. I just wanted to stop and offer my congratulations."

Not a soul in the room believed that line, but no one wanted to chance the ordeal being prolonged, so none of the Westons replied. And thankfully it was over. Mrs Rooke came to her feet and made her goodbyes. Lenore saw her out.

When the room emptied except for Weston and Anne, they stood looking at the door before turning to each other.

"Are you all right?" Anne asked.

"Why wouldn't I be all right?"

"I don't know. Maybe the memories are painful for you."

Weston's look was unreadable, and Anne wondered if she'd hit rather close to the mark.

"I'm going to finish my dinner," Lenore poked her head back in long enough to say. "Does anyone care to join me?"

"I will," Anne replied without hesitation.

Weston watched his wife walk away, desperately wishing he could explain what was going on inside of him but convinced that it was too soon.

With no desire for anything else to eat, Weston took some time in following the women—too much time. He found the dining room empty. Betsy said his mother had gone next door.

"And my wife?"

"She didn't mention her plans, Mr Weston."

"Did she go out?"

"Not to my knowledge."

Weston left the dining room and started for the stairs. It was a big house, and he'd only given Anne one tour. He assumed she'd gone to her room.

❧ ❧

Norwood Place

"Are you all right?" Louisa asked the moment Lenore stepped inside the huge mansion whose property adjoined her own.

"Yes. We had an unexpected visitor."

Lenore's color was a bit high, and even though Louisa had guests, her neighbor was more important to her. She led her friend to her husband's study, just off the foyer, and shut the door.

"Can you tell me?"

"Victoria Rooke."

"Oh, Lenore, what did she want?"

"Mostly to get a look at Anne, I'm sure. I lost track of how many times she told Robert that her Henrietta had made a terrible mistake."

"And Anne was listening to all of this?"

"Yes, she was right in the room."

"How is she?"

"That's just it—I can't tell. We had a few minutes alone while we finished dinner, but there was something so vulnerable in her gaze that I couldn't bring myself to ask."

"Where was Weston at that time?"

"Still in the other room."

Louisa gave her friend a hug.

"We'll pray that the two of them can talk it out. It might turn out for the best."

"In what way?"

"Well, if Weston hasn't shared much about Henrietta, he'll need to now. And there's no one better to do that with than his wife."

∾ ∾

Berwick

Weston stood in the upstairs hallway, his mind doing a mental walk-through of the house. Anne wasn't in her room or in the upstairs sitting rooms or salons. The downstairs salons were very large, and while he couldn't picture her comfortable all alone in such large rooms, he still headed in that direction. It wasn't until he was descending the last steps that he remembered the library.

Anne was buried in a deep chair, shoes kicked off, her legs drawn up beneath her, the lantern high as she gazed absently at the book in her lap. She looked up when she heard the door.

"I thought you might have gone to bed."

"I had quite a long nap."

Weston nodded. "I'd forgotten about that."

"Weston," Anne said, putting the book aside, actually quite glad to see him. "May I speak with you?"

"Of course."

Weston took a nearby chair, one that allowed the light to spill onto both their faces.

For Anne, the conversation from the night before concerning Francis Cavendish was completely forgotten. Right now she had one question for her husband, and she desperately needed it answered.

"Weston, what's in this for you?"

Weston blinked and asked, "What are we talking about, Anne?"

"Our marriage. What's in it for you?"

Weston looked so surprised that Anne rushed on.

"It occurred to me after Mrs Rooke's visit that if you had married Henrietta it would have been for love. When you married me, it was a rescue. I know why *I* married. What I don't know is why *you* did."

Again Weston could only stare at her, so Anne went on.

"I should have asked this during those long talks at the manse, but I didn't think of it. Mrs Rooke's visit has prompted the question, and now it's all I can think about. Please tell me, Weston, what's in this marriage for you?"

"Many things," Weston responded, finally finding his voice.

"Can you name some?"

"Certainly. Companionship. I so enjoy having you at Brown Manor and sitting beside me in church. Even the ride to London seemed faster and easier because you were there with me."

"What else?"

"You draw me out of myself, Anne. You force me to think of someone else. I've been alone for a long time. Your presence has helped me to be more caring and concerned about others."

"And you truly don't regret having not married for love?"

"No, Anne," he told her sincerely, desperately wanting to handle this with tact and honesty. "I think someday we will love each other, but I can't help but wonder if more marriages shouldn't start as ours has."

"What do you mean?"

"I mean, we both came into this with our eyes wide open, not full of romantic notions and unrealistic dreams. If we have romance someday and talk about our dreams, I'm sure the timing will be just right, but it didn't have to happen before the marriage. It didn't have to be before we made this lifelong commitment in front of God and man."

Anne looked thoughtful. She couldn't have agreed with him more, but why hadn't they talked of this before? Or had they, and she hadn't understood or fully taken it in?

Weston sat in his chair, taking in her expression. That his feelings were swiftly changing toward Anne did not alter the truth of the words he'd just spoken, but they did make him feel as though he must wait to discuss them with her. He found himself praying for ways to gently show her how much he cared without pressuring or scaring her.

"Did that answer your question?"

"Yes, thank you."

"Did I do something that caused these thoughts to come up, or was it just our visit from Mrs Rooke?"

"Well, after she left, you did seem reticent to tell me if you were all right."

"I can assure you, Anne, I am not longing for Henrietta Rooke. Not even hearing from her mother and having her voice such regret has affected my heart. I hope Henrietta is well, but I do not wish her to be my wife."

"Did I sound jealous and silly just now?"

"Not in the least."

"It's occurred to me," Anne went on as though he hadn't answered, "that one has so much to learn to be a wife. I don't know how to do it all! I don't know what all your looks mean. I'm sure in time I'll have some memorized, but it might take years for me to be the wife you need."

"You're already the wife I need, although I appreciate your wanting to know me better. I certainly want to know you better."

Anne's face softened as she looked at him. She'd never known anyone so easy to talk with. He said she helped him be more caring, but it seemed to her as though he cared even before they spoke of marriage.

"Why do I get the impression that I did or said something right?"

Anne's warm gaze turned into a smile, but she didn't answer. Weston might have pressed her, but his stomach growled just then.

"Did you get enough dinner?" he asked.

"Yes, but I wouldn't mind having a little something sweet. How about you?"

"I'm still hungry. I believe I'll ring for Betsy and see what she can drum up."

And that was all it took. Betsy was serving food in the library just 20 minutes later. Time slowed to a relaxed pace as the twosome talked and ate. Anne found herself with questions about Berwick—the home her husband had lived in from birth—and the closest neighbors.

"We should pop over to Norwood Place tomorrow," Weston said at one point. "The house and grounds are stunning, and I'm sure Louisa would love to show us around."

"I would enjoy that. I would also enjoy some time in your mother's garden."

"I thought you might feel that way. We can also plan on seeing Coventry Gardens. The late summer flowers should be splendid just now."

"I won't argue with you about that idea."

"Actually," Weston said insightfully. "I don't believe you argue with me about much of anything."

"Did you think I would?"

"No, but what I find most interesting is that you do have a mind of your own. You're quite willing to follow my lead, but you're no one's floor mat."

"That was a nice compliment."

There are more where that came from, was the next thing to pop into Weston's mind, but he kept that thought to himself, saying only, "It's one you deserve."

The two talked until Lenore came home. She hadn't expected to find them up, but when she sat with them in the library and saw that all was well between them, and especially with Anne, she was relieved.

Lenore was the first to excuse herself, more than ready to lie down in bed. When she was finally settled, sleep crowding in swiftly, she had a final thought. For some odd reason she had the notion that her son not marrying for love would be less of an emotional drain for all of them, but it simply wasn't so. For one thing, Weston was on his way to loving Anne, if he didn't already, and for another, whenever humans were involved, there was always some expense of emotions.

I'm old enough to know that by now, she told the Lord, wondering at her own lack of acumen, and promptly went to sleep.

The trousseau began to arrive on Friday morning. Accessories that had been picked out in the shops on their day in London were delivered, as well as the first items from Mrs Martin. In silent awe Anne looked at the beautiful clothing in her room.

She might have gone on looking, staring in wonder as Jenny unwrapped one item after another, but Weston knocked on the door. Jenny went to answer it and slipped out when the new husband walked in.

"I understand Saint Nicholas paid you a visit," he teased.

"Oh, Weston, have you ever seen such lovely things? How will I ever thank your mother?"

"You won't need to. She'll take one look at your face and have all the thanks she needs."

Anne barely heard him. She was inspecting a pair of shoes they'd ordered at the cobbler's, a pair of evening slippers that would be beautiful with several of her gowns.

"They're so pretty."

Weston had come to her side. He took a shoe and held it in his palm.

"Your feet are quite small. I've never noticed that before."

Anne looked over at her husband to find him staring down at the hem of her dress, as though trying to view her feet. Anne felt a slow blush that started at her neck and moved upward.

"Why, Mrs Weston, I do believe my attention to your feet has made you blush."

Anne turned her head and tried not to smile.

"I didn't know anyone could turn such a pretty color," he went on without mercy.

"Oh, do stop."

"I can't stop until you tell me I'm incorrigible."

"Well, you are! Make no mistake about that."

Weston laughed as she turned to him, red face and all.

"You're enjoying this way too much."

"Indeed, I am."

The laughter fell away just then, slowly, like a sunset. Anne and Weston looked at each other, their thoughts growing quiet.

"How many weeks have we been married now, Mrs Weston?" her husband asked softly.

"Almost three." Anne's voice was just as soft.

She seemed soft and inviting to him just now, but he couldn't be sure. They had decided on their wedding night to find another time for intimacy, but it probably wasn't fair to initiate such an action, or even kiss her, until they'd spoken of it. Anne was, however, so sweet and approachable just now that Weston could not keep his hands to himself. He reached up and stroked down her smooth temple with one finger, finishing the caress on her cheek.

His voice still just as quiet, he said, "You might feel wonderful in your new clothing, and I'm sure everything will be beautiful on you, but never forget that I find you completely lovely right now."

Anne's heart pounded almost painfully within her. No one had ever spoken to her in such a way. Had this been a suitor, Anne would have been wise to turn away and not encourage such advances, but this was her husband. This was the man who cared enough to marry her, to rescue her.

"Thank you," Anne said, hearing the breathlessness in her own voice but still going on. "It occurs to me that you might be correct. I may feel wonderful in my new clothing, but having you find me appealing is what matters the most to me."

"Never doubt it, Anne," Weston said this time, his gaze intense as he studied his wife. He was ready to broach the subject that was often on his mind lately, but he caught a slight tremble as Anne stood before him. He didn't know

her well enough to gauge if she was fearful, nervous, or perhaps excited, so with an effort he pushed the matter from his
mind.

It was with relief that his mother knocked on the door,
Jenny behind her. More clothing had arrived, and Weston
cleared out to let the women explore. He prayed for
patience as he ordered a horse to go riding in the park.

Chapter Eighteen

The first day of September found Anne in church with her husband and mother-in-law, dressed in new clothing from her hat to her shoes. She met Pastor Crawford and his wife at the door as they arrived, enjoying their warm welcome and obvious good friendship with Lenore.

The sermon was like one she would hear at home, causing her to be very thankful for the upbringing her husband had known. Not until they were in the carriage and headed back to Berwick did Anne realize she didn't know Lenore's story of salvation. She didn't even wait to arrive back but asked her right away.

"Robert's father believed first," Lenore explained, her eyes alight with the memory. "We were newly married, and I thought all this searching he was doing was a reflection on me. I thought he was unhappy in our marriage and regretted it. I was crushed, and although he tried to explain it to me, I didn't understand, and he only grew frustrated. That upset me more.

"Then he trusted Christ to save him, and the change was remarkable. He had always been a kind, caring man, not easily angered or put out, but after his conversion he was unlike I'd ever known him. The frustration he'd exhibited while trying to explain his need to me was gone. He took all the time I needed, sometimes answering the same question over and over again. I still tried to accuse him of being unhappy with me and our marriage, but he just became more loving, so that argument died.

"Then I was expecting Robert, and James told me in plain terms that he was going to raise this child to love and follow Christ. I was terrified."

"Why was that?" Anne asked, completely rapt.

"I felt I would be left out. I knew what an influence James would have on our child, and I was certain I would be all alone, left outside of this experience they shared."

"What did you do?"

"I began to attend church with James. I knew our friends were talking about us, but James only quoted to me from 1 Peter 4, where it says that old companions will speak evil of you when you don't run and sin with them any longer, but they will have to someday give an account to God for their choices.

"Those were the words that got my attention. I was no longer afraid of being left out, I was no longer afraid of anything except having to give an account to God. I knew I was a sinner, although I'd never admitted it to myself, and suddenly I was desperate to have God save me."

"And He did," Weston put in, his face content as he listened.

"Yes!" Lenore exclaimed. "I'll never forget the day. We had just arrived home from church, and usually I needed to eat right away or the pregnancy would give me an upset stomach. But this time all I could think about was my sin. James knelt with me in the library, and I confessed my sin before God. I asked for His cleansing and healing hand in my heart, and then I vowed my life to His Son, Jesus." Lenore smiled again. "I can't say that I've never gone back on my promise, but He always forgives me when I fail Him. By the time Robert was born, I was as committed to raising him to love Christ as James was."

Anne smiled at her husband, who was looking very pleased.

"I'm glad you told your story, Mother. It's been a while since I've heard it."

Lenore shook her head. "I was very stubborn and full of pride for a time, but God broke through." This said, Lenore reached over and touched Anne's arm. "Tell me your story, Anne."

Not leaving out any detail, Anne filled her in. Weston enjoyed hearing it again, remaining quiet so his mother could catch all the details.

"And your father, Anne?" They were at Berwick now, walking to the front door, and Lenore had slipped her arm into Anne's. "Did he never make a commitment?"

"Not that I know of. He was always willing to have my mother read to us from the Bible, but he never yearned for God or studied the Word on his own. Such a lack of interest has never given me much hope."

"We will pray, Anne," Lenore told her sincerely. "If God can break through my stubborn heart, I know He can reach your father, no matter his present emotional state."

Anne nodded, asking God to help her believe this. Her father did have moments when he was lucid, and her God was a saving God. Anne knew she needed to remember this more often.

~ ~

The days passed swiftly. The threesome had shopped a bit more, visited gardens, and had a thorough tour of Norwood Place, but now, in just two days' time, Weston and Anne would be leaving London. For this reason Lenore felt a small sense of urgency as she looked for her son. He had been in the garden with Anne, but Anne now picked flowers alone, and Weston was not to be found. She couldn't ask her new daughter where he was—that might rouse her interest—but she was most determined to find him.

"Well, Mother," Weston said calmly, having come up behind her in the hallway. "You look as though you've lost something."

"Robert," she said on a laugh, "I've been looking everywhere for you."

Weston frowned. "You knew I was in the garden with Anne."

His mother took his arm and urged him toward the privacy of her room.

"I can't ask you about this in front of Anne."

Weston went along, fairly certain he knew her topic. The subject had passed through his mind on several occasions, but he'd still not seen to it.

"Have you spoken to Anne about Jenny?" Lenore asked the moment they were behind closed doors.

"No."

His mother's look was pointed.

"When did you plan to take care of this?"

"Today. I'll do it today."

"Good. Let me know how it turns out."

"I will. And thank you, Mother, for seeing to it."

Weston wasted no more time. He moved back to the garden, but Anne was not there. Not many minutes or inquiries later, he found her arranging flowers in the dining room.

"Very nice," Weston complimented when he saw her arrangement. "You should do flowers for Brown Manor."

Anne's hand came to her mouth, her eyes dancing with merriment, and Weston knew he'd misstepped. Floral arrangements were probably all over Brown Manor, and he'd never noticed.

"I think I'll go back out, come in, and try this again."

"No, don't," Anne said, taking his arm. "I didn't expect you to notice. It doesn't matter."

"Well, I shall notice when we arrive home; I can assure you of that. But that's not why I came in. Can you arrange flowers and listen at the same time, or shall we take a seat?"

"How serious is it?"

"It's not serious at all."

"Then I'll keep working."

"You can take Jenny back to Brown Manor with you when we leave."

Anne immediately stopped working and turned to her husband in surprise.

"Uproot her? Take her out of London? She's not going to agree to that. We've gotten on very well, but I can't expect that of her, Weston."

"Jenny used to live in Collingbourne. It was some years ago, but she still has friends there. Mother hired her with the express intention of having her as your maid, not just here but at home. You need a personal maid, but I didn't think you were comfortable finding one on your own." Weston paused when he noticed that Anne no longer looked surprised, but neither was she responding. "You do like Jenny?"

"Very much."

"Then it's all settled."

Anne continued to stare at him. "Why didn't you think I could choose someone on my own?"

Weston shrugged a bit, starting to feel ill at ease with how he'd handled the situation. "I don't know. I assumed you wouldn't be all that comfortable with the matter and, well, you didn't take care of it, so I asked Mother to help out."

"We were married for two weeks and then left for London," Anne calmly pointed out. "When was I supposed to do this?"

Had Weston been able to find any words just then, he would have told her she had a very good point. As it was, he stood quietly, measuring his wife's mood and working on his own response.

"And if I might also inquire, we never did speak of your statement concerning Louisa's brother-in-law. Were we going to cover that?"

It took less than a heartbeat for Anne to see she'd taken him completely off guard. She was debating whether to speak up again when Mansfield entered. He was looking for Weston.

"Excuse me, sir."

"Yes, Mansfield." Weston turned to him with far too much enthusiasm.

"A gentleman is here about the work on the conservatory. I thought it might be urgent."

"Thank you, Mansfield. I shall be right along." Weston turned back to Anne. "I hope you'll excuse me."

Anne couldn't stop her smile. "For needing to leave, yes, but not for looking so relieved about it."

Weston's own grin peeked through. "I will admit that I am, but we will speak of these things. It may not be possible before we leave, but the ride home should surely afford a time. If not, we'll speak of them once we get back."

Anne nodded in swift agreement, somewhat relieved herself.

Glad to be ending on a good note, Weston bent and kissed her cheek. He also gave her hand a squeeze before turning to follow Mansfield.

ॐ ॐ

"You're certain, Jenny?" Anne pressed the young maid one more time. "It's not as if the situation were irreversible, but I don't want you to feel pressure."

"Thank you, Mrs Weston, but Mr Weston's mother explained it all to me. And I'm sure."

Feeling comfortable enough to ask such questions, Anne studied the maid's eyes in order to assess her true feelings.

"I'm glad you're coming with us, Jenny. You are aware that we leave in the morning?"

"Yes, ma'am. I'll have all your things ready."

"And yours," Anne reminded her, smiling a little.

Jenny smiled and bowed with respect before leaving Anne alone for the night. Anne climbed into bed, but she didn't sleep for some time. Never had so many changes come upon her in so little time. It was as if she'd stepped into someone else's life. She found herself a bit shaken by it all.

When she did drop off to sleep, it was not with a peaceful heart. She felt anxious about the future, and then felt anxious about being anxious. Not at any time before she slept did she begin to think well about her situation. And in the morning she would start a two-day ride home without enough rest.

❧ ❧

"It was such a lovely time," Lenore told Anne, tears standing in her eyes. "You must come and see me again."

"We certainly will, and I hope you will come to Brown Manor very soon."

"I'll plan on it."

The older woman stared at her new daughter for several heartbeats.

"Did I tell you how thankful I am for you? Did I tell you how precious you are to me, how swiftly you walked into my heart?"

Anne hugged the older woman.

"I was most eager to meet you," Anne admitted, close to Lenore's ear.

"Why was that?"

"I wanted to know the woman who could raise such a special son."

Lenore didn't try to stop her tears. She hugged Anne all the tighter before releasing her with a teary smile.

Weston was next. His mother hugged him warmly and told him of her love. He thanked her for the wonderful time and repeated his wife's invitation to visit soon.

By the time the newlyweds climbed into the coach to leave, they were both a little emotionally spent but very content with the way things had gone.

With a wave from the window and a word to the coachman, the carriage left Berwick for Collingbourne. The day felt as if it could grow warm, but right now they were comfortable. Husband and wife sat across from each other, each with his own thoughts. Anne thought back to all the lovely things they'd done and what a delightful person Lenore Weston turned out to be. She thanked God for saving Weston's parents so he could know Christ in his own life.

Sitting catercorner from her, Weston's mind was on the various subjects that had come up with Anne during their two-week visit. He shook his head a little at how often conversations were started and not finished. Had they been small matters, he might have dismissed it, but they weren't. And if he was going to have success in his marriage and truly know his wife, he needed to think of a way to communicate his heart.

For a time Anne didn't notice Weston's intense mood. She was quiet, taking in the countryside once they'd passed out of the city. Only when she turned and found Weston watching her did her mind move in the same direction his had. Anne waited to see if he was ready to talk. It didn't take long for her to learn that he was.

"I made the most awful blunder when I asked you about Francis Cavendish," Weston began quietly. "I made it sound as though it was your doing when I was the one with the problem. I somehow thought that our marriage made you off-limits in other men's minds, but of course it doesn't. I found myself wondering what I would do if some other chap came along and you fell in love with him. Cavendish's attention to you raised all sorts of demons in my mind."

"So you don't believe I took my vows to you seriously?"

"Yes, I do, but just as you worried that I might regret not marrying for love, I felt fear that you would be stuck with me while in love with someone else."

"Thank you for telling me," Anne said sincerely, realizing it must have been hard to admit this to her. "I think it's fair to assume that I would have to be looking and interested in giving away my heart for that to happen, and I can tell you that I'm doing no such thing. I am committed to this marriage and to you, and I plan to stay that way."

Weston acknowledged this with a slight bow of his head, very thankful that she had understood.

Anne wondered if now was a good time to mention the decision about Jenny, but Weston beat her to it.

"Are you truly pleased that Jenny is coming back as your personal maid, or did Mother and I pressure you into it?"

"I'm very pleased, but I'm still not sure why you handled the matter through your mother. You've come to me on other issues. If you had wanted me to acquire a maid right away, why did you not take the matter up with me?"

"I should have. I think I was being protective of you."

"In what way?"

"I didn't know how accustomed you were to dealing with such issues. It might have been years since you'd had any servants in your home, let alone interviewing and selecting a personal maid. I wanted that for you but wasn't sure if I should expect you to take care of it."

Anne nodded but didn't comment.

"What are you thinking?"

"I'm only asking myself the same questions. Would I have been comfortable finding a maid on my own? I'm not sure."

"But you would have enjoyed trying?"

"Possibly." Anne was still thoughtful. "I honestly don't know."

"Well, in the future I shall work on coming directly to you."

"Just work on it, not do it?" There was a slight tease in her voice.

Weston gave a small shake of his head. "I would be a fool to promise you anything, since my first inclination is to protect you."

"I'm tougher than I look," Anne told him and then watched as Weston's gaze grew intense.

"I won't ever see you as tough, and you may save your breath telling me not to be protective of you. That will never happen."

Anne didn't know how to respond. His eyes seemed to be telling her things, things she wasn't ready to hear. Feeling flustered, she tried to calm her restless hands by folding them in her lap. When she looked back up, Weston's gaze had softened.

The moment was over but not forgotten. Anne fell asleep a short time later, and when she woke, she found that Weston had moved to her seat so she could sleep against his chest. She fell back to sleep, thinking that having his arms holding her was one of the loveliest things she'd ever known.

~ ~

Brown Manor

Anne was surprised at how much she had missed Brown Manor. It hadn't been her home for very long, but it felt wonderful to return, as though she'd been away for much longer than two weeks.

The staff was on hand to greet the returning couple, and Anne's smile for them was most genuine.

"Welcome home, Mrs Weston," Cook greeted her.

"Thank you, Cook. Has all been well?"

"Yes, ma'am. Very well."

"I'm glad."

They spoke for a moment about the menu, and then Anne went to her room to freshen up, Jenny on her heels. At one point she turned to find the younger woman gawking at her surroundings and smiled in memory of her own first response to Brown Manor.

"I'll let you put everything away, Jenny, so you can become acquainted with where things go."

"Yes, Mrs Weston. Are there certain clothes you want set out for dinner?"

"You may pick something nice, Jenny, but don't spend too much time. You can always finish tomorrow. Go soon and see to your own room and belongings."

Jenny did set things out for Anne and saw to some other needs, but she did as her mistress bid and soon went to settle her own belongings. Anne had no hesitancy about dressing herself for dinner—she had done it often enough—but with all of her lovely new things to look at and enjoy, she dawdled long past the time she needed.

For this reason, Weston found Anne in her underclothing when he innocently joined her from the adjoining door.

"Oh, Weston!" she froze.

He did the same.

"I'm not dressed," Anne stated the obvious.

"I see that," Weston said, his voice so comical that Anne felt laughter coming on even as she blushed.

Weston looked in no hurry to avert his gaze, and Anne refused to act like a schoolgirl trying to cover too many parts with only two hands.

"I need to get my robe," she said at last.

"All right," Weston said, his hands going behind his back and seeming quite content with the view.

Anne wanted to laugh again.

"Will you turn around?"

"If I must," Weston said with a smile and turned away from her.

Anne went directly to the bed and scooped up her new robe. She slipped it on and belted it into place, repeatedly checking the front for gaps before looking up at her husband's back. What she saw caused her mouth to open a little.

Weston was directly in front of the mirror he'd purchased for her at Benwick's and had calmly witnessed her the entire time.

Weston turned slowly, his eyes catching Anne's, his gaze clearly intimate. His words, though softly spoken, were not of an intimate nature at all.

"I was coming to escort you to dinner, but I can see you need more time. Shall I wait in the hall?"

"Yes, please."

Weston allowed his gaze to touch her a moment more, nodded his head, and exited to the hall. Anne flew from her robe and into her dress. Jenny had already fixed her hair, but Anne fixed a few spots that suffered from dressing in a hurry before joining her husband.

A strange and exciting feeling had spiraled through her before he left the room, and for that reason she didn't meet his gaze as he escorted her to the dining room. When she did look at him, his eyes were normal. Indeed, Anne found him to be his old self for the rest of the evening.

❧ ❧

Weston climbed into his own bed, more than ready to be there, but with Anne heavy on his mind. He was ready for changes in this marriage—much sooner than he'd anticipated—but ready nonetheless.

Sore from two days in the carriage, he took a few minutes to settle on the pillow, but as soon as he was comfortable, he began to pray.

Thank You, Lord God, for Your provision and Your great love. Thank You for the wife You've given me. Please help me, Father. Help me to be the kind of husband Anne could love. My heart is already so involved, but I sense that she is holding back. Help me to lead us to this next step without causing fear or guilt. Help Anne to trust me to be the man she needs.

Sleep was crowding in fast, but Weston had one more plea: He asked God for patience. He was tired of being alone in his bed and having Anne in the next room, but it had to be God's timing, not his. He might never win his wife's heart if he ran ahead of his God.

❧ ❧

"I'm going to go see my father this morning," Anne told Weston over the breakfast table the next day.

"I rather thought you might. Did you want me to join you?"

"I think I'll go on my own, but thank you."

"Why don't you invite your father to dinner? We can send a coach."

"I'll try, but I don't know what he'll say."

"All right. I don't wish you to do any cleaning."

Anne looked very innocent on hearing this remark, but Weston wasn't fooled.

"Either take a maid with you, Anne, or plan not to clean," he reiterated. But the lady of the house didn't reply.

"I don't think I'm being listened to."

"I heard you," Anne told him, but her voice revealed that she was still not willing to burden the staff at Brown Manor with matters at Levens Crossing.

"It looks as though I'll need to come along."

Anne felt guilty and gave in, knowing he had other things to do.

"I won't clean."

Weston heard her tone and felt his own guilt. He didn't want to bully her, but he was not about to let her clean when there were servants who could see to that.

"Do you find me unfair?"

"No, I don't, but the staff here—" she began.

"Is only too willing to serve," Weston finished. "Mansfield and Cook see to that. In fact, the maid who would go to clean at Levens Crossing would probably enjoy the change."

Anne nodded, more convinced, all the while realizing it wasn't worth quarreling over.

"When will you leave?"

"As soon as I've eaten."

"Mansfield," Weston spoke to the man who was standing nearby. "Ask Cook to pack some baked goods for Mr Gardiner, will you?"

"Right away, sir."

"Should I see how he's fared, Weston?" Anne suggested. "Pastor and Judith were to see to things. Maybe he has plenty."

"Leave the baskets in the coach and make your decision when you arrive, but at least take them with you."

Anne thanked her husband and finished breakfast just after. She was on the road a short time later, praying for her father and wondering what she was going to find at Levens Crossing.

ॐ ॐ

The Manse

"Anne!" Judith said with delight when Phoebe showed her into the dining room. "Welcome home."

"Thank you. It's lovely to be here."

The women embraced before Judith held her friend at arm's length.

"A new dress. You look beautiful."

"Oh, Judith, I have so much to tell you. But first of all, how is my father?"

"He wasn't home just now?"

"No."

"Your father is very well," Judith said, linking her arm with Anne's. "But let's head to the church. Frederick has things to tell you."

Judith let Phoebe and the children know where they were headed and took Anne across the grassy expanse to the church's side door. It was cool and quiet inside, and because Pastor Hurst heard the door, he met them as they covered the distance to the office.

"Welcome home, Mrs Weston," Pastor said after he'd hugged her. "You must be here about the Colonel."

"He wasn't home, but Judith said he's well."

"He is well, but not long after you left he fell and gave himself quite a bump."

"Oh, no. How long was he alone before you found him?"

"Not long. We sent for Dr Smith, who patched him up and told him to stay in bed. He did that for several days and grew more steady on his feet every day."

"Do you know why he fell?"

"No. Smith thinks he might have had a slight stroke, but the Colonel doesn't seem any worse for wear since then, so it's hard to tell."

Anne's sigh was huge. "I'm so relieved you were there. Thank you so much."

"I have better news."

"What is it?"

"We spoke of spiritual things."

Anne's mouth opened.

"The Colonel doesn't come with you to church, Anne, because the high ceiling makes him dizzy."

"That's what he told you?" The Colonel's daughter looked as amazed as she felt.

"Yes, but I told him I still wanted to speak to him about the Bible, and twice he's come to the side door and knocked. I go outside to sit with him, and we've spoken of Scripture."

"What do you speak of specifically?"

"Jesus Christ. He listens well and even asks questions for short intervals. He tells me he thinks a lot of Jesus Christ."

Anne felt as though she needed a chair. This was nothing less than a miracle.

"I've explained the way of salvation to him, Anne. He understood that he was a sinner and that Christ came to die for sins."

"Did he understand that we're lost until we accept that gift?"

"I'm not certain. He drifted before we could speak of eternity, but," Pastor added, "he knows that you believe. He said you had taken care of things with God and that he should get to that some day soon."

For a time Anne couldn't say anything. She felt elated and drained all at the same time.

"I prayed for him every day." Anne began to speak, her eyes not looking at anyone and her voice full of wonder. "Not for his spiritual well-being, although I thought of that, but more for his physical health and safety." She finally looked at the Hursts. "Thank you. Thank you so much for being here and giving him all he needed."

"You're welcome," Pastor said, and he meant it.

Eager to have some time with her father and to report to Weston, Anne didn't stay long. Her heart still filled with the wonder of it all, she hugged her friends, thanked them once again, and hurried on her way.

Chapter Nineteen

Brown Manor

"So did you ever have a chance to speak with your father?" Weston asked when Anne explained the entire story. She had paced her way all over the salon as she talked. Weston had never seen her this way.

"No. I asked the driver to stop again on the way back, but he still wasn't home. I left him only some of the food Cook prepared because his stores are in good shape, and I wrote him a short note."

"And how do you feel about all of this?"

"My mind hasn't slowed down long enough to deal with it."

Weston couldn't stop his smile. Anne was still on her feet, walking to and fro. It was easy to imagine what her mind must be doing.

"Do you think I should try to bring the subject up? Should I speak of it to him?"

"If he's lucid when you see him, I don't know why you shouldn't."

Anne nodded and then caught herself. She came to a stop and looked a little sheepish.

"I've been pacing this whole time. I'm not anxious, just excited."

"As well you should be. You've prayed for your father for many years, and this gives you reason to hope that he might be ready to listen."

"Yes, it does. That was well put."

Anne forced herself to calm down and even took a seat. Weston sat next to her, turning slightly to look at her.

"How are Pastor and Mrs Hurst?"

"Doing well. I'm so glad they were there for Father."

"He's a blessed man to have all of you."

"And you."

Weston acknowledged this compliment with a nod.

"And the church family? All is well?"

"I believe so. We talked only of Father."

Anne's mind was still mulling over the morning's activity when her husband interrupted her with a compliment.

"That dress is nice on you. I like the color."

Anne looked down at the dark blue print as though just noticing.

"Thank you. I think this might be one of my favorites."

"I also like the other blue one."

"Which one?"

"I think you wore it the last day at Berwick."

"Oh, yes. I like that one too." Anne suddenly looked at him. "Not every woman has a husband who notices clothing. I rather like that about you, Mr Weston."

"Not every man has the lovely wife I have, Mrs Weston, whose clothing only compliments her."

The two laughed at their own silliness, but it didn't take long to die away. As Anne was coming to expect, her husband's eyes grew serious and warm all at the same time. She wished she knew what he was thinking, but he didn't share.

"I imagine that lunch will be ready soon," he voiced quietly. "Shall we go find out?"

"Yes, please."

Once again the moment was over. Anne asked herself for the rest of the day whether she should have questioned him or not.

Mansfield handed Weston the post very early on Tuesday morning. He studied the details in a letter from his solicitor and knew a sinking heart. He told Mansfield of his plans and went to find Anne. She was in the salon writing thank-you notes—several gifts had arrived while they were away—her head bent in concentration.

"May I interrupt?"

"Certainly." Anne set her pen aside and stood.

"Don't stand. I'll join you."

"I have to make a trip," Weston said as soon as they were both seated.

"To where?"

"Banbury. My grandmother had some property there I've been attempting to sell. Now things have gotten a bit muddy with an adjoining property owner, and my solicitor thinks it would be best if I was on hand."

"When must you leave?"

"Today, as soon as I can get ready."

Anne was surprised by this. She did her best to hide it but didn't do a very convincing job.

"I would take you with me, Anne, but it's going to be rushed and uncomfortable."

"Oh, don't feel like you must explain. Of course I'll stay here."

"Will you be all right?"

"Yes," she said honestly. "It just took me a moment to get used to the idea."

"All right. Mansfield will be staying to look after you, so if you have any needs, go to him."

"Weston," Anne protested, "you need Mansfield with you."

"I will be fine. I will travel easier knowing he's here seeing after you."

"Please do not leave Mansfield for my sake, Weston. I will be fine."

Weston only smiled at her—clearly his mind was made up.

"Do you know that you like having your own way?" Anne pointedly told him.

Weston's brows rose, not just at her words, but over her tone. Unless he missed his guess, his wife was flustered with him right now, and he didn't want that. His mind scrambled to give her an explanation.

"I don't take Mansfield everywhere, Anne. Truly I don't. And this isn't about wanting my way."

Anne looked so skeptical that Weston laughed, an action that made things worse.

"This is not funny, Robert Weston! I'm here with all the comforts of home. You need your manservant with you!"

Weston studied her, not sure why this was so important. That action—his lack of response—only made matters worse.

Anne stood and faced him. "I can see there's no talking to you about it. I'm sorry I tried." With that she turned to leave.

"Anne, don't go," Weston urged, still in his seat but managing to catch her hand. "Tell me why this is so important to you. I want to understand."

Anne studied him, seeing that her actions had been odd and knowing he deserved an answer.

"It's all so one-sided. You give and give, and I take and take. The least I can do is be strong enough to stay here so you can have Mansfield with you."

Weston released Anne's hand and stood, his eyes flashing a little.

"This is utter nonsense! Where did you get the foolish idea that all you do is take and take?"

Anne didn't care for his tone and felt her own temper rising. She knew she should bite her tongue, but she didn't.

Her brow lowered in very real anger, she asked, "What else would you call it? I come penniless to this marriage;

your mother spends a small fortune on me; you give, give, and give some more; and you even support my father!"

"And why is that a problem?"

"Because you won't let me give anything back. Not even Mansfield for your trip!"

For a moment the two stood staring at each other, eyes angry, breathing hard, and trying to make sense of it all.

Weston was the first to calm down. He moved until he stood directly in front of Anne, taking her hands in his.

"Thank you."

"For what?" Anne's voice was calm, but her emotions were in turmoil.

"For caring enough to want Mansfield with me."

Anne stared up at him.

"We quarreled, and I don't like that."

"I don't like it either." Weston studied her eyes, wanting to stand and drink in her sweetness for more time than he had. "Do you know who Oliver is?" he finally asked.

"The young man who assists Mansfield?"

"Yes. He's worked long enough with Mansfield that he understands my needs. I shall take him along and have my every comfort seen to."

Anne nodded, pleased with this alternative.

"Are we settled now, Anne? I don't want to leave with you angry at me."

"I'm not. I'm sorry I was so cross."

"I'm sorry I'm so accustomed to having my way that I tell you things without discussing them with you, without giving you a chance to give to me."

"Some of it is my pride, but some of it is more than that."

"Such as?"

"I'm not sure I can explain it right now." Anne shrugged in apology as new emotions continued to bombard her.

Weston didn't question her again but just followed his heart. Raising his hands to hold Anne's face, he bent to kiss her gently on the mouth.

"I must go," he whispered, still close to her lips.

"Hurry back," Anne said, and Weston kissed her again.

With great reluctance Weston released her and went on his way. Anne was on the drive when his carriage pulled away, but she was in something of a fog as she waved him on. She couldn't wait to be alone with her thoughts, for just now they were quite tortured.

❧ ❧

"You're looking pleased about something," Cook teased Mansfield when he entered the kitchen a short time later.

"Am I?" he asked, his voice vague, but Cook wasn't fooled. She snorted in mock disgust, telling Mansfield she was willing to wait for her answer.

At any rate Mansfield wasn't worried. It wasn't anything he could discuss, but in time everyone would know what he'd known all along: Mr and Mrs Weston were going to fall in love. Some might have been put off by their argument in the salon before the master left, but not Mansfield. These two were on the way to love. He'd known it all along.

❧ ❧

Just admit it to yourself, Anne's mind tormented her. *Just be brave enough to say it, out loud even.*

But the scolding did no good. Anne continued to pace the floor in her bedroom, her mind running with all that had transpired that day, not to mention the past weeks.

"He kissed me." She said this out loud and then shook her head and paced a bit more.

Of course, he was leaving, her soliloquy continued. *It was a natural thing. You mustn't read things that aren't written.* But all of this had no effect. Anne finally stopped midstride, her hands balled into fists in front of her.

"I'm falling in love with my husband," she told the empty room, as though it would help to voice it. "I've no true idea what he's feeling toward me. Now he's gone and I don't know when he's coming back. How could I have been so foolish?"

Anne wrapped her arms around herself, suddenly feeling very cold and alone. She went to her bed and lay down, asking God to help her faithless heart to trust Him for her future. She fell into a fitful sleep for the next hour, her heart still uncertain about what she should do.

๑ ๑

The nap, fitful though it may have been, was just what Anne needed to clear her head. She awoke and confessed her anxiety and desire to control everything. She spent more than an hour studying her Bible, as well as praying for her future with Mr Weston and asking God to help her give her heart unconditionally. She didn't wish for her husband— whether he loved her or not—to return and find that she'd done nothing during his absence. After her Bible study, she wrote invitations for the little girls to come for tea at the end of the week.

"This letter goes to Penny Jennings, and this one goes to Emma and Lizzy Palmer. The last one is for Margaret Hurst."

"Very good, Mrs Weston. Do you wish Bert to wait for replies?"

"Please. He probably should speak with Mrs Palmer, Mrs Jennings, and Mrs Hurst for those replies, but yes, that would be a good idea."

"I shall see to it directly."

"Thank you."

Anne left Mansfield in the hallway and made herself walk to the spacious room next to the library. She was aware of this room—she'd been in it twice—but never for any length of time. Today she was going to go inside, shut the door, and stay.

After Anne shut the door, she leaned against it. Her eyes traveled the walls and furniture, drinking it all in, before coming to rest on the piano that dominated one corner. Anne moved slowly toward it, seeing that it was thoroughly dusted and ready for use.

She sat on the bench and lightly rested her hands on the keys. A frisson of fear raced through her. What if she couldn't remember? What if it had been too long? Anne stiffened her spine, telling herself she wasn't going to know unless she tried. Reaching to open the music in front of her and adjusting the bench a small bit, Anne began to play. Her playing wasn't without a few missed notes, but the more she concentrated the more it returned to her. At times tears ran down her face at the memory of her mother's playing and teaching, but all in all, Anne was having a wonderful time.

Unbeknownst to her, servants that passed anywhere near the vicinity of the music room stopped to listen, their eyes showing surprise and pleasure at the mistress' accomplishments. Mansfield himself lingered now and again, utterly captivated with the unfolding of this young woman who had come into their midst.

At last he got on with his work, but not before thinking: *If Mr Weston doesn't discover the treasure he has in his wife, he has no one to blame but himself.*

❧ ❧

Levens Crossing

"Well, Anne," her father greeted her in delight the next morning, "you're back from your honeymoon trip."

Anne laughed as she accepted his hug, thinking that some things never changed.

"How are you, Father?"

"I'm well, very well. My ship just returned, so I'm still finding my land legs."

He chuckled at his own little joke as Anne joined him at the table. It didn't look as if this was the day to question him on spiritual matters. She wanted to leave this with the Lord, but her heart knew a moment of disappointment.

"Where did you go on your trip, Anne? I can't recall."

"London," she answered, even though they were not talking about the same thing. "We visited Mr Weston's mother."

"How is that dear lady?"

"She's very well." Anne ignored the fact that the two had never met. "How is your head, Father? Is it mended?"

The Colonel gave his daughter a look that said she'd lost him, so she dropped the subject. A noise came from the other room right about then, and the Colonel stood.

"Do we have company?"

"It's just the maid, Father," Anne said and then held her breath.

"Oh, very good. Maybe you and I could have a drop of tea while she cleans."

Anne was more than happy to make it and pour out. The two of them talked while they drank, two hours passing very swiftly, and all the Colonel did was ramble. When Anne finally took her leave, the house was cleaner, but there had been no occasion to ask her father about his trips to see Pastor Hurst. Anne was forced to leave the business of her father's eternity in God's more capable hands.

❧ ❧

Brown Manor

Mr Weston was still not home on Friday. Anne did not actually expect him, but she was hopeful. The little girls, however, were to arrive at any time. Cook was working on a splendid tea, with special food planned with children in mind, but first they would start in the garden, each with a basket, to pick flowers to their hearts' content. Anne could hardly bear the excitement and found herself even more excited when the girls' fathers dropped them off and each one stayed for a moment to visit.

"How are you?" Palmer asked, once he'd kissed Anne's cheek.

"I'm very well. Weston is traveling, and I wanted some company. I do thank you for loaning me the girls."

"Our pleasure. Liddy wants you to visit soon."

"Tell her I shall. I'm going to drop Penny home last today so I can see their baby, but I'll come to Tipton to visit soon."

When the fathers had gone their way and the young ladies were in the garden, the laughter and fun began. Flowers were delighted over and traded, plans were made for nosegays for their mothers, and sighs could be heard from Margaret, who thought Anne's gardens were the most beautiful in the world.

Their tea was an unqualified success as well. The girls were good eaters, and after a tour of Brown Manor, all loaded into the carriage for the ride home. Anne was good at her word, taking Penny home last. Jennings met them at the door of Thornton Hall, distracted Penny, and allowed his wife and new baby to have Anne all to themselves.

❧ ❧

"Oh, Marianne, she's beautiful."

Marianne smiled as she watched Anne holding her four-week-old daughter, knowing she couldn't disagree.

"I can tell she's a good baby."

"She is. She only fusses when she's wet or hungry. She doesn't even demand to be held."

"Which means you'll have to find other excuses."

Marianne laughed because it was quite true.

"How were the girls today?"

"Adorable. We had such fun."

"Did Penny remember to thank you?"

"She certainly did. We ate some fruit from the compote she picked out, and I could tell she was delighted to see me using it."

"Lydia had just the medicine that day to take Penny's mind from Catherine's imminent birth. When they arrived back, all Penny could talk of was how Lydia had allowed her to pick out your gift."

Anne looked up at her friend. "We've had so many gifts, Mari—not just from the church family but from townspeople. I've been surprised."

"But pleased too?"

"Very pleased, but I somehow thought that everything I did lately met with the town's disapproval. It's been a *very* pleasant surprise."

"I'm still not getting out much yet, but when I do venture, I plan to visit you and see all your gifts."

"I would love that, Mari. Please plan on it."

"How long will Weston be away?"

"He didn't say, but Banbury is a good journey, so it might be several more days."

"Do you miss him?"

Anne studied the baby's small head, stroking her smooth, tiny brow before looking up.

"Very much."

"It's startling when your heart becomes involved, isn't it?" Marianne read correctly.

"Yes." Anne was so relieved to have someone understand. "Everything takes on a new meaning, a new dimension."

"But your situation is far harder, Anne. You're already married to Weston and living together. With Jennings I could go home and have peace and privacy to iron out my thoughts and emotions. You might not have that luxury."

Anne looked thoughtful. "Maybe his absence has been good for that. I have done a good deal of thinking with this time on my own."

"Is there fear, Anne? Are you afraid to fall in love with him but not have that love returned?"

"Yes, but I've asked the Lord to help me not hold back. I might end up having my heart bruised, but I can't use that as an excuse."

"So you think you love him?"

"I don't know. I don't know what it feels like. Does your heart ache and feel elated all at the same time? Do you feel frightened and ready to take the world on all in one moment? Do you feel more vulnerable than you have in all your life?"

"Yes, Anne. All that and more."

Tears rushed to Anne's eyes. "Please pray for me, Mari."

"I do, my friend, every day."

Marianne leaned close and hugged Anne, baby and all. The two visited for the next hour, Anne with questions, and Marianne with as much help as she could give. By the time Anne left Thornton Hall, she was more determined than ever to give her whole heart to Weston. Indeed, she knew nothing else would work.

න ග

Anne felt something akin to sadness creep over her as the carriage took her home from church. She had honestly believed that Weston would be home before now, and she was growing a little blue over his absence. For this reason Anne wasn't paying much attention as she entered the front door and walked through the large foyer. She mounted the stairs for her room, her mind far away. She was almost to her room when she spotted him.

"Hello," Weston said softly. Having arrived tired and dusty, he'd been home only an hour, immediately calling for a bath. He meant to be on the drive when Anne's carriage pulled up, but he'd not made it downstairs in time.

"You're home," Anne approached, doing nothing to disguise her pleasure.

"I'm home. How are you?"

"I'm fine. How was your trip?"

"It turned out very well. Both property owners are happy, and I sold my land."

Anne smiled. "I'm glad."

Weston's heart thundered over what he read in Anne's eyes. He picked up her hand and led her to the nearest door, his own bedroom. He took them inside and shut the door.

"I missed you," Anne said, barely aware that they had moved.

"I missed you," Weston told her, both hands now holding hers.

"Did you really?"

"I thought of you constantly."

Anne gave a little laugh.

"All these servants, and the manor was lonely without you."

"Newbury Inn felt empty without you."

"You stayed there?"

"Yes." Weston's gaze had taken on an intense gleam and his voice dropped. "I couldn't help but remember the night we shared a room. I recalled how soft and unbound you felt when I lifted you from the floor to put you in my bed."

Anne's gaze softened.

"I never did find out how long your hair was."

Anne bit her lip in a moment of insecurity and then grew bold. Using both hands she reached up and pulled the pins from her hair. She let the tresses fall around her shoulders and back as her husband watched.

Weston's sigh was audible as he touched her long, dark hair, circling around to her back to finger the thick length. And then with his chest to her back, he put his arms around her and whispered close to her ear.

"Anne, I'm in love with you."

Anne wasted no time in turning to him. She looked up, searching his eyes closely before putting her hands on his chest and entreating, "Will you kiss me goodbye again?"

Weston's laughter sounded in the room before his head lowered to find her lips with his own. In but a moment Anne was swept into what felt like a vortex of excitement, emotion, and pleasure. Between kisses, husband and wife confessed their love to each other over and over again, laughing over how it had happened and how swiftly the time had come.

There was so much they would share in the days and months ahead, but not just now. Now was a time for discovery, just between the two of them, husband and wife, in love and delighted with the wonder of each other.

Chapter Twenty

"Good morning," Anne said to Weston from the edge of his bed.

Weston who had been stirring, smiled as he opened his eyes all the way. The two looked at each other for a moment.

"Was it just yesterday afternoon that I told you I loved you?" Weston asked, his voice holding that early morning growl.

"Yes."

Weston took her hand. "It feels much longer."

Anne smiled at him, but he noticed her dress before she could speak.

"What time is it?"

"After ten."

"That late? Are you headed out?"

"I didn't see my father all weekend, so I thought I should check on him."

"Have you eaten?"

Anne laughed. "Long ago. You were sleeping soundly when I left."

"I was tired," he told her with an inviting gleam in his eye.

It was all so new for Anne that she blushed, but she was pleased nonetheless.

"Shall I come with you?" he offered, taking pity on her red face.

"No." She stood but kept holding his hand. "I won't be long, and you haven't eaten."

Weston pulled her close to kiss her.

"I love you," she told him, still marveling at how sweet it was to say.

"Hurry back," he told her, and Anne exited with plans to do just that.

※ ※

Levens Crossing

The carriage driver helped Anne from the interior of the coach and handed her the food basket he'd taken up top with him.

"Do you wish me to take that inside for you, Mrs Weston?"

"I have it, Bert. Thank you. I won't be long."

Bert began to work on his lines as she walked away from him. One strap was a bit twisted, and Dodger had been living up to his name on the ride over. Bert was still adjusting the strap, working near the horse's head, when Anne rushed up to him.

"Please," she gasped, clutching at his arm desperately. "Please find Mr Weston, please!"

"I will, Mrs Weston!" Bert began to turn away but thought better of it. "I don't want to leave you, Mrs Weston. Will you come?"

"No. Please, Bert, just find my husband."

Bert read the pain in her eyes and did as he was told. He worked Dodger as he'd not worked him before in an effort to reach Brown Manor in a hurry.

Anne watched him drive away and in a daze headed for the small stone bench at the front of the house and sank onto it. It had rained earlier that morning, and while she felt the damp seep into her dress, she didn't give it a thought.

Time ceased to move. Anne's thoughts traveled in every direction in the next 30 minutes. Without a clue as to how long she'd been sitting there, she stared in wonder as the coach pulled up and her husband bounded from inside. He was at her side in an instant, seeing his wife cry for the first time.

"Anne, what is it?"

"My father, Weston," she cried softly. "He's dead."

Weston's eyes closed even as he pulled Anne from the seat and held her in his arms. He stroked her hair and kissed her brow before helping her to sit back down.

"Stay right here," he commanded before going into the house on his own. He wasn't gone long, and when he exited, he went directly to Bert with instructions.

The manse was closer than Brown Manor, so Anne was taken there. Weston saw her settled with Judith before both he and Pastor began working on the arrangements.

"I can't stop trembling," Anne said as Judith wrapped another quilt around her.

"It's all right. Phoebe is making tea. You tremble and cry all you wish."

"Judith, do you think…"

"I don't know, Anne," she gently told her when Anne let the sentence hang. "I only know that God wanted your father to come to Him far more than any of us did."

The younger woman nodded, huddling into the blanket a little deeper and asking God to help her think clearly during this time, to remember all the blessings in her life and all the years she shared with her father.

Thoughts of her father caused fresh tears to flow. Judith sat with her, not talking overly much but being close and praying out loud every so often. Anne dozed after a time, waking when Weston arrived back and put his arms around her. They were alone in the room, and Anne stared at him for a moment.

"Do you think he had been gone very long?"

"No, and neither does Dr Smith. He thinks it was some time just last night."

Anne nodded, fresh tears coming to her eyes.

"I'm glad he was safe in bed, Weston, and not fallen and helpless."

"That is a comfort. I didn't tell you how sorry I am. If it wasn't for your father, I might not have gotten to know you. I'm very sorry you've lost him."

Overcome, Anne let Weston hold her for a long time. She sobbed against him, but then she felt as if she would choke on her own tears and tried to stop.

"My heart feels broken in two," she admitted, tears still on her face. "I didn't know it would feel this way. I mourned my mother as a child. This is so different."

"I imagine it is, and someday you'll need to comfort me in the same way for my mother."

"Weston!" Anne said suddenly, grasping his coat front with urgency. "What would I have done if you hadn't been here? What if we hadn't married?"

Weston held her close.

"You need not worry about that. You do have me, and you're going to have me for a very long time."

Anne realized the foolishness of her questions and knew her emotions were on the verge of spinning out of control. Another change had come into her life, not one that was comforting and lovely like being married to Weston and living at Brown Manor, but one that made her feel as vulnerable as a child.

"We need to talk with Pastor about what day you want the funeral. Shall I get him?"

"Yes, please."

In the hour that followed plans were made. Anne held together very nicely, but by the time she arrived back at Brown Manor, she had a headache and was ready to lie down.

Not until she rose from her nap did she find out how swiftly word had traveled. Notes—with more servants arriving each hour—were delivered from the church family and townspeople all day. Anne would often cry at the sweet memories that were shared or on hearing that someone was praying for her.

That evening the Palmers came, and Anne was ready for the company. Lydia hugged her and began talking about the girls.

"They had such a good time with you last week, Anne. It was all they could talk about."

"We did have fun," Anne admitted. "They all love flowers, which endears them to my heart."

"Your gardens are spectacular," Lydia said. "I'm jealous of your kitchen garden."

"I'm so glad you said something, Liddy. We have a wealth of herbs just now. May I send some with you?"

"Yes, please. We would enjoy that."

"I'll tell Mansfield right now so I don't forget."

While Anne went to ring the bell, Weston caught Lydia's eye and spoke softly.

"Thank you for not talking about her father."

"Did she get our note earlier today?"

"Yes, thank you."

"What day is the funeral?" Palmer asked before Anne could come back.

"Wednesday."

As Anne returned to the group, Weston asked how schooling was going for the Hurst, Palmer, and Jennings children. The report was all good, with the occasional mix of humor, which was always to be expected with children.

The friends didn't stay much longer, but their visit was the tonic Anne and Weston needed. They were tired and emotionally worn. Having Palmer and Lydia come in an undemanding way and visit for a time without mentioning the

Colonel made it easier for Anne to retire. Her father was on her mind, but not in an all-consuming way.

Jenny settled her in for the night, but she was still awake when Weston entered from the adjoining door. When he climbed into Anne's bed and put his arms around her, Anne held him right back and fell sound asleep.

∾ ⟋∾

"Thank you for coming. Thank you."

Weston and Anne uttered the words over and over again on Wednesday morning in the churchyard to the folks who had gathered for Colonel Gardiner's funeral and burial. He had been dressed as he ever was: full regimentals, his hat in the crook of his elbow, his sword at his side.

As planned, Pastor Hurst handled the sermon. He did so with honesty, tact, and compassion. Anne thought she would never forget his closing words.

I don't know about you, my friend, but I find it such a comfort to know that God alone holds the keys to life and death. But that's not all. He loves and yearns for me, for all of us. And if I will only follow His plan, the one He fulfilled when His Son died to take away my sins, then I can enjoy Him for all of eternity.

"How are you holding up?" Lydia was suddenly at Anne's side, taking her hand, her eyes full of compassion.

"I'm all right, Liddy. Thank you."

"I so appreciated some of the things Pastor Hurst said."

"I was just thinking of that. You knew that he'd had some conversations with my father?"

"Yes. I was so excited to hear it and feel confident that God's will has been done, Anne. He loves us so greatly that we need never doubt His plan."

"I'm certain I will need to remember that in the days and weeks to come."

"Don't ask yourself to mend too swiftly, Anne. It takes time to feel less of the hurt, and it's all right if a little bit of it always stays with us."

"Thank you, Lydia."

Others were waiting to talk to Anne, so Lydia moved on. Weston stayed within arm's reach, keeping a careful eye on his wife.

The Hursts served lunch for the grieving couple when everyone left the church, but Anne was rather drained by then. It helped to have the children join them, especially with eight-year-old Margaret in a talkative mood.

"You have prettier flowers than we have."

"Do you think so, Margaret?"

She nodded. "But I'm supposed to be thankful."

"And how are you doing with that?"

Margaret shot a glance at her mother, who kept silent. Only just that morning there had been some grumbling over the shoes she had to wear.

"I'm working on it," the little girl volunteered.

"I'm glad, Margaret. That's what I do when I struggle with sin too."

"Maybe I could come and pick flowers again some time."

Before her parents could protest her boldness, 11-year-old Jane spoke up.

"Margaret, the Colonel just died and Anne is sad!"

"But flowers could make her cheery again. I'm sure of it. I would do all the work, and she would need only to hold the basket."

Pastor cleared his throat and both girls turned to him.

"Thank you, Jane, for being sensitive to Anne's feelings right now. Thank you, Margaret, for wanting to cheer her with flowers, but we will not be making plans today. Mr

Weston is going to want to take Anne home soon so she can rest, so let us not dawdle over our meal.

"Jeff," he said, turning to his oldest. "Will you tell us how school is going—some of the things you're working on with Palmer and Jennings?"

It was the perfect diversion. The meal passed without Anne having to contribute, something she was too tired to do. There was much on her mind, but not even when she and Weston were alone in the carriage could she muster the thoughts into words. Her father was gone, dead and buried.

Weston was equally tired but kept himself going until Anne was resting on her bed. It was only just now occurring to him that when you married a woman, you also married her family; all the joys and heartaches became yours as well.

I feel as though I've taken this marriage seriously, Weston prayed as he sought some solitude in his own room. *But there's still so much for me to learn. Help me, Father, to be the man Anne needs right now. Help me to lead in kindness and strength. Help us to accept this death, be thankful, and to keep growing in You.*

Weston's thoughts turned to his mother just then. He would lose her some day as well. There was no use worrying about it—that was a waste of time—but someday she would be gone. Just as Anne had recalled, Weston was thankful for Pastor's reminder that God alone held those keys.

❧ ❧

The letter started, *My dearest Anne.* Lenore wrote to her new daughter the moment she received word of the Colonel's passing. Anne found a quiet spot in a comfortable chair and settled in to read.

What words are needed at a time like this? Even having experienced loss in my life, I'm not sure. I didn't sit and think about what I wanted to say; I've simply begun my letter so you can know all my thoughts.

First of all, I love you. You are beyond precious to me. It is for this reason that my heart breaks for your pain. I so wish the journey was a bit shorter. Do know that I would have come if I could have made it in time.

What will the days be like for you now? I know that I can speak to you as a sister in our Lord, and although He fills our every need, you will know a certain emptiness, Anne. You will experience a void that will last for a time. There might be a measure of relief. Do not fight this— it's normal. But mostly you will be reminded again and again that he's gone. In time this will lessen for you. In time the pain will fade. Do not rush your heart. Do not make yourself bear up and be brave. If you need to cry, indulge yourself. Robert will always understand.

I wish I had known your father, Anne. You expressed wanting to know me because of the son I had raised. I know your father was not well in these last years, but I too would have enjoyed meeting the father of my precious Anne.

The comfort that I have knowing God and Robert are with you is indescribable. I pray that you will be comforted as well. God's will and timing are always perfect, even when we wish to argue. Ask Him to keep your thoughts clear of bitterness or anger, and be thankful for His

*timetable. I will pray that very thing for you
every day.*

*If my timing is not all wrong, I would love to
come and see you. Will early October work?
There will be no wounded feelings on my behalf
if you wish me to delay this visit. I will come at
your discretion and will wait for your word on
the matter.*

Please greet Robert for me.

Love to you both,
Mother

Quite confident as to what his answer would be, Anne
did not even seek her husband out. She immediately started
a letter back to London, one telling Lenore to come whenever she liked.

✿ ✿

"Do you know what your mother likes to eat?" Anne
asked Weston a week before she was to arrive.

"Everything we like."

"That was vague."

"Was it?"

Anne smiled, now having caught on to what he was
doing.

"I want to make it special for her."

"I know, love, and it will be special. Just her visiting will
make it special. She won't care what she eats."

"But we could surprise her with one particular meal."

"True," Weston agreed, thinking maybe Anne did need
this diversion. She had been drawn and pale lately, and he
didn't want her overly burdened with anything.

"Can you think of one thing?"

"She's fond of chocolate and cocoa."

"All right."

Anne was ready to ask for more, but Mansfield came to the door.

"Your guests are here, Mr Weston."

"Thank you, Mansfield. Please tell them I'll be out soon."

"I didn't know you were expecting company," Anne commented.

Weston stopped himself from telling her that they had talked of it.

"It's Jennings with Jeffrey, Thomas, James, Frank, and Walt. As part of their course on mathematics, Jennings wants them to measure and study the construction on the conservatory."

Anne nodded as it came back to her. Not wanting to keep her husband or his guests waiting, she didn't ask any other questions, but the matter was not really settled about what his mother liked to eat.

Weston had no more left her when Anne felt too tired to care. Wanting to enjoy her mother-in-law's visit, Anne wondered when she would ever feel lighthearted again.

ᔛ ᔜ

"She sleeps quite a bit."

"I think that might be normal, dear," Lenore tried to reassure her son, even as she felt her own sense of worry.

"I'm hoping your being here will cheer her some."

Lenore nodded, not able to promise him anything, even though she wished for the same thing.

The door to the salon opened, and Anne came in. She smiled in true pleasure at the sight of Weston's mother.

"I'm sorry I wasn't here to greet you."

"Robert did the honors, dear. Don't give it a thought. How are you?"

"Doing well, I think. Better when I rest. I must admit that I nap most days."

Lenore had taken her hand.

"You need that right now. Don't worry about entertaining me. We'll just visit or do whatever you like."

Anne's heart lightened at the prospect. It had been many years since she'd had a mother, and Weston's mother was so fun and easy to be with.

Lenore's visit signaled a period for fun. The three of them shopped a bit and even dined out, but most of the two-week visit found Lenore and Anne walking, talking, reading, or puttering in the garden. Anne was able to put some of her mourning on the shelf and enjoy this visit.

Lenore enjoyed it as well and left with the promise that she would come again for Christmas.

๑ ๑

Weston was headed to town. His mother had been gone for a few days, and his wife had held up beautifully during this time, but he could see that her heart was still broken. He wanted to find her a gift, something that would make her smile.

After breakfast he had been vague about where he was headed or how long he would be gone, and he did not invite her to go with him.

"Are you all right?" Anne questioned him, a little concerned.

"Yes," he told her, punctuating his words with a kiss. "I just have a bit of business on my mind."

Weston told himself he was being truthful: It was the business of finding his wife a gift, and not just any gift but one she would treasure.

"Did you need me to pick anything up?"

"No, I shall be fine, thank you."

Weston kissed her again, and with a good deal of enthusiasm took his leave. Anne wondered at his business and wished she'd asked but decided not to worry about it. In truth, she'd realized in the night that she hadn't played the piano for weeks and headed to the music room immediately.

It didn't take long for Anne to forget Weston's trip to town. One of her favorite pieces of music was still on the piano, and in moments the room filled with the sounds of her playing. She was deep into the melody before she realized she was being watched. Hands still moving, she glanced up to see her husband coming toward her, his face showing surprise. Anne came to an awkward halt, not sure what was wrong.

"You play the piano." Weston stated the obvious.

"I thought you were gone." Anne said the first thing that came to mind.

"I forgot something and had to come back. Why have you not played before?"

"I do...I have..." she began, stumbling a bit. "I guess you weren't here."

Weston's brows rose in surprise. He wasn't away very often. How could he have missed this?

Seeing Anne look uncomfortable, Weston immediately tabled his plans to leave. He went to his wife, joining her on the piano bench. Things were coming back to him now. The look on Anne's face the night at Berwick when they'd listened to Louisa Cavendish play, the interest she'd shown in the music at the bookstore—clear indications he'd totally missed.

"I need to ask you some things," Weston said quietly.

"All right."

"When did you first play this piano? When I was on my trip?"

"I think that was it, yes. So much has happened since then."

"Is that why you haven't played since, or have I made you feel as though you mustn't?"

"No, nothing like that. I hadn't played in many years, so I guess the first time I wished to be alone, but not now. It only just occurred to me last night that it had been some time since I'd come back to this room."

"When did you learn?"

"As a girl." Anne smiled at the thought. "My mother taught me."

"Did you have your own piano at one time?"

"Yes."

"And it had to be sold," he stated more than asked.

"Of course."

Sitting side by side staring at each other, the two laughed.

Weston watched her, never growing tired of her nearness. "Have you ever thought about how blessed we are?" he asked.

"Often."

"We could have gone for years without this level of care and commitment to each other, this love for each other, but we grew into it rather soon, didn't we?"

Anne put her hands on his face, touching him gently and marveling at the special man he was.

"God must have prepared our hearts, do you not think?"

"It's the only thing that makes sense."

"I was embarrassed in front of you after the ordeal with our first 'marriage,' but after we talked at the manse, I knew such a peace."

"With the occasional doubt creeping in," he teased her, thinking of the times she'd asked him if he had regrets.

Anne kissed him.

"Play something."

In an instant she was shy.

"I thought you were going to town."

"I will, but play something first."

"Don't watch me. I really am quite rusty."

Anne took on a case of the giggles when Weston stayed on the bench but turned his back to her.

"Go on now," he said, his back still to her and the piano.

Anne took a moment but eventually began to play, softly at first, wanting to keep laughing at her husband's broad back, so close to her shoulder. But in time the music took over. When Weston did turn back around, Anne didn't notice. She played with complete concentration, making herself repeat parts that were anything short of perfect. When the piece ended, she again turned to the man next to her.

"You peeked."

Weston didn't answer. He stared at her for what seemed like minutes before placing his arms around her. The two enjoyed a long and tender kiss and the piano was forgotten. Indeed, Weston never did leave for town that day.

Chapter Twenty-One

The door to their bedrooms was left open now. Neither Weston nor Anne felt any need for privacy from the other, so the door lay back against the wall in Weston's room most of the time. For this reason, Anne was nearly to Weston's shoulder before he realized she had entered. He was reading his Bible but put a hand out to catch hers.

"Here, sit on my knee a moment and listen to this."

Anne slipped an arm around his neck to get comfortable and noticed that he was in the book of Jeremiah.

"This is from chapter 9. 'Thus saith the LORD, Let not the wise man glory in his wisdom, neither let the mighty man glory in his might, let not the rich man glory in his riches: but let him that glorieth glory in this, that he understandeth and knoweth me, that I am the LORD which exercise lovingkindness, judgment, and righteousness, in the earth: for in these things I delight, saith the LORD.'

"I thought of you as I read that," Weston told her when he finished. "On days when you might be tempted to question God's timing, you can remember this verse. You can remember that our God is loving, a righteous judge who only does what's best for us."

"Thank you," Anne said sincerely. She hadn't even taken the time to open her Bible that morning. "I grow discouraged too easily these days. My father's interest in Christ was such a lovely surprise, and the instant I heard about it I determined that God was going to save him before he died."

"And He may have, Anne. Your father may have repented. What we need to remember is that we are not lost in the last moments of life. Most of us have years to accept or reject God's offer. He never forces it on us, but it has to be on His terms."

Anne nodded. "Which is only right, considering that He's the potter and we're the clay."

Weston kissed her cheek.

"Did you come in for something in particular?"

"Just to be near you."

Weston put both arms around her. "Are you a little down this morning?"

"I am, yes. I have much to be thankful for, but all I can think about is my hurting heart."

"Can you do both?"

"How's that?"

"Can you be thankful and still having a hurting heart? Can you have a hurting heart but not be consumed with it?"

Anne had to think about that. It was a challenging idea. She knew that Christ Himself understood mourning, so there certainly must be a righteous way to go about it.

"Another passage just came to mind," Weston continued, paging in his Bible to the book of Matthew. "Remember the man in chapter 12 who had an unclean spirit? It would seem that he got rid of it but didn't replace it with anything, so the spirit returned with seven other spirits, even more evil, and the man was in worse shape than ever before.

"I think believers do this. They try to overcome a sin without putting something else in their heart. You've lost your father, but you have the ultimate Father in God Himself. Fill your heart with God's Word. Don't let there be an empty space inside of you, and God will see you through every moment of pain."

"Oh, Weston," Anne breathed as she wrapped her arms tightly around him. "Thank you. Thank you so much. I haven't known quite what to do. I do feel empty. I read my Bible and still feel so sad—not a righteous sadness, but one where I want pity. Now I know what to do. Now I can mourn but have joy and thankfulness in my tears."

Anne buried her face in his shoulder. Weston smiled. She was trying to choke the life out of him, but it was worth it. To see her face light up with a plan to keep molding herself to Christ as she mourned was worth every second.

Tipton

"You don't think it too soon after my father's death, do you?" Anne asked of Palmer and Lydia.

"No, Anne, we don't," Palmer said immediately.

"And from what you've said, you're not planning an overly large affair," Lydia put in.

"That's true."

"So what can we do?" Palmer asked.

Anne lit up at that moment. The Palmers learned in an instant that she was very well organized and knew exactly what she was looking for. They listened, growing excited with her.

"What do you think?"

"We think it sounds wonderful."

"It's not a large group to invite, but do you think you'll be able to keep it a surprise?" Lydia asked.

"I don't know, but I'm going to try."

"We won't speak of it to the children," Lydia said. "That will certainly help."

"And you can tell Weston that you're invited to dinner that evening," Palmer put in. "Everyone can be here ahead of time, and he won't suspect a thing."

"That's what I'm hoping."

The three ironed out a few more details and Anne took her leave. She knew she'd been moping around Brown Manor long enough. Weston hadn't said it in those words, but it was time to stop wallowing in her misery, replace the pain with Christ's love and His Word, and stop thinking about only herself. As the carriage pulled away from Tipton to take her home, Anne was reminded of how wonderful it was to put others ahead of herself.

ૹ ૹ

Brown Manor

Mansfield had all he could do not to laugh. The mistress of Brown Manor was nearly beside herself with excitement. She had given him a list of things she needed done, food she wished to have prepared, and instructions on how the evening should go.

"And it's a surprise, Mansfield. We must do our best to keep it quiet." This was all said very softly, even though they were quite alone in the kitchen.

"I shall do my best, Mrs Weston. Do you need me to devise a plan to get Mr Weston to Tipton?"

"No, I shall tell him today that we've been invited to dinner. Everyone will be there ahead of time. But now, Mansfield," the lady went on. "His actual birthday is a few days later. I also want to have a special dinner that night. Ask Cook what she recommends, and please check back with me."

"Very well, Mrs Weston."

Anne watched him take a few more notes, waiting until he looked up.

"Do you think I've forgotten anything?" she asked, seeming younger than her years.

The servant looked thoughtful and then asked, "Do you have a gift in mind?"

Anne's eyes grew large before she thanked the manservant and hurried on her way.

Alone at last, Mansfield gave in to the urge to smile. If he had to enlist the help of every servant at Brown Manor, this would be a party Mr Weston would never forget. And all the credit would go to his lovely wife.

ร ร

Collingbourne

"I'm going to go to Benwick's on my own," Anne informed her spouse just as they came into town the next afternoon.

"Is there a reason?"

"Well, you said you had business with Mr Vintcent, so I thought I would head directly to Benwick's."

"All right. I'll join you when I finish."

"Why don't we meet at Gray's?"

"Oh, there's no need for that. I'll come and fetch you."

"I have business at Benwick's. There's no need for you to come."

"What business?"

Anne saw no help for it. "Weston, your birthday is this month."

He looked stunned.

"It is, isn't it?"

Anne had to laugh at him.

"Nevertheless, Anne, I don't relish the idea of your going to Gray's on your own."

"It's only across the street, Weston," Anne pointed out. "I'll just walk over as soon as I'm finished."

"But if I finish first, I'll come and find you at Benwick's. I won't come in, I'll just wait for you outside."

"But if you do that, you won't know if I'm inside or already waiting for you at Gray's."

He hated to admit it but she had him. Anne hid a smile from her protective spouse and waited for him to speak.

"All right," he agreed at last. "I'll go to Gray's and wait for you."

Anne kissed his cheek and assured him, "I will be fine."

Weston had no real reason to doubt that, and with a clear mind left her and went on his way.

In the shop, Anne browsed for a gift. She had some vague ideas but rather hoped she would spot something and know it was just right. She was still at a complete loss when someone called her name.

"Anne, is that you?"

"Lizzy!" Anne exclaimed with delight as she rushed to hug the friend who had entered the aisle. "How are you?"

"I'm very well," Elizabeth Steele told her, smiling in delight of their meeting. "How are you?"

"I'm married," Anne told her, her smile lighting her whole face. "I'm Mrs Robert Weston."

"Oh, Anne, I'm so pleased for you."

"But tell me, Lizzy!" Anne rushed on. "Are you visiting or have you moved back?"

"I'm back."

"How long have you been here?"

"Only a week."

"And what brought this about?"

"Several things, but mostly that my brother has left England to travel for a time."

"Which brother?" Anne's brows rose in surprise.

"Edward. He left in August, but it feels like forever. I told Henry that I was returning to Collingbourne, and surprisingly enough he wanted to move as well."

"And is it just Henry, or are all your siblings back?"

"Everyone save Edward," Elizabeth said with a smile. "A little peace and quiet in Newcomb Park would have been lovely, but we're all home."

"It's so wonderful to see you, Lizzy. Things are busy just now, but when the holidays are over, I want you to come and visit."

"I want you to do the same. I want to meet your Mr Weston."

"And you shall. We'll be in church tomorrow."

"I shall seek you out."

The two hugged again and parted. For a time Anne couldn't think. It was so lovely to see her friend. They had not stayed in touch over the years but had been very good friends as girls.

In the midst of this rambling, she spotted it. Anne walked toward the shelf that held the perfect gift for her husband, picking it up with gentle hands. Benwick chose that moment to join her.

"How are you faring, Mrs Weston?"

"Very well, Mr Benwick. I'll take this. And when you deliver it, please instruct your man to leave it with Mansfield."

"Very well."

Her step light and wanting to fly to Gray's in her excitement, Anne made her way across the street some ten minutes later. She had spotted two other needs before exiting the shop but was now done and ready to join her husband.

Weston had ordered and was waiting for her, standing as she took her seat and then adjusting her chair.

"Dare I ask how it went?"

"It went very well." Anne looked downright smug. "And I refuse to give any hints, but I will tell you that I met a friend I hadn't seen in years. She just moved back into the area. You shall meet her tomorrow."

"I look forward to it," Weston said as Anne poured the tea. "Will we be visiting Lucy Digby today before we leave town?"

Anne stared at her husband, marveling all over again at his kindness.

"Weston, that's a lovely idea."

"I'm glad you think so. I look forward to meeting your friends."

And that was just what they did. From Gray's they made their way to the small house of Anne's longtime friend. Weston was at his most charming, and in a matter of moments Lucy relaxed and enjoyed his visit. The little girls—especially Meg—were delightful, and Anne could see that Weston found them adorable. Billy came in early from work and Weston was able to meet him.

"Where are you working these days, Billy?"

"I'm at Ashridge right now, but I'll be coming to your church soon."

"Does the church need masonry work?" Weston asked.

"The manse does," Billy told him, relaxing with this man as his wife had.

The men continued to speak of Billy's work for a time, genuinely enjoying one another, before the baby began to fuss.

"Thank you for coming," Lucy told Anne when she walked her to the door and hugged her goodbye.

"We'll visit again," Anne assured her as the men shook hands.

"I wanted to invite them to church," Weston said the moment they were in the coach, "but I thought it might be best to wait for our next meeting."

"I've invited Lucy over the years, but I don't think anyone has ever reached out to Billy."

"I'm glad to know that, and I'll be sure Pastor knows about it before Billy starts the work there."

Anne kissed his cheek. Weston took her hand, and they rode home in silence.

≈ ≈

"That's a nice coat," Weston complimented his wife as they settled in the carriage for the ride to Tipton.

"Thank you. Your mother picked it out."

"She has good taste," Weston said as he picked up his wife's hand and kissed the back. "And speaking of taste…" he let the sentence hang as he turned her hand over, shifted the sleeve of her coat and kissed the inside of her wrist.

Anne took her hand away.

"I think you need to behave."

"It's not my fault."

Anne fought laughter.

"How do you figure?"

"It's your skin. It's so soft that I lose my head."

"That was a charming thing to say."

"Does that mean I can have your wrist back?"

Anne could only laugh.

They arrived at Tipton a short time later, spirits high. Anne was certain that her face was red with excitement and was thankful for the cover of darkness.

"Welcome." Palmer was on hand to see them in, Lydia close behind. All seemed quiet and normal, and Anne thought they must have succeeded with their plan. A glance at her husband told her he didn't suspect a thing.

"Shall we start in the salon, Liddy?" Palmer asked with all the unconcern of an actor.

"Indeed. You go right ahead, Anne and Weston."

Moments later the doors were opened and ten friends came from behind chairs and curtains to shout their greetings of surprise. Weston's mouth opened and closed, but no words emerged. The party-goers gathered around him, wishing him well with handshakes and hugs, and Anne stood back and smiled.

"Where is my wife?" Weston was finally heard to say.

The crowed parted until Weston could see Anne.

"You, madam..." he began, still shaking his head, but he never got any further. The group was too busy laughing, and Anne had come up to take his hand. Weston dropped a kiss on her cheek, amazed that she'd pulled it off.

Games were played and food was enjoyed. Weston was blindfolded and made to guess the name of the person addressing him, even though the person was allowed to disguise his voice. Dessert was eaten and gifts were presented. Weston spent the entire evening laughing at how easily he'd been fooled.

As the evening ended and Anne and Weston made their way home, Weston turned in the carriage to stare at his wife. She was already watching him.

"I did it," she said. "I fooled you."

"You did that." He shook his head a little more. "All this talk about finding me a gift at Benwick's. I had no idea you were so deceitful."

Anne only laughed, more than a little pleased with herself. Weston put an arm around her and pulled her close.

And that's not the end of it was Anne's thought as she snuggled against his side. *You'll find out just how sneaky I can be. Your real birthday isn't until Tuesday, and I have a few more plans.*

જ઼ જ઼

Levens Crossing

"We don't have to do this," Weston said, standing with Anne in the front yard of her old home. "We don't have to let it or sell it."

"Isn't that rather a waste?"

"If it's still standing empty a year from now, it would be a waste, but there's no hurry to do this right away."

It had taken weeks of slow work to go through everything. Anne had found things belonging to her parents she hadn't known existed. She had read letters and studied papers that gave her special glimpses into her past. The overwhelming tone of it all had been that her parents had been very much in love, but life had changed forever when her mother died and her father grew ill.

Much of the sorting and reading had been done at Levens Crossing, but now it was complete. Most of the furniture had been sold or given away; a few pieces were moved to Brown Manor. Repairs had all been made and now the house stood clean and empty, ready for occupancy.

Anne didn't think she would be this attached, but suddenly the thought of having strangers living there was sad to her.

"You're right. It is too soon," she said, thankful that Weston had given her a few moments to think. "Maybe in the spring I'll think about it again."

"That's a fine plan. It's not as if we know someone who's in need just now."

Anne's face changed.

"What is it?"

"I was just thinking of Billy and Lucy. Their place is so small. Do you think they would ever desire to get out of town?"

"I don't know. We can ask them."

"They would be fine tenants, Weston. Billy is such a hard worker."

Weston put his arm around her.

"You don't have to convince me, love. If they want to live at Levens Crossing, that's fine."

"Thank you, Weston."

"For what?"

"I don't know. Always being so supportive, I guess."

"Well, it's a good start to the idea. I think maybe we should pray about it, ask God to lead, and watch for an opportunity to talk with them. What do you think?"

Anne nodded, feeling very good about the whole thing. Just looking at the house and thinking about her time there made her want to stay a bit longer, but the rain was coming back. Before they could even move to the carriage, the sky started to pour. Anne looked out the window as the coach pulled away, gaining a final glimpse and doing as her husband suggested: praying. If God wanted the Digbys to occupy Levens Crossing, He would show the way.

◦◦◦

Brown Manor

"What's this?" Weston asked when Anne set a wrapped box next to his plate at the end of dinner. They were alone in the dining room, and it was Weston's actual birthday.

"Your birthday gift."

"I thought the party was my gift."

Anne didn't comment. A smile in her eyes, she just watched him.

Weston gave her an indulgent look and tore at the paper. A moment later his look turned to one of excitement.

"Do you like it?" Anne asked anxiously.

"Yes!" Weston exclaimed as he brought out an enamel pocket watch. It was Swiss-made, beautifully painted, and when he pushed the pendant, a tiny bird sprang up and sang.

"Where did you find this?"

"Benwick's."

Playing with it like a child, Weston suddenly remembered to kiss and thank his wife.

"I didn't expect this."

"I didn't expect you," Anne said.

Weston's eyes warmed when he looked at her. He set the watch aside and went to take her into his arms. Anne forgot all about the fact that a cake had been prepared and would arrive any moment. She went into her husband's arms, wrapping hers tightly around him.

"I love you."

"I love you."

The two broke apart when they heard footsteps. They enjoyed the cake Cook had made, but as soon as they could manage, they retired in order to be alone.

Before they slept that night, Weston decided that the sweetest gift he'd ever received was having Anne for his wife. He would enjoy the watch and treasure it, but if he never had anything but Anne, he would know nothing but contentment.

Epilogue

Brown Manor
Christmas Day

"Happy Christmas," Lenore greeted Weston and Anne when she arrived downstairs on that morning.

"Happy Christmas!" they greeted her, hugs and kisses all around.

The gift opening did not take long to commence. Everyone was as excited as children to give the gifts they had selected, and in order to start they were even prepared to forego eating.

"Weston!" Anne exclaimed when she unwrapped the first package he'd handed her. "These were my mother's," she said, her hand touching the linen tablecloths and napkins.

"Were they?" Weston said, working to look innocent.

Anne flew to his side, her arms going around his neck, while Lenore laughed in delight.

"He's been so excited about that gift, Anne. He told me the moment I arrived."

And that wasn't all. Weston had also recovered a set of silverware, some silver serving dishes, and a small stack of music. Benwick thought he might have more in the storeroom, and would continue to look, but for now Weston's surprise had been complete.

Anne had a few surprises of her own before the morning finished, and Weston and Lenore had their own hugs and thanks to dispense.

The day was spent in a relaxed fashion. It was cool outside, so the fires were kept high.

The three Westons sang around the piano, Anne played, and they visited and ate all during the day.

That evening they went to the Hursts' to have a celebration with them, making the day complete. Anne couldn't remember a sweeter time, but long and tiring as the day had been, she still had one more gift to give.

Back at Brown Manor, Jenny had helped her with her gown and brushed her hair—they had not rushed—but Weston had still not made an appearance. Anne crept to the door to see what he was about and found him reading a portion of newsprint. She came up and slipped her arms around him from behind, her cheek laid against his back.

"Something interesting?"

"Yes, I never did take the time to read this today, and there's a new bank scandal in London."

"Does it involve our bank?"

"No, but I wonder if it might eventually."

Anne held him for a moment and then spoke.

"I have one more Christmas gift for you."

"Do you?" Weston sounded as distracted as he was, but Anne kept on.

"A little news of my own."

"Um-hmm."

"We're going to have a baby."

She knew the moment she had his attention. It took a few heartbeats, but he stopped, his head coming up as though he could see her in front of him.

"What did you say?"

Anne stepped back and waited for him to turn and face her.

"I said we're going to have a baby."

Weston was the most flustered she'd ever seen him.

"Are you all right?" he finally managed. "Do you feel all right?"

"I feel fine. Are you pleased?" she asked, feeling unsure over his reaction.

Weston took her in his arms.

"I just had a moment of fear was all. I'm delighted, but I can't stand the thought of anything happening to you, and for a few seconds my thoughts ran wild."

Anne put her hands on his cheeks.

"We won't worry about that. It's not our job. We'll just trust that God has a baby for us, and we'll both be here to raise him."

Weston nodded, still a little in shock.

"It could be a girl," he suddenly said.

"It could be," Anne agreed with a smile.

"*Or one of each!*" he now suggested, warming to the subject.

Anne began to laugh.

The full truth of it hit him a moment later, and he lifted his wife and spun her around.

"A baby! We're going to have a baby!"

Anne laughed, even as he tried to kiss her.

"My mother!" Weston stopped and said. "I've got to tell her."

"She's probably in bed, Weston."

"That doesn't matter," he declared, his eyes wide with the wonder of it all. "She's going to become a grandmother. There's no time for sleep!"

Anne's sides hurt from laughing as she watched him dash to the door and fling it open. He was calling to his mother long before he reached her room.

A huge smile on her face, Anne stayed where she was, her arms wrapped around her middle, thinking about the little person inside of her and the special father he would have.

"Or she," Anne said out loud to the empty room, her heart full of peace and confidence that whomever God put in their future, boy, girl, or *one of each*, it would be perfect.

After all, God had sent Robert Weston to rescue her. He could do anything!

About the Author

LORI WICK is a multifaceted author of Christian fiction. As comfortable writing period stories as she is penning contemporary works, Lori's books (6 million in print) vary widely in location and time period. Lori's faithful fans consistently put her series and stand-alone works on the bestseller lists. Lori and her husband, Bob, live with their swiftly growing family in the Midwest.

To read about other Lori Wick novels, visit **www.harvesthousepublishers.com**

Books by Lori Wick

A Place Called Home Series
A Place Called Home
A Song for Silas
The Long Road Home
A Gathering of Memories

The Californians
Whatever Tomorrow Brings
As Time Goes By
Sean Donovan
Donovan's Daughter

Kensington Chronicles
The Hawk and the Jewel
Wings of the Morning
Who Brings Forth the Wind
The Knight and the Dove

Rocky Mountain Memories
Where the Wild Rose Blooms
Whispers of Moonlight
To Know Her by Name
Promise Me Tomorrow

The Yellow Rose Trilogy
Every Little Thing About You
A Texas Sky
City Girl

English Garden Series
The Proposal
The Rescue
The Visitor
The Pursuit

The Tucker Mills Trilogy
Moonlight on the Millpond
Just Above a Whisper
Leave a Candle Burning

Big Sky Dreams
Cassidy
Sabrina
Jessie

Contemporary Fiction
Sophie's Heart
Pretense
The Princess
Bamboo & Lace
Every Storm
White Chocolate Moments